AN EXMOOR HARBOUR TALE

Trouble in Combe Tollbridge

ROSEANNA HALL

Farrago

This edition published in 2024 by Farrago,
an imprint of Duckworth Books Ltd
1 Golden Court, Richmond, TW9 1EU, United Kingdom

www.farragobooks.com

Copyright © Sarah J. Mason, 2024
Map © Hannah Marchant

The right of Roseanna Hall to be identified as the author
of this Work has been asserted by her in accordance
with the Copyright, Designs & Patents Act 1988.

All rights reserved. No part of this publication may be reproduced,
stored in a retrieval system, or transmitted, in any form or by any
means, without the prior permission in writing of the publisher.

This book is a work of fiction. Names, characters, businesses, organizations,
places and events other than those clearly in the public domain, are either the
product of the author's imagination or are used fictitiously. Any resemblance
to actual persons, living or dead, events or locales is entirely coincidental.

A catalogue record for this book is available from the British Library

Printed and bound in Great Britain by Clays Ltd, Elcograf S.p.A.

Print ISBN: 978-1-7884-2508-7
eISBN: 978-1-7884-2509-4

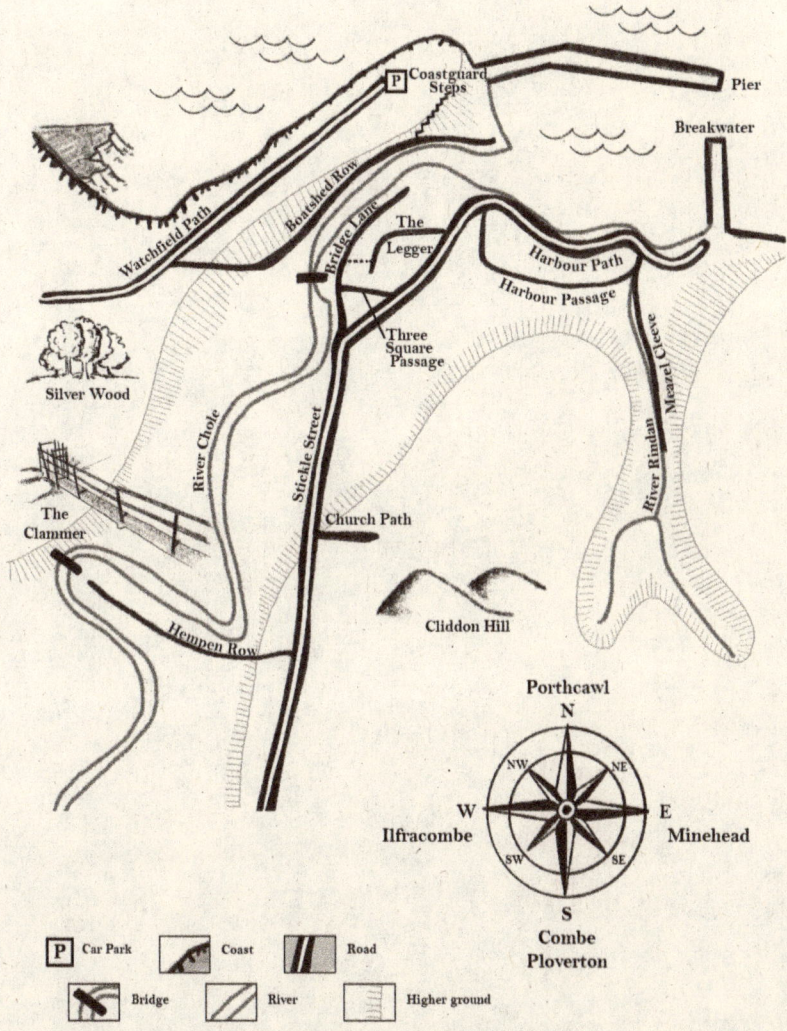

Chapter One

Jane Merton woke muzzily, took a few measured breaths and, without opening her eyes, stretched under the duvet and gave a little wriggle. She lay still, listening. At her side she heard the quiet snuffle that showed Jasper hadn't yet woken, but continued to swim several fathoms deep in dreams.

Jane blinked as realisation dawned. She could hear her husband sleeping – and that was all. After three days and nights of what had felt like solid rain, the rain had finally stopped. She gazed at the ceiling. As she had hoped, it was bright with reflected light from – she turned her head – yes! a cloudless, clear blue sky, and the rising sun's glimmer on the waters of the Bristol Channel. Could this be another lucky day?

To make sure, she rolled quietly out of bed and padded to the window. There was no rattle of curtain-rings to disturb the dreaming Jasper: Clammer Cottage, at the end of a one-and-a-half-car-wide lane that went nowhere, needed no blinds or curtains. No passers-by could be startled by Jane's colourful nightshirt, for nobody ever passed by. The narrow Hempen Row came to a decisive halt at the steep bank of the River Chole, bubbling and rushing in the near distance.

Jane sighed with lazy content, listening to the river as she looked out to sea, watching distant white horses prance towards the little harbour and mute their plunging gallop to a steady trot. Yes, she might be in luck. From the height of the sun and the shadows of the headland it was an hour or so past dawn. She would let Jasper sleep, remembering how very late he'd stopped work the previous night, or maybe it had been early this morning; it wouldn't be the first time she'd gone off to try her artistic fortune without him.

A quick wash and brush-up, then Jane slipped into her clothes and left her nightshirt on her side of the bed, its arms curled round a sketchbook and pencil. Jasper would understand, when he finally woke, that his wife had been struck by inspiration and was off about her business. One day (she insisted) she would capture exactly the image she wanted, even if none of her previous attempts had ever been closer than almost...

Seagulls wheeled and screamed as she shut the door and, with camera and sketchbook, made for the small plank footbridge (locally a clam, or clammer) that crossed to the old hemp garden on the far side of the little River Chole. Here in centuries past Combe Tollbridge cultivated hemp for cordage, sails and clothing; in more recent days village elder Elias Budd, retired from fishing, had used the land as his private vegetable patch.

Mr Budd's clam, perhaps a hundred years old, was no longer deemed safe but survived, a few yards from its replacement, as a witness to history. From mediaeval times there was always a bridge over the Chole at the end of Hempen Row. Constant exposure to Atlantic weather systems meant that these primitive structures had been often replaced. The latest model, in fibreglass rather than wood, was almost its neighbour's twin – apart from bigger gates at each end. The woods and cliffs above and around Combe Tollbridge are the undisputed territory of a reckless and irresponsible tribe of feral goats. While these for the most part keep themselves to themselves, being generally omnivorous and virtually unstoppable they have few manners, and scant regard for public opinion. Village memory can charge them with some legendary breaches of the peace.

But now it was high summer. With plenty for the goats to forage in the woods and on the cliffs, Jane thought she could relax. She walked to the middle of the new clam and looked down on the rushing Chole in its steep, narrow bed as it boiled and eddied its way from the high moor to the harbour, and into the wider sea. On such days as this she never could decide whether it looked more like chocolate sauce or burnt caramel, but the swirl of off-white foam always made her think of whipped cream.

Yet again she leaned over the handrail and took photographs. Yet again she was disappointed: they were too dark, too uninspired. She opened her sketchbook.

Several pages in, she emerged from her creative daze. This wasn't what she'd meant to do! She shut her sketchbook, slipped it in the tote bag to join her camera, and hurried back across the clam towards Hempen Row.

Near the corner where Hempen Row joined Stickle Street, a movement caught her eye. A squawk overhead made her hesitate. She couldn't help it: she stopped, and looked up.

On the pocket-sized plot squeezed from the garden of a cottage abandoned about the time Queen Victoria went into mourning, stood the pint-sized tin tabernacle erected by a small band of nonconformist brethren. As songs of dissent faded through generations to silence, the meeting house became ownerless, its corrugated iron panels in need of paint, its roof in need of repair. It was gradually adopted by Combe Tollbridge, earmarked for the village museum – One Day. Until that day came it was used to store such items as the Octopus Fire Pump, which sucked water from the Chole through canvas hoses, and similar paraphernalia of defunct or moribund local heritage that Tollbridge felt ought not be forgotten – if only someone (but of course, it must be someone else) could arrange these memories in some sort of order within the dilapidated little building.

This bijou example of nineteenth-century flat-pack ingenuity had first been assembled by the Brethren in accordance with the manufacturer's instructions. Exmoor rains, however, can be heavy. A metal roof reverberates and distorts, drowning out the voices of even the largest congregation. The Tollbridge Brethren were earnest, but never numerous. Local thatchers were approached; the original roof was replaced. Worship continued in relative peace to the end, though there was always the regret that neither a bigger building nor even renewal of the thatch had ever been possible.

Among the penultimate worshippers was a farmer from Combe Ploverton, higher up the valley. He demolished a barn, producing a quantity of unwanted corrugated iron. The Brethren capped their thatch under a makeshift scaffold and left the outcome to providence.

Local wildlife, especially nesting birds, deemed the decaying thatch providential indeed.

Jane stared now at a tangled silhouette of straw dragged by beaks and recent storms into a strange, distorted shape. That might be the profile of an old man with a hooked nose, shoulders hunched under his hat, drip on the end of his nose – another squawk, as another bird flapped out from under – no, once there had been a drip, and a nose, but now... Jane reached for her camera before further images should be lost.

The crunch of heavy feet at last broke into her concentration. Her pencil staggered a little on the page, and she closed her sketchbook as the footsteps drew near.

'Oh!' She focused on the newcomer approaching in his sea-boots, knitted jumper and dark blue beanie cap; took a closer look at his face, and ventured a smile. 'Good morning.' The answering nod and smile seemed a little forced. Strange: and not a good start. Hastily she stuffed pencil and sketchbook back in the bag with the camera. 'I must say, this sunshine makes a welcome change.'

After a pause: 'That it do,' agreed Gabriel Hockaday, slowly.

Combe Tollbridge and Combe Ploverton seldom look further than Mr Hockaday when Father Christmas is required to make a public appearance. In and around the twin villages the splendour of Gabriel's white whiskers has few rivals, though the glorious 'full set' sported by his brother-in-law and chief crony Mike Binns comes close. The whiskers of Mr Binns, however, rejoice in a suspiciously auburn hue. As the brothers-in-law are of a similar vintage, in rare moments of family tension remarks can be passed about dye, and doubts expressed over a certain locked compartment in the Binns household's bathroom cabinet to which not even Mike's son Mickey has a key.

Mike and Gabriel were among those village elders who first approved civic adoption of the sadly redundant tin tabernacle. Much later, when a young ex-librarian came to live in Tollbridge, it was Gabriel who persuaded the others that One Day had at last dawned. On behalf of the whole community, after much argument, he drew up a job description, and Angela Lilley was pleased to accept the part-time post of museum curator.

Angela had struck up a friendship with fellow incomers Jane and Jasper Merton, so Jane might surely be excused some mild interest in her friend's place of work – or perhaps this interest had seemed to Gabriel like impertinence. He wasn't usually so... tetchy. It was weird to meet Father Christmas in a bad mood.

Then the old gentleman smiled a proper smile. Jane relaxed. Their encounter must have interrupted some attempt of his to recall more dialect words, or dream up more tall tales, for the entertainment of such visitors as came to Combe Tollbridge. Visitors and their money were always welcome in a small village so far from the usual West Country tourist trail, whose population grew ever smaller as younger generations drifted away to the town.

Jane and Jasper, happy to move away from the bright lights towards Combe Tollbridge, had fully embraced working from home. They relished the calmer lifestyle their move had achieved, gladly accommodating themselves to the sluggish habits of electronic communication in the neighbourhood. Jasper had seriously considered the merits of promoting Tollbridge as the latest Digital Detox haven, but Jane pointed out that as things currently stood the village would doubtless be overwhelmed in the general stampede: they must find some scheme with rather more balance. Meanwhile, let Gabriel, Mike and the others strut their tourist-trapping stuff at a rather more manageable pace.

Now Gabriel smiled at his young friend, his black eyes twinkling under bushy white brows. 'Sunshine? And high time too, midear. If such powerful sladdery weather was to hold up much longer, why, they pesky stares – that'd be starlings to you, young Jane – they'd grow webs to their feet and be diving in the river after fish, so cunning as any shag – which in more civilised talk you'd say, a cormorant.'

Relieved that it was nothing she'd done that had upset him, Jane risked a pleasantry. 'It's rather early in the day for tourists, though of course I don't mind if you want to practise on me – but do let me show you.' She reached in her bag for her camera. 'It just happened to catch my eye – look, isn't this a comical shape? Almost like a man's head, at first, but then some more thatch came out and if you turn it sideways…'

She adjusted the camera and Gabriel peered at the little screen as the images scrolled past, nodding politely as she discoursed on various ideas that were starting to develop.

'You could do worse than have further speech with my grandson,' he said as she ran out of breath. Christopher Hockaday was building a reputation for excellence in wildlife and nature photography, and in a recent international competition his bird pictures had come runner-up to acknowledged genius. Combe Tollbridge and Combe Ploverton, where most inhabitants were cousins in a greater or lesser degree to at least half the rest, deemed in these circumstances second place equal to an outright win. His grandparents were not alone in their pride at this local boy making good.

Jane was about to agree, when it struck her. 'Oh dear – Chris! Yes, of course – but I keep forgetting...' Again she put away her camera; it was clear she was now eager to be off. 'When I came out early on purpose! Do excuse me, but I want to catch the light before the sun gets right above the cliff. Full sun's too bright to see how the river fans out into the harbour and stains it with everything washing down from the moor. Last time Chris dropped by we saw those marvellous images he'd got with his drone. He's so good at seeing things – that clever way he *looks* – and I promised myself I'd try for something similar, with paint – only I do have to see it in real life first.'

Gabriel's whiskers quivered as his broad grin broadened. It was of course his grandson's right to have his work admired, and doubly right when it was an artist all the way from London – but by Tollbridge standards this former townie was indeed up early, and Gabriel thought it only fair to return the compliment. 'Ah, he's a clever boy – yet no more so than you, midear, if you take my proper meaning, as o'course you do. Such as they clever drawings you made on behalf of Susan and the rest, if we're to speak of – well, of tourists.'

For all her wish to be away, Jane had to grin back. Local author Susan Jones, between books and in collaboration with Jane (scenes from history) and Chris (photos of the present) was slowly refurbishing the series of Local Interest booklets produced years ago by Tollbridge's small printery. Susan was known to a large and admiring readership as bestseller Milicent Dalrymple; Jane and Chris still had their names to make, but all three professional creatives gave their services at no cost. Printer Sam Farley asked nothing beyond basic expenses for paper and ink. The pub, post office and bakery gladly found room for a display box or revolving stand, and did not grudge the space; village elders, when time permitted, would lurk at the harbour looking picturesque, having brushed up on local history, folklore and the more respectable words and phrases of local dialect. The greater the number of visitors who came to Combe Tollbridge and found the experience worthwhile, the bigger the boost to general funds.

'Mmm,' said Jane. 'Yes, tourists – well, I'm glad you approve of what we've done so far. But if you don't mind, I'll leave you to your rehearsal.' Thinking it a good exit line, with a laughing wave she hurried away, while he laughed with her before making for the cottage he shared with his wife Louise. The Hockadays had been married long enough to justify a Local Interest leaflet of their own. Louise, he was sure, would be as pleased as himself that young Jane thought so highly of their Chris.

Young Jane had resolved that nothing and nobody else should further distract her from reaching the end of the breakwater, where worn stone steps rose to the top of the protecting wall on which a sturdy metal lattice supported the harbour entrance light, accessible via a rather less sturdy ladder. From time to time, blown bulbs needed changing; after severe storms glass, obscured by windblown salt, must be cleaned. To perform either task required not only agility, but also a steady head for heights.

Jane was endowed with both, and knew that there was space – barely, but enough – by the lantern for her to stand and take photos. No, call them reference shots, which sounded better. She knew she was no Chris Hockaday, waiting hours to capture the perfect photographic image: it was only a general impression she was after. True inspiration came once she put pencil to paper, which common sense and channel breezes would make impossible until she descended the lantern ladder to the shelter of the breakwater wall.

She hurried on down Stickle Street and turned into Harbour Path, another car-and-a-half wide lane that came to a sudden end, though not at a riverbank but a cliff wall. In the shadow of the cliff squatted Trendle Cottage, which overlooked the turning circle worn by decades of people who either hadn't believed or hadn't observed the road signs that warned of a No Through Road. Jane and Jasper had rented Trendle for a few months before their move to Clammer Cottage. They'd been dismayed by the number of drivers with apparently poor eyesight who couldn't even manage a respectable three-point turn when required.

A curious sound – whine? whistle? – erupted nearby, accompanied by a light, rhythmic rattle. Jane shook her head, stared round, saw nothing, and walked on. Cliffs, cottages and corners made Tollbridge a misleading echo-trap. Sound carries over water. Might this be some new kind of marine engine? In the distance a fishing boat was heading for harbour, but this seemed an unlikely source. Perhaps – she glanced up – it was an experimental helicopter from HMS *Whirlybird*, the 'stone frigate' further along the coast? Fleet Air Arm pilots with a sense of humour might think an unusual 'buzz' at this hour an amusing way to wake retired submariner Captain Rodney Longstone, who lived close by. A scandalous and very embarrassing divorce had encouraged the captain to leave the service early, but some of his peers not only continued to serve, but also knew his address.

Yet nothing but gulls currently flew anywhere near Combe Tollbridge. The sound stopped. The rattle pattered to silence.

Jane shrugged, and hurried on.

All she heard now above the waves was the song of the river, pouring from Exmoor to the sea across the clattering shingle. Tollbridge shingle is less famous than Chesil Beach, and while sharing the name insists on spelling it 'chezell'. Unlike its Dorset counterpart the beach is overhung by tall cliffs, and washed by the waters of two rivers, the larger Chole and its smaller sister Rindan.

One bank of the Rindan is precipitous, the other merely steep. Only on the steep bank was it possible to construct the modest homes of Meazel Cleeve, yet another ultimate dead end that, just beyond the home of Captain Longstone, vanished into the tangled woods above the tiny Rindan Valley. Angela Lilley, part-time museum curator, rented a cottage halfway up the cleeve and said that living there beat any gym subscription for keeping fit.

Jane heard a different sort of clatter, and a muttered oath.

This was too much. She swerved in her course to look over the rough harbour wall. Bright eyes above a splendid set of auburn whiskers smiled up at her from the chezell piled by the storms of many years high above the tideline.

'Morning, midear! You'm up bright and early.' Mike Binns brandished a black-and-silver box as he waved at her.

She remembered Gabriel Hockaday. 'Well, I'm not the only one.'

'No, but tidn like you in the general way. Nothing wrong, I hope?'

'Oh, no, everything's fine, thank you.'

'No need to thank me, midear. I had nothing to do with it!' He chuckled richly.

Evidently he was in one of his more mischievous moods. 'Thank you for asking, is what I meant. Appreciating a nice, neighbourly gesture.'

'No offence.' Again he waved the black-and-silver box. 'Taking advantage of the dry weather, no doubt, for at a guess you've your sketching gear in that bag you carry.'

'Ye-es – but I think I've left it a little late to catch the view I wanted.' To retreat from a second village elder, so soon after leaving the first, would be a poor return for the courtesy and many kindnesses she'd known since her first visit to Tollbridge, as a child. 'Once the sun's over Cliddon Hill there's too much dazzle on the water – too many reflections. Shall I take a few snaps of you, instead? What are you doing, anyway?'

'Taking advantage of the dry weather,' said Mike, with another chuckle. 'Same as you.'

He gestured to his feet, where something bright green and yellow was half-hidden by his boots. 'From Mickey, and only arrived yesterday for all he put the order in at least a month ago.' He beamed. 'My birthday present.'

Jane replied warily. 'It – it doesn't look very much like a drone.' All Tollbridge had heard the hints dropped by the old gentleman to his son (and any other interested parties) from the day news of Chris Hockaday's inclusion on the competition shortlist reached his family. Michael Binns, Senior was a born inventor, tinkerer and enthusiast for technology even when he didn't fully understand it. He held that instruction manuals, carefully read, could reasonably inform a sensible man as well as any expert – and having thus informed himself, he would proceed to engineer improvements that few experts would have imagined possible. Sometimes they worked, sometimes they didn't, but Mike and his son Mickey always had fun thinking things through.

'No, tidn a drone,' agreed Mr Binns. 'More a consolation prize, me having realised at long last I'm getting too old for this modern world.' He gave his audience no time to utter the cheery disclaimer he would normally expect. 'Can you credit it? Every idea I'd had for making better use of a drone than photographs – which idn to talk down young Chris, by no means – but I cottoned to the whole notion far too late, and that's the truth. No matter what I'd thought of, someone else had thought of it first, though 'twas the lost dog that finally made me see sense and Mickey, he had to agree.'

It must have been one of the few occasions when the younger Binns had succeeded in deflecting his father from anything on which he'd set his heart. Jane was impressed, but puzzled. 'I haven't heard of anyone losing a dog,' she began.

'No, not here, 'twas in the paper backalong.' Mike, born and raised a Cockney, was evacuated at an impressionable age from London at the start of World War Two, adapting to his new life with no regrets. 'Didn you spot the story, midear? On television, too. I forget where it happened, but the poor thing was frightened by fireworks where fireworks had no business to be – children bunking off school, so 'twas said – and she panicked, and bolted, and couldn be found for days, poor thing.' Mike Binns was very much a dog lover.

'Poor thing,' echoed Jane. 'How awful! What happened?'

'Maybe 'twas the Norfolk Broads.' He frowned. 'Somewhere marshy underfoot, a nature reserve and few paths, so that the wildlife shouldn't be disturbed, though in such a case they'd have made an exception, only she kept running further towards the sea – or it may have bin the river – and hungrier by the hour, which is how they got her in the end.'

Jane was shocked. 'They waited till she was too weak to run?'

He chuckled. 'They found where she lay hid, and took a chunk of the richest, most characterful sausage the local butcher could supply, and tied it to a long piece of string and let it hang from a drone. And then a park warden with binoculars guided that drone with its tasty morsel right over that little dog's nose until they'd roused her interest, and they tempted her to follow that smell right to the spot where her owner was waiting!'

He beamed, nodding at Jane, who looked as pleased by the happy outcome as he could have wished. 'But,' he went on, 'for all it's a smart notion, I doubt it's one I'd ever think of myself. I'm a practical man, requiring some foundation for building my ideas, not hope for them to come out of the blue – and a sausage on a string needs the sort of brain such as I know I don't possess.' He paused. 'A man has to know his limitations, and must accept them.'

This last was said in so meaningful a tone that Jane knew it was her job to draw him out. 'I can't imagine you or Mickey being limited by – well, by anything. Not once you've found out all about it—'

'Aha!' The crow of triumph told her she'd been right. 'Once we've found out, you say. Very true, midear – which is why you find me here, ensuring that when the time comes for me to reveal this-here scrambling device to the world, I'm able to show sufficient skill not to make three kinds of fool of myself.' He sniffed. 'Unlike some folk, who'd try to make a man run afore he can walk – or be a damsight too eager to try running on their own account.'

Light dawned. Gabriel Hockaday's mild tantrum was explained. Father Christmas had no doubt accompanied his brother-in-law to the harbour that morning, seizing the earliest opportunity to play with the birthday present – and Mike hadn't played fair. Small children were taught they must share their toys, but those approaching second childhood didn't always hold to this teaching, especially when there was a remote control in hand.

The spring-green and sunshine-yellow Scrambler Tank was a popular electronic toy with caterpillar tracks, multiple arms and a powerful motor. The Scrambler ate batteries for breakfast, but its fans ignored the cost and rushed to buy each new upgrade as it came on the market. A village further up the coast had this year organised a race meeting on its long, sandy beach bringing punters and spectators by the thousand – and a noticeable boost to community funds.

Mike Binns was only starting to learn how to control his new toy on chezell, a very different prospect from driving the thing on smooth golden sand. Having his brother-in-law hovering to give advice no better than guesswork wouldn't take long to annoy him. Small wonder Gabriel showed signs of temper when Jane met him in Hempen Row – but at least the delay as they chatted had given Mike time to calm down before their own encounter.

'I know Jasper joked about hanging an aerial from a drone to make the internet faster, but I'm glad you didn't take him seriously.' Or had he? Jasper, egged on one night in the pub by local entrepreneur Barnaby Christmas, after a second mug of scrumpy (only genuine locals could cope with three) had discoursed at length on the benefits and requirements of modern technology. The high cliffs and deep valleys of Combe Tollbridge make cyberspace accessible only through broadband which, squeezed into vintage telephone wires, is likened by its (few) users to swimming in treacle. WiFi is little more than a word. While most of Tollbridge remains happy to live without technology, it is generally agreed that one day, when funds allow, a trench might be dug and a cable laid of whatever length and quality will be needed to bring the village into the twenty-first century. One day.

Nobody knows how Barney Christmas made his millions, but having once made them this son of Tollbridge came home to retire. Soon he grew bored. When Jasper Merton arrived from London, Barney recognised in the founder of the small but well-regarded Packlemerton's Publicity a kindred spirit, though there was more than half a century between them; and after a wary start they warmed to each other. Jane wondered if Mr Christmas might be lonely. In more ways than the financial he'd clearly outgrown his fellows, few of whom had moved for long in the outside world. Tales of Barney's achievements must sound more like boasting than the gleeful reminiscence the Londoners could understand.

Mike looked thoughtfully at his companion. 'Now you bring it to mind, I reckon there'd be no particular harm in asking Chris if such a thing could be done—'

'Please don't!' begged Jane. 'I was joking, too!' Then she saw the gleam in his eye and smiled, ruefully. 'And I do know what you mean about limitations.' She waved the bag she carried. 'Chris Hockaday's photos are something special, and although I find it inspiring I couldn't hope to do anything like his work, even with a top-flight camera. Of course I use a camera, but it's nowhere near as smart – anyway, I'm far more comfortable with paper and paint. Each to his – her – own, is my motto.'

'Feet on the ground,' Mike agreed, laughing again. 'Or me, feet on deck – save that this morning they're Mickey's.' He pointed out to sea, where the distant fishing boat had all the time been coming closer. 'I'm waiting for him to fetch in the *Priscilla* with whatever the pots might hold, then he's to get ready for another fishing party while his poor old dad does the selling. The van's already down at the Anchor, then if nobody's waiting from the village I'll be upalong to the Pig, and beyond if Tom Tucker don't buy what's left of today's catch.'

Tom Tucker was the landlord of Ploverton's Slandered Pig, an ancient hostelry thatched at correct intervals by local experts, whose expertise added, on the roof-ridge, a straw 'dolly' in the form of a lordly porker. Jan Ridd, landlord of Tollbridge's Anchor, silently regretted that his own pub was roofed in slate. Each time the Pig's thatch or the dolly had to be renewed, Jan was quick to have his inn sign repainted.

'Busy, busy.' Jane admired the old gentleman's stamina. 'Will you be joining him tomorrow? Mickey, I mean. I suppose it depends on how many anglers are in the party?'

'Tidn a day for the minibus, so unless Jerry's any taxi-driving to do he'll be out with his cousin to help keeping an eye on the townies. I might go along, might not. Depends.'

Which Jane interpreted as, he hoped that by tomorrow his differences with Gabriel were sorted and the two old salts could be at their favourite harbourside spot, looking picturesque as ever, telling tall stories to such tourists as might appear, and accepting tips without even the hint of a blush.

Chapter Two

Mike bent to pick up the Scrambler Tank, set it straight, walked a few yards in the direction of the slipway and fiddled with the control box. He turned, pointed the aerial, and adjusted something else. The green-and-yellow toy began to stir. There came again the same strange sound that first alerted Jane to the invisible presence over the wall so early in the morning: the eldritch whine of the motor, the mysterious accompanying rattle.

Many-jointed arms opened their claws to snatch at smooth, heavy pebbles, but were too slow to take proper hold. Mike muttered; Jane held her breath. The claws slid and fumbled; then the motor whined less harshly and the caterpillar track at last began to roll in synch with the claws. Jane relaxed. For a few moments from her vantage point on the road she could admire the Scrambler's trundling passage down the beach... until it reached a spot where wind or tide, or both, had piled the chezell in uneven mounds it didn't seem to like.

It struggled, tipped up and fell on its side, tracks churning, arms waving, claws groping.

'Damnation!' cried Mike.

Inwardly Jane rolled her eyes: boys of any age took their toys so seriously. 'Hey, language,' was all she said aloud, knowing she must say something. 'Look, I'll leave you to it. You won't want to be bothered with photographs now.'

'That-there brochure,' said the exasperated Mike, 'and being a practical man I've studied it with care – that brochure holds to it there's no difficulty with rough ground, grass, a bit of a hill – but it stayed silent on the matter of pebbles rounded by the sea.' He sighed. 'I'd thought we might try a tournament of our own here. Races on the beach, handicap according to size, prizes – a bit of fun sure to encourage folk to visit. The Chezell Challenge was what I had in mind for a name, but now I've serious doubts.' He shook his head. 'Seems that close by the sea a sandy surface has to be the preference, or anyhow smaller pebbles than Tollbridge chezell – and laying overall a sight less bumpy than this.'

'Shells, you mean?' Jane had consulted various guidebooks before the move from London, and was thinking now of one place in particular.

'Woolacombe.' Mike knew the same place. 'Barricane Beach. Mickey went with the Sunday School as a child, and it helped sparking his interest in geological doings – but a fisherman has little time to gallivant, midear. One day, maybe, I'll visit, but when all's said and done it's nought but shells, carried across the ocean from the West Indies, smashed small by the journey and the tide and rocks that surround the bay. No doubt it makes an uncommon sight to bring the trippers, but tidn here, is it?'

Then he brightened. 'Up and down Stickle Street, now that'd make a grand race-track had we sufficient numbers to put on a good show! Your Jasper would have his chance to spread the word, and there'd have bin visitors by the score.' His eyes gleamed.

'But if you race on the public highway you could hardly call it the Chezell Challenge, could you? And then what a waste of a catchy title. We'll have to put our thinking caps on and come up with something to fit.'

'Glad you like it.' She didn't know if her words had pleased or peeved him. 'No sense in the might-have-been, however – and Mickey's almost here.' The little fishing boat had chugged past the narrow breakwater and was slowing as she neared the beacon at the entrance to Tollbridge's tiny harbour. Before very long, Mickey Binns would be securing M.V. *Priscilla Ornedge* against the short stone pier to unload his catch. 'I'll get across,' said Mickey's father, 'and meet him by the van. You want to come along with your camera?'

'If you don't mind. But if you're going to be in a hurry—'

'Ah, life's too short to waste in hurrying.' He cleared his throat. 'No sense to be out of breath with rushing, being all too soon you're out of breath for good.' He grinned up at her. 'What you might call, a thought for the day. Reckon 'twill do?'

'Well enough. You could always have a sideline in Christmas cracker mottos.'

'And so I might.' Mike Binns didn't mind being teased by a personable young woman. 'Wait you there, midear, while I gather my traps, and then we'll be on our way.'

Jane went to meet him at the top of the breakwater slipway, waiting in quiet sympathy as he stumped glumly towards her over the municipally-flattened area of chezell that had proved too great a challenge for the Scrambler Tank. Strangers to Combe Tollbridge, with its huddled cottages, narrow lanes and cramped corners, always had to ask where cars might be parked. The official choice lay between going 'back up roundabout' to the unsurfaced Watchfield car park on the headland, or driving down Harbour Path to the slipway and the stretch of chezell that, twice a year, was levelled by a county council bulldozer. Between times, Tollbridge called in favours from farming cousins in Ploverton who had tractors.

But (the timid visitor might enquire) isn't the Bristol Channel notorious for its high tides? Surely there's some risk my car will be washed away?

The reply was always dramatic, but ultimately positive. The village wanted to encourage visitors, not scare them away before they'd spent any money. 'High tides? Famous, they are, second highest in the world, twice a day so regular's any clock – but the most notable wave this region has seen was back in the days of Robinson Crusoe!' Knowing laughter. 'And the man who wrote about *him* likewise wrote a famous book about that same great storm, hundreds of years long since. More-and-so, in these modern times we've the weather forecast to warn of coming trouble, not forgetting tide tables, for sale in Farley's shop, should you wish to check for yourselves, though you've no particular cause for concern – always excepting the gulls.' A rueful look into the busy, quarrelsome sky; a jerked thumb, a chuckle. 'But they dratted birds fly over the Watchfield, too. Your paint's at risk no matter where you choose to park! Still, you've nothing to pay in either place. Time and to spare to enjoy yourselves with no worries.'

Gabriel Hockaday and Mike Binns, the most successful double act in Tollbridge, were often asked to pose for selfies with tourists who'd been reassured by their cheerful patter and had swallowed, with willing suspension of disbelief, even their tallest tales. Jane smiled to herself as, camera at the ready, she and Mike made for the pier and *Priscilla Ornedge*. Any little coolness between the brothers-in-law never lasted: they'd be back at their old tricks this afternoon, probably, once Mike had returned from selling the day's surplus catch to the Slandered Pig, or wherever. He might even inveigle Mr Hockaday into joining him on his travels to help with the fetching and carrying.

'Let's hope they've done well,' she said aloud.

'Not too bad,' said Mickey Binns to her enquiry, after greetings had been exchanged. 'The usual, of course – a couple of fine lobsters to suit Tabitha Ridd...' The Anchor's landlady had a jealously-guarded family recipe renowned through the twin villages. 'That bass I'll ask you to take straight to Tom Tucker,

Dad. The Ridds can have first refusal on everything else, but Dora wants to try out a way she's been told of baking them in salt – from young Angela, I believe.'

'Or 'twas maybe her mother.' Mike's air of innocence almost convinced.

'Susan? Never!' Mickey was usually deaf to the teasing of his father in the matter of Milicent Dalrymple, but his silent worship was not blind. As Jane giggled, he roared with laughter. 'You know very well Susan's not half the cook her daughter is – a quarter, if so much! Moreover, she's working on a new idea, she told me the last time we spoke. You know how she battens down the hatches when she's seized with a new idea. There's no time for giving recipes to the Pig, or to anyone else.'

There was a glint in Mike's eye. Quickly Jane changed the subject. 'I wonder if I could get a shot or two of your Scrambler alongside one of the lobsters? For the contrast – nature and technology, both with claws – the old and the new, that sort of thing.'

'Pity they can't run a race.' Mike still lamented his thwarted hopes.

'Just a bit of fun,' begged Jane. 'It wouldn't take long.'

Mickey Binns was happy to oblige the young artist, while Mike kept close watch, offered much advice, and dropped hints about portraits of working fishermen from different generations offering yet another contrast, such as in years and experience.

'And beards,' added Mickey, whose handsome dark whiskers were the gift of his long-dead mother's Huguenot ancestors. Middle age, sea spray and weather had begun tinting those whiskers with frost. Tollbridge frequently debated the odds that Susan Jones might pause from her typing long enough to accept the poor chap before he grew desperate, and a second locked drawer appeared in the Binns bathroom cabinet.

After some minutes of busy snapping and a few afterthought sketches Jane thanked her friends, and headed for Widdowson's

Bakery. Bakers and those they employ start work early, and master baker Evan Evans employed as his assistant Angela Lilley, one-time librarian, part-time museum curator. Angela, recovering from a broken relationship, was Tollbridge's most multi-part employee. Keeping so busy kept her sane, she said. Variety of jobs was the spice of the working life; besides, she needed the money.

'You'm out and about early, midear!' Evan welcomed Jane with a wide smile. 'Coffee? Tea? Hot chocolate?'

'Chocolate, please, and is there any gingerbread? I didn't like to disturb Jasper banging around in the kitchen, when his work kept him up so late last night.'

'You'm well ahead of him this morning.' Evan indicated the sturdy tote bag in which she carried her camera, sketchbook and pencils. The handwoven fabric was a first attempt by Angela, who was also a part-time apprentice to Evan's cousin Miriam. Miriam Evans was an expert textile worker who'd shown Angela how to spin yarn, weave cloth – and cook up natural dyes. Angela would always prefer the cooking of comestibles, but agreed (eventually) with Miriam that you did get used to the smell of colour.

Since moving to Combe Tollbridge and making new friends, Angela had left London and most of her previous life behind. It had helped greatly that, after a shaky start, she'd always managed to keep busy and earn money, though finances remained tight and it fretted her that all she could offer her friends in the way of thank-you gifts were home-made cakes, sweets and handicrafts.

Angela was too modest. Her break with the treacherous Paul might have shattered her confidence, but she was a better cook now than she'd ever been and her cakes were making a name for themselves locally. Evan Evans wouldn't have said he was worried there might be any threat to Widdowson's Bakery, but having chatted once or twice with her he did the sensible thing and offered Angela a part-time job. The recipe for Widdowson's gingerbread was as closely guarded as that for Tabitha Ridd's celebrated lobster. With her first bite Angela correctly identified the secret ingredient as liquorice, and when Evan bet her she couldn't work out the exact proportions of what he knew as 'lickerdish' she had accepted the bet – and won.

Angela herself now appeared from behind the huge oven installed almost two centuries before by the son of the original widow. She dusted her hands and smiled at her friend.

'Morning! You're up with the lark, like us!' She turned to Evan. 'The timer's set, the cooling racks are ready. Okay to go home and start the rest of the day?'

'Suits me, so long as you'm here again same time tomorrow.' He gestured to the plate and mug he was preparing for Jane. 'Young madam here's asked for gingerbread with her chocolate and you know how 'tis, once the first slice is cut then the rest follows in a twink. Mickey Binns has another party booked tomorrow and there'll be the shop to manage, too.'

Angela was being given the choice: another early start, or— 'Would you like me to bake a couple at home this afternoon and bring them in tomorrow? At a more civilised hour? I'd hate Mickey's anglers to starve, but I can't face two dawns on the trot.'

The baker winked at Jane. 'Drives a hard bargain, your friend.'

'Will it make things better or worse if I take a slice home for Jasper?' Jane handed over the money, smiled, and produced the camera. 'Angela, I know there's nothing to be done just yet, and the sheet-iron gives some protection but for how much longer nobody seems to know... Well, the birds have been at the museum thatch again. I wondered if you'd like a print of this to help persuade the committee to put it higher up the list of – of whatever's in line for a share of Prue Budd's legacy.' Living now in the late Mrs Budd's cottage, knowing how much she and Jasper had paid for it, well aware that the old lady's will bequeathed her entire estate to be used for the good of the community, Jane thought that the village elders were taking far too long to make even the smallest decision.

'Huh.' Evan peered over Angela's shoulder. 'You know what's said of a camel? 'Tis a horse designed by a committee. And cooks? Too many of 'em will spoil anyone's broth. Now, had old Prue, bless her, only made her wishes more exact, so there could at least be priorities settled, we might yet live to see the old meeting-house roof made good – or a new lifeboat shed, with a new boat to go in it—'

'Or a new village hall,' suggested Jane quickly, with a sideways look at Angela. Evan's views on committees and Authority, if allowed free rein, were known to be expansive.

'Hall?' He didn't make the connection at first. 'Oh, yes – well, some folk say that's a rather different case, seeing how 'twas after Prue died the Jubilee Hall burned down.'

'And thanks to Angela that it wasn't worse,' said Jane. 'If she hadn't raised the alarm when she did—'

'More thanks to Rodney Longstone,' broke in Angela with a faint blush, looking up from her absent-minded scroll through the other photos on Jane's camera. Mobile phones (as phones) didn't work in Combe Tollbridge, and at the time of the fire the cottage Angela had just begun renting hadn't acquired a landline. Captain Longstone lived a few doors away and was an established resident: she'd felt sure he would have a landline, and he had. The captain praised her quick thinking when she raised the alarm and went at once to action stations, leaving her breathless in his wake as he helped coordinate rescue efforts in the next valley, halfway up Cliddon Hill. Angela had been impressed by his quiet efficiency, and wanted Tollbridge to give him all due credit.

Neatly deflected, Evan prepared to cut and bag a second slice of gingerbread. 'Thanks due to both, midear. You, young

Angela, for being so poor a sleeper that night – and the cap'n, for being a man of orderly mind and quick thinking. Doubtless from living so long in a submarine, but he always seems to know what to do.'

'And does it,' said Angela. 'I had no idea there even was an Octopus pump, but the captain knew at once to warn Gabriel and everyone else, and they did the rest.'

'Teamwork,' said Jane, sipping chocolate. 'You can't beat it.'

Evan snorted. 'A committee's no team, just a load of talk. More-and-so, th'old pump's put out so many blazes large and small over the years, it could near as ninepence find its own way to the river and let down its own hoses. But working together to pump water or carry buckets when the need's immediate idn the same as a party of folk gathered round a table jangling over every little point that's raised for their consideration, taking all the time in the world to make up their minds – which even when they do, they still don't do aright.'

Jane and Angela exchanged glances. Evan, in general a genial old party, from time to unexpected time was prompted to recall his long-ago clash with the county council's planning department. Inheriting Widdowson's Bakery from a relative too old to recognise its commercial potential, Evan had applied for the relevant official permissions. After a wait of several months and the completion of far too much paperwork, a newly promoted officer arrived to admit, grudgingly, that there should be no difficulty (subject to Health and Safety regulations) in adding a small table and some chairs, but now that he'd seen the oven door at the back of the shop (which had not – and why not? – been mentioned on any of the forms submitted by Mr Evans) this was an ironwork masterpiece of obvious historic importance. Mr Evans was on no account to replace it, and certainly not permitted to sell it.

Mr Evans growled that he had no intention of selling the oven door. He'd seen no need to mention it because, why should he? This was a working bakery, and a bakery's oven was in use every day and needed its door 'as any but a born fool did ought to know!'

'There's no need for insults, Mr Evans—'

'So who began it? Telling me not to sell what's my own when I'd never a mind to do so in the first place! I'll allow it to be a handsome – a very handsome – piece, which my intention was to display to best advantage once I've found a match for the damaged tiles, but these days tidn so easy and I've better things to do with my time.' The oven's brickwork boasted a spectacular surround of dark green, finely glazed painted tiles embossed with ears and sheaves of wheat. 'And any half-hearted affair would be wrong for the look of the thing. I'd soonder have it stay chipped and crackled as buy any cheap modern doings.'

'You can't do that! You must use the original supplier.'

'Gone out of business fifty year since, give or take.'

'There must be others.'

'None in these parts. Think I've not made enquiries? I'm not daft – unlike some.'

The planning officer struggled with his better nature. Despite that recent promotion his better nature won, and the skirmish had no serious consequences: even some long-term benefits. Evan's modest tea-and-buns corner kept its licence. In warm weather a few extra chairs might spill over into the Legger, but a tactfully blind official eye was always turned. The Legger was a crooked lane with a No Through Road sign at its Stickle Street entrance. It was so narrow there was no room for any footway, and only strangers tried to negotiate its corners in a car: trying to do this had been the planning officer's original mistake. He and Evan Evans both learned something from their brief, but memorable, encounter.

Angela paused in her scrolling to chuckle. 'I'd rather cook that lobster than waste time racing it against that green and yellow spider thing. Whatever can it be?'

'Mike Binns's birthday present.' Evan had the answer before Jane could draw breath. 'Worth more than any lobster, I'll wager, him being disappointed of the drone on account of others proving far more ingenious ahead of him. So Mickey said he'd happily lash out with a similar sum of money so long as his father didn expect no more'n a token gift at Christmas, and Mike was entirely agreeable.'

'Oh, by Christmas Mickey will have forgotten and buy something splendid,' said Angela.

'Of course he will,' said Jane.

'He's a good son,' said Evan, who was unmarried. 'Always looks out for his dad, Mike being inclined to be carried away with new ideas. But Mickey can handle him. Told him it was for his own sake he'd rather he didn buy a stunt kite, when they were very much on the telly, but Mickey said he'd not know a minute's peace for fearing the line would tangle round Mike's feet and break his leg, or round his neck and throttle him, or pull him over the top of the headland and wash him out to sea.'

His audience laughed.

'And it worked?' said Jane.

'So what did he buy instead?' asked Angela.

'A ride in a hot air balloon, with photographs in an album. Mickey's a good son,' repeated Mr Evans, looking at Angela. 'A decent chap – a great pity his marriage didn work out.' The younger Mr Binns had grown weary of travelling the world with the geologist wife he'd met at university. After several years of peripatetic togetherness, she had wanted to keep on moving while Mickey began to feel it was time to settle down. The parting was amicable and, a true son of Combe Tollbridge, he'd been happy enough with his career change from mining engineer to fisherman. Regarding matrimony, he always said he kept an open mind but if he found the right person...

Tollbridge explored various ways of hinting to Angela that she might one day find herself with a stepfather. Susan Jones was known to have lost her husband so young that Angela didn't remember him. Susan was very well-liked; Mickey Binns, all agreed, was a very likeable chap. Angela, while anti-man herself at the moment, when pressed would say that Mickey and her mother were both old enough to make up their own minds, and that she planned to let them.

'It's a great pity,' she now said firmly, 'when anyone's marriage – or relationship – fails to work out, but these things happen.'

'They certainly do. Life's rich tapestry, and all that.' Jane retrieved her camera with a smile. 'Talking of relationships, Gabriel and Mike seem a bit cross with each other this morning. When I was taking photos in Hempen Row Gabriel was nothing like as bright as usual, or anyway not to start with – and then, down by the breakwater Mike was dropping hints I thought it much better to ignore.'

Evan laughed. 'Won't let him play is all, midear. Honest, like a couple of chillern they two can behave sometimes, and both old enough to know better – but 'twill soon blow over. That pair have bin thick as thieves and falling out again since childhood.' Their first falling out, in Mike's first week at school, had seen the older Gabriel trounce the young upstart Binns for cheek but, pleased with his cock-sparrow chirpiness, swearing eternal friendship; the friendship was crowned by a double wedding when the two married the dark-haired and popular Jerome sisters, Louise and Marguerite. Marguerite's death in childbirth had devastated Mike Binns, but with Gabriel's help and support he had survived.

'Soon blow over,' said Evan again, to allay any possible concern.

'Oh, I know, but you're right, it's just like children. What's the betting Gabriel will want a Scrambler Tank of his own, if Mike doesn't give in quick!'

'How soon is his birthday?' asked Angela.

'Who – Gabriel?' Evan stared, then chuckled. 'Why, Louise would never consent to give him anything o' the sort. She'd say 'twas only to spoil the man and make him soft! Five chillern – five sons, all needing boots and clothes, appetites like young horses – that's no encouragement towards softness and spoiling when money's tight, as it was – and such a habit as folk find hard to break, in later life. No, Louise wouldn allow it.'

'A box of chocolates,' suggested Jane idly.

'Or toffees, if his teeth aren't a problem,' said Angela.

Chuckling again, Evan nudged his assistant in the ribs. 'I'd recommend a few peppermint creams, to Prue Budd's special recipe!' Though the old lady took her culinary secrets with her to the grave, after some trial and error Angela had successfully reproduced the recipe for peppermint creams to general satisfaction. Angela wasn't slow to acknowledge the benefit of living halfway up the steep Meazel Cleeve, and dashing from part-time job to part-time job: for all her enthusiastic testing – and tasting – her weight had remained almost the same.

'O'course,' added the old man with a wink, 'I'm not so sure how Captain Longstone, for one, might take to that particular notion.'

'I'll make double the amount that week, if I'm asked,' was all Angela said in reply.

Chapter Three

The little van was ancient but roadworthy: like all fishermen, Mike and Mickey Binns knew about engine maintenance and emergency repair. As owners they did most of the work, but in Tollbridge work was often a family affair. The Hockadays shared the fishing, just as Mike and Mickey shared the driving of minibus or taxi, while anyone who could mucked in with spanners, wrenches and skilled brute force as required. M.V. *Priscilla Ornedge* was a stately old lady, even older than the busy little van.

Gabriel Hockaday's middle son Jerry, short for Jerome, had a keen sense of colour and a generous hand with a spray gun. His mother Louise, defying arthritis, walked with the aid of a hollow-handled thumbstick, in which she carried a small flask of brandy 'in case I might fall'. Jerry had sprayed the stick, at her request but his suggestion, a lively yellow. 'Should I tumble over in the dark I'll be easier to see,' declared Louise.

Jerry had never liked the dull but trustworthy shade in which the Binns mainly-fish-but-general-carriage-too van had been painted. He said he would accept muted indigo or navy for a taxi 'for dignity, when driving folk to funerals', but insisted on a rich crimson livery for the minibus; he thought that a van selling fish should do so in a more appropriate colour than grey, and kept saying so until Mike Binns, for the sake of family peace, conceded that his nephew might – *might* – just have a point.

This grudging concession was enough for Jerry. Left one day to his own devices by his trusting relatives, who were fishing the Severn Sea with a party of anglers, enthusiasm and temptation got the better of him. On their return, Jerome Hockaday presented Mike and Mickey Binns with a fait accompli.

The little van that now drove from Tollbridge's Anchor to the Slandered Pig in Ploverton was cheerful in sea green and ice blue, and bore an impressive legend. This was neat, clear, and not in the least vulgar; nor was it entirely truthful, but Jerry said he had worked hard, and it looked good, and family was family. They should at least give it a fair chance. It paid to advertise.

Thus it was that into the small yard of the Slandered Pig rumbled a van advertising *Ornedge, Binns and Hockaday – Purveyors of Fresh Fish* in long banners, black letters on white, down each blue side; the doors and bonnet were green. As the Pig's other visitor was the scarlet Post Office van, the yard became bright with colour.

Landlord Tom Tucker was leafing through a sheaf of envelopes, shaking his head. He glanced up, nodded vaguely to Mike as the fisherman brought his van to a halt, and returned to sorting letters while delivering an apparently irritable monologue to the weary postman.

The Slandered Pig, a more venerable building than the Anchor, is not as old as its story, which dates from the fourteenth century. A certain John Doget, known in Ploverton for his short temper, was more than usually short with his neighbours after a storm dragged half the thatch from his roof and destroyed the fence of one Martin Southmoor. Martin's cottage, like many in the village, lost some thatch; Martin's wife had toddler twins, a newborn baby, and an understandably sharp tongue. Repairs to the Southmoor roof were therefore effected more quickly than those to the Southmoor fence – with the result that Martin's pig was caught red-trottered, enjoying a hearty meal at the expense of John Doget, whose plot of land lay next to that of Martin.

The village court had to fine Martin one penny for the broken fence, but said that if within seven days he repaired it and replaced, from his own vegetable patch, the cabbages and onions eaten by the pig – which everyone knew to be ringed according to statute, meaning 'the beast couldn possibly have done so much damage as John Doget claimed' – he would be excused payment. The Southmoor fence was not the only one to have suffered in the storm; more-and-so, the Southmoor baby had suffered worse, being born 'on the very night and still not properly recovered, nor its mother neither.' And 'bad weather being famous for bringing down the goats from the woods and cliffs, who was to say twadn the goats to have grubbed out they roots, rather than Martin's pig?'

Martin's many friends helped with the repairs, and drank deeply in the alehouse to his good health. The manor court rolls for the next session record a fine of sixpence imposed on John Doget for 'slandering a pig belonging to Martin de Southmoor, while he was selling it, whereby he lost the sale' – and a subsequent entry listing fines of one penny each against both Martin and John for common assault after 'a mutual drawing of blood'.

'What these days we'd term a punch-up in the pub,' Tom always said when asked what lay behind the Pig's unusual name. 'And small blame to Martin Southmoor for losing his temper, with Doget forever trying to do him down. More like sympathy, him having paid his dues and the pig unable to speak for herself!' Laughter. 'There's her likeness on the roof and that's the why-for, a commemoration of the slander, woven in reed from each renewal of the thatch down the years – though the alehouse, o'course, be long lost to history.'

'Like the pig,' was usually added by one or other of his audience. 'Can I buy you a drink, landlord?'

Tom would smile his thanks, explain that he must keep a clear head, and suggest instead the purchase of a raised pork pie decorated with a pastry portrait of Martin Southmoor's pig. His wife Isadora made them, and they were highly regarded in the two villages. Vegetarian customers he encouraged to drop coins in the Air Ambulance box; those enquiring about a Lifeboat Fund were encouraged to make their next port of call Ploverton's sister pub the Anchor 'in Combe Tollbridge, down to the coast, where –' a broad smile – 'a lifeboat's a greater requirement than up here.'

This morning Tom was neither smiling nor in the mood for anecdote. Whatever it was he'd been telling the postman had been more serious. At Mike's approach, he thrust the letters in one pocket of the brown canvas apron he always wore in an attempt to disguise his stomach – without success: where big Jan Ridd was mostly muscle, Tom Tucker's bulk hinted at a surfeit of the proverbial brown bread and butter – and he seemed to be making an effort not to scowl at the newcomer.

'Morning, Tom,' said Mike. 'I'll not say *Good morning* as it's evident, to me, that for you it isn't.'

'Morning, Mike.' Tom pulled himself together. 'No, tidn.' He frowned at the postman. 'And I'm so much the more put-about on account of Dora saying at least to take the number of the car, but 'twas such a hurry-skurry day in general, I never did.'

'So now she've got the whip hand of 'ee, Tom.' The postman grinned. 'That is, should she want it – but when did a woman never not want to crow over her man?'

'Not often, I'll grant, though you could say the same of the menfolk, too. Human nature, is all.' Sighing, the landlord plunged his hand back in the apron for his correspondence, shaking the envelopes into a fan. 'You sure you've no more for me in that sack?'

'I'm sure.' Exasperation made him brisk. 'And I'll be on my way, having heard more than sufficient of your complaints.'

Then, turning to leave, he relented. 'Tell Mike about it. He'll maybe find some argument Dora would accept, if required.'

With an airy wave he climbed back in his red van, and skilfully edged past the Binns blue-and-green out into Ploverton's main street.

Mike's curious gaze followed him. 'Trouble?' he enquired.

Tom Tucker sighed again. 'Cheatery. Oh, the trick's known in the trade, and warnings given, but tidn such a thing as I'd thought to see in these parts, being generally quiet, and never have before. Only, Dora's bin saying these past few days, with so many strangers visiting after the helicopter and the crane and the television and reporters, we did ought to have expected it might happen and take precautions...'

When Jane and Jasper Merton, moving to Combe Tollbridge, installed their fibreglass footbridge across the River Chole, the crane hired to manoeuvre the structure in place had fallen over. Two helicopters from HMS *Whirlybird* attended the scene, restoring order in a manner both expert and photogenic. It was the silly season; the crowd of journalists was followed by a rush of trippers. Tollbridge's overspill was to Ploverton's benefit. The positives were many: the negatives were just starting to be understood.

'Oh?' prompted Mike, as Tom paused to shuffle again through his fan of envelopes.

'Cheatery,' reiterated the landlord. 'To be kept watch for in future, but a sad lesson to learn. 'Twas a busy day, like I said. No time for stand and chat – more, take the order and ask who's next; rushed off their feet in the kitchen, too. So in comes a pair, nice and quiet and polite, meal ordered, drinks, all still quiet – then, seems the drink goes to their heads as they empty the bottle, and they fall to bickering. Voices raised. Then he calls for the bill, quick, and his credit card won't pay, and she's well-nigh screeching at him now – which no man of sense would find acceptable, in public, with everyone trying far too hard not to listen but in truth hanging on every word – so he grabs her, gives her a shake and pulls her away, and says he'll send a cheque in the post with something extra for the trouble, and off they drive.' A pause. 'Ten days since, that was, if not more.'

'Oh dear,' said Mike.

'And every morning since, each and every endilope received at this address, the same – postmark, handwriting all known. Nothing slipped tactful under the door, nor through the slit. Dine and dash, that's the name of the game, and enough to make a saint swear!' The landlord fell silent, brooding. He looked at Mike. 'I feel a right fool – but it could've bin far worse. They might've bin four, not just two.'

'Money lost is still money lost – but Dora's a good-hearted soul, with little inclination to bullyrag.' Mike pondered. 'So, then.'

Tom brightened. 'Yes?'

'So, she's just a touch inclined to blame you for not taking the number of the car?'

'I said it was far too busy a day, remember.'

'So you did, which by logic follows Dora had no time for the taking of it, neither. Rushed off their feet in the kitchen, you said, same as the bar. The way I see it, deep down she feels every bit so much of a fool as you – and,' he added hastily as Tom glared – 'and blaming herself likewise, only she don't care to own it. She puts it all on you to – to spread the trouble! A trouble shared is a trouble halved, right? So I say, you both agree to keep better watch from a lesson learned, and remind her of both parties being equal in marriage – for better and worse, as worse this is – and tell her,' Mike drew a deep breath, 'that in my van I've the finest bass waiting the old *Priscilla* ever landed. She'd best get busy cooking it afore the freshness is entirely lost – and help take her mind off of your troubles,' he finished, in a triumphant rush.

* * *

Down in Combe Tollbridge the bell jangled over the door of Farley's General Stores and Post Office. Louise Hockaday, stepping confidently with the yellow thumbstick, entered with a quick glance about her to judge the size of her audience. She had news to impart, and didn't want to waste the first impact on too few people.

Like her schoolfellow Louise, Olive Farley was well into her ninth decade, yet remained Tollbridge's official postmistress. Today Olive was all present and correct, which sometimes she was and sometimes, depending on the weather, she wasn't. One long-ago artificial hip, and two more recent knees, had failed to work as well as everyone had hoped, and there were days when she found it impossible to hobble on her two sticks even as far as the main shop to sit behind the counter and supervise.

Louise, trying not to look smug, raised her thumbstick in greeting as she came in and hardly missed a step at the end of her journey from far-off Hempen Row. The only way poor Olive could move about Combe Tollbridge now was by car.

Also on duty were Olive's twins: divorced Debbie Tucker and widowed Tilda Jenkyns, both very busy. Debbie and Tilda took turn and turnabout between the post office and the shop, where Louise was glad to observe Captain Rodney Longstone, near the sweets. She thought the captain a quiet young man, and polite – he turned as she came in, and raised his hat – and she knew he dropped by every day for his paper and a 'twist' of the ferocious peppermints whose secret recipe, created by Prudence Budd, had after Prue's death been successfully recreated by Angela Lilley, of Evans Gingerbread fame.

Louise would have preferred a larger crowd, but—

'Morning, Louise!' cried Olive. 'You'll never guess what's occurred upalong to the Pig!'

Louise thought quickly. Her glance flicked past Tilda and sideways, to Debbie. Hmm. From Debbie's expression most likely it was through Dora Tucker they'd heard of the cheatery (if such indeed was Olive's meaning) with Tom a cousin to Debbie's ex and, knowing the truth of the breakup, bearing no grudge. Debbie's husband left Ploverton the very day the papers were signed, which showed it was no blame of Debbie's; and if the connection was kept up, family stayed family. Tom Tucker was a friendly chap but, for all he kept a pub, had otherwise small inclination to gossip, especially on the telephone. Dora's tongue had been hung in the middle from birth, more than ready to wag at both ends. Dora, decided Louise, was the one to blame for her stolen thunder.

She did some more quick thinking.

'You mean the dine and dash?' She spoke airily, saw Olive's expression change, and smirked. 'I met Mike Binns back from his rounds, and he told me. Disgraceful. Tidn at all the sort of thing to which we'm accustomed in these parts. On account of so many visitors lately, I don't doubt.'

'Mike Binns?' Olive, balked of her story, had to be affronted at something. 'And how should Mike Binns have aught to say on the matter? Why, tidn five minutes since Tabitha Ridd popped across on her way to the bakery, on account of Evan's phone's playing up, and the Pig unable to get through and Dora naturally thinking, with him serving cakes and drinks, he did ought to be warned to be watchful same as the Anchor.'

So guessing 'Dora' had been right, but that Dora had told the Farleys had been wrong; she'd told the Ridds, who also kept a pub – and no more than fair, to let others know what might happen. Louise looked very pleased with herself. 'Oh, Mike told me he'd just took a fine bass upalong for Dora – to be baked in salt,' she added kindly, in case they didn't know. She cleared her throat to make sure Captain Longstone continued to pay his usual polite attention. 'A salt crust, and flavoured with herbs. Tom said she's bin mad to try, ever since young Angela spoke of it and give her the recipe.'

'Ah.' Olive subsided. After eighty years of petty squabbling she and Louise knew when a point had been decisively won.

'Angela's shaping to be as fine a cook as Dora or Tabitha, in time.' Tilda was keen to pay tribute. She knew it had been Angela's quiet friendship with the former submariner that had encouraged her peppermint experiments. Like many in Tollbridge, Tilda hoped for an appropriate outcome between the two. The age difference wasn't so very great; but it was feared their mutual reserve would need some prompting. Angela probably wouldn't stay anti-man for ever, but might leave any change of heart rather too late for Captain Longstone.

The captain's divorce had made headlines one August – it always puzzled the Farleys that he was happy to buy a daily paper – and Tollbridge, having with the rest of the country devoured and laughed over the scandalous details, found that on his early retirement from the Royal Navy to settle in Baker's Cottage, at the top of Meazel Cleeve, Rodney Longstone was every inch the gentleman they had supposed (from what they'd read) he always was. As for his wife, it was a puzzle why he'd married her in the first place, but no doubt they'd both been very young. News coverage of the time suggested such a woman was never worth all the upset, but you couldn't say that to a man as private as Captain Longstone. Still, by now he ought to know the laughter had long since died away, and all Tollbridge wished him very well indeed.

Debbie Tucker, likewise an innocent party in divorce, was less romantic than her twin and, if asked, would suppose the peppermints had been seen by Angela as a challenge 'same as the gingerbread, for Evan, Evans bet her, and she took him up on it, as would anyone. More-and-so, had she any serious intention towards the cap'n he'd not be in here every day, buying them twists of his. He'd have no need. Angela would give him some for himself each time she mixed another batch for the shop.'

'No, she wouldn't want to do us out of the business.' Tilda always tried to see the best in people. Some might shake their heads at her for being soft beyond common sense, but the loss of her husband at sea, and the village's whole-hearted response, had only reinforced the general optimism she'd shown from childhood.

Now a tactful change of subject seemed wise. There had been hinting enough to the captain for today. 'Do mind yourself around that bucket, Cap'n!' as Rodney Longstone moved along the shelf in search of bread and biscuits. 'Can't have you breaking your neck all through a leak in our roof!'

'Thank you, Mrs Jenkyns.' He glanced down, sidestepped neatly and moved on.

Louise clicked her tongue. 'Loose tiles, Olive? Dear, dear. Well, I'd feared it might be something of the sort when first I sighted that bucket.'

'No great surprise after the last few days,' returned Olive. 'Nor idn our roof the only one to suffer. The wind's bin terrible rough, gusts fit to rattle a body's teeth from their head – but putting up a ladder's heavy work, plus it's finding someone with the time. We're none of us so young and spry as once we were, Louise. And you've your Gabriel to help – sons and grandsons, too – while we're not so fortunate, the three of us here.'

'Well—' Louise began, but Debbie broke in with: 'As if we hadn enough—' and Tilda uttered a quick 'Oh!' looking reproachfully at Louise.

Once an officer in the Royal Navy, always a naval officer. Captain Longstone could see trouble brewing on the lower deck. As he carried his purchases to the till he coughed. So rarely did he involve himself in local affairs that all four ladies at once subsided.

'If,' he said, 'a suitable ladder could be borrowed, Mrs Farley, I'd be glad to help as far as my capabilities allow.' He smiled. 'What a shame the repairs on the fallen chimney are now complete. The last few days of work involved a scaffolding tower, remember – rather more to my taste than a ladder! You see, submariners aren't really used to heights. With us, it's depths.'

He chuckled. Debbie at the till had to smile back, her twin relaxed, and the increasingly scratchy atmosphere became a little smoothed over.

The fallen chimney to which the captain referred had been an incident almost as dramatic as the Mertons' fibreglass clammer, and the helicopter rescue of the overturned crane. In Tollbridge, many cottages are ancient structures built of cob: which is clay that has been puddled thoroughly with straw, then built up in careful layers, and packed firmly as each layer is added to a wall easily three feet thick. A cob wall, properly built, can last for centuries. In mediaeval times smoke from the hearth would dissipate slowly through the roofing thatch, but when chimneys came into fashion they weren't easy to construct through a cob wall. Their huge brick bulk would be added, a fire-resistant afterthought, to the most convenient outside wall: usually at the front of the cottage, crowding narrow horse-and-cart-wide lanes still further. Thick walls and low roofs require a chimney to have height in order to draw properly; for safety, a tall chimney needs a large footprint on the ground.

It is inevitable that certain of these chimneys, erected for the convenience of Tudor and Jacobean cottagers, should five hundred years later find themselves getting in the way of twenty-first-century traffic.

A van driver misjudged a critical manoeuvre near Farley's General Stores. What began as a loud crunch of metal ended up a torrent of demolishing brickwork. Nobody had been hurt but, while the insurance claim had been fairly soon settled, repairs took longer. People with the skills necessary to rebuild such a chimney were in short supply, and only after some spirited nagging on the part of the owner (and rumours of cash in hand) did the edifice stand once more proud and massive in the crooked Legger lane.

'That's very kind of you, Cap'n.' Olive was pleased by the unexpected courtesy. 'Very kind, and thank you, but I reckon us can spare you the bother of a ladder. Tabitha Ridd said she'll get Jan to come over in a bit – only, this morning the delivery's due from the brewery. Being up on a roof's no place for checking paperwork down on the ground.'

'And Tabitha's busy in the kitchen, not wanting interruptions.' Tilda couldn't help herself. 'She said Angela's helping out with the rooms to give her the time, on account of some lobsters Mickey Binns just brought in—'

'—and Tabitha,' broke in Debbie, 'still hoping to keep her special recipe secret! As if that's likely with young Angela around!'

Even Louise joined in the general amusement. Captain Longstone smiled, but said nothing.

Olive felt a little sorry for him. 'Or there's Mickey himself or Mike could help us, if Jan's not able. This afternoon did ought to see it sorted, one way or another, so you've no cause to fret yourself on our account. The bucket's there now more for show, even if –' she glanced at Louise – 'the dratted clinkum-clankum would have driven a body mad. For 'cause, while I may be getting on in life, my hearing's little worse than ever it was – *and* my eyes.' Louise had undergone cataract surgery at the age of seventy-two. It was successful, but had added a point to Olive's side of the invisible score-sheet. Four months later, however, Olive made an unexpected trip to a Minehead optician and came back with reading glasses in an entirely new style. Tollbridge seethed with curiosity and suspicion. The lenses, when she wore them in the shop, looked little different from her old pair, but the arms were far thicker: clumsy, some might think. Was Olive trying to hide that she'd been forced to buy a hearing aid? Oh, the twins might say their mother had sat on her old specs when her knees gave way suddenly – but who apart from them had seen it happen?

When Olive removed her glasses to greet a customer, or to indicate something on a distant shelf, Tollbridge took to whispering. When she managed to reply without hesitation, the village wondered how and when she'd learned lip-reading.

It was Louise who pointed out that Olive found no difficulty in conversing sensibly even when her back was turned. For Christmas that year Mrs Hockaday gave her old friend a handsome and elaborate spectacle chain, in eighteen-carat gold.

The glasses bumped now against the counter as Olive leaned forward, laughter in her voice. 'And just supposing Jan idn able for the job – why, we'll ask young Angela when she expects that friend of hers with the green hair to come calling again!'

More general amusement. The sight of Andromeda ('but I prefer Andy') Marsh, with her motorbike, black leathers and stylish pink-streaked emerald locks pixie-cropped, had startled Tollbridge on the occasion of her first visit. Andy had brought Angela, with basic essentials crammed in the panniers, as a pillion passenger 'home to mother' even though Susan Jones didn't move to Corner Glim Cottage until long after Angela set up house with Paul. Susan lived, very happily, alone; but family was family. Susan's heart ached for her suffering child. She duly accepted her maternal responsibility; and found the acceptance hard. All too soon Milicent Dalrymple was unable to work, while Angela was unable to relax, and kept trying to be helpful. Fortunately it dawned on both parties at about the same time that it suited each far better to live completely independent of the other. Angela moved to Meazel Cleeve, and all was well.

Angela enjoyed her new life in Combe Tollbridge and gladly forgot most of the old, but she didn't entirely forget those friends who'd been most supportive in her hour of need. Andy Marsh soon discovered that the motorway journey was exactly right for her cherished Triumph Bonneville's regular workout, and the self-styled 'Jill Of All Trades' would cheerfully invite herself to stay at The Old Printery and swap a few days of scenery, sea breezes, and good company for the assembling of flat-pack furniture, a little light plumbing, or – with caution and constant googling – medium-hard work out of doors. Flat-dwelling Londoners don't always make the best gardeners.

The owner of Angela's rented cottage was local printer Samuel Farley, who'd found the larger windows of the old coastguard station better suited to his growing business. Bachelor Sam had been very helpful to Tollbridge's newest inhabitant, and his cousin Tilda at once began to cherish hopes on his behalf, but before friendliness had a chance to blossom the young man, dropping by his former home to collect the rent, met Andromeda Marsh balanced on a plastic crate, fixing a wobbly bracket on the downstairs curtain rail.

The village, having discussed this meeting at some length, finally agreed that it might be all to the good. Sam, as a child, had been thought 'overmuch inclined to devilment' and even now was 'maybe still a touch too spirrity' for Angela, who (even when you got to know her better) could hardly be thought outgoing – very like the captain, indeed, though it was wonderful how he seemed to be emerging from his shell since Susan Jones's daughter came to Tollbridge.

'Ah yes, Miss Marsh.' Rodney Longstone, packing away his purchases in a neat canvas tote, smiled a general farewell. 'Is that enterprising and delightful young lady coming to visit her friend Angela?' The smile broadened. 'That's good news, though she, too, dislikes ladder-work, she told me once. I do hope your problem is fixed before she comes…'

It was afterwards hotly debated whether or not the captain, at this point, winked.

'…but I'm sure Sam Farley will be glad to see her again.'

He tipped his hat, smiled once more, and was gone.

Chapter Four

After two weeks when Andy Marsh and her Triumph were neither seen nor heard in Tollbridge, Angela, delivering peppermint creams, was quizzed in Farley's by Debbie Tucker on the non-appearance of her friend.

'Yes,' said Angela, 'Sam mentioned it, too. I've no idea how the rumour started.' She couldn't say it might be wishful thinking on the part of Debbie's cousin. The young printer's interest in machinery was mainly professional, but embraced motorbikes too. The Triumph under its waterproof cover at The Old Printery had caught his eye; Andy's ability to do most of the maintenance herself met with his respect. Angela had smiled inwardly, and left them to it. 'We've got nothing immediately planned, and I doubt if she'd just turn up without warning, though we've known each other for yonks.'

'She keeps busy, I've no doubt, with her odd-jobbing all over the place.' Debbie raised weary eyes to the ceiling. 'We need more like her, seeing how long it's taking to get to the bottom of our leak.' She sighed. 'Believed it was fixed, didn we — but oh, no, 'twas all drip-drip-drip in that bucket again so soon as that last lot of rain started.'

Angela regretfully shook her head. 'Andy doesn't do ladders, I'm afraid. No head for heights at all — though if it was a pipe leaking, not a roof, no problem.'

Debbie sighed again. 'Tidn right to keep asking Jan Ridd or the Hockadays, busy about their own affairs as everyone is, taking advantage of their good nature. If Barney Christmas hadn had the lads busy upalong to the old school these days past I'd know where to ask, except – well, now I'm not so sure.' She lowered her voice to a conspiratorial level, though the two were for once alone in the shop. 'If you ask me, Barney's getting extra done far over and above weather repairs to an empty building. I'd say there's that old gleam starting back in his eye, which always used to mean he'd some new scheme in mind. I wonder if young Jasper's bin putting a few London notions into his head? You know anything, midear? You and the Mertons being such pals, I mean.'

Angela confessed to a lack of knowledge, reminding Debbie that various part-time jobs restricted her general socialising, though of course she saw her friends on the nights she worked in the Anchor 'and I can't say I've noticed anything then. No huddling in corners, or cryptic whispers. Everyone seems to hang out together in pretty much the same old way, although of course Barney's not there every evening. Perhaps he's just making up for all the refurbishment time he lost when the chimney had to be rebuilt—'

'More like making up all the money!' Mrs Tucker cocked a knowing eye at her young acquaintance, and both ladies began to giggle. It was often said of Barney Christmas (who would cheerfully accept any slander, no matter how outrageous) that it was 'worth eighteen pence to get a shilling out of the man' and, as Tollbridge had not been slow to point out, 'if the council hadn started getting on to him so hard about it, why, he would surely never have bin willing to pay overtime to fix that fallen chimley'.

What the village didn't know was that Mr Christmas, successful businessman, understood rather too well how slowly, without appropriate encouragement, the mills of reconstruction can grind. He swore his workers to secrecy and agreed more than generous terms for weekend working – unless word got around, in which case there would be no bonus for anyone. Mr Christmas enjoyed having the last laugh against his fellows, if only in private.

'I'm at the pub most evenings this week and a few days, too, next week,' Angela said. 'If Barney comes in and they stay in the bar, rather than heading out to the skittle alley, I'll try to keep my ears open. Somebody might say something.'

'Tabitha Ridd was saying you'm all extra watchful these days, and small wonder. Dora Tucker says they've heard no more of that dine-and-dash pair – only to expected, I suppose – and for all it's a crime the police have nought to say on the matter, beyond tidn the only place in these parts this sort of thing's happened. Why, we'll have security cameras in here next, taking folks's likeness just in case.' Debbie sighed, and the connecting door to the domestic part of the building clumped open to allow Tilda to enter with a tray, two mugs and a plate of biscuits. She caught her twin's sigh, and put the obvious question.

'Something wrong?'

'Human nature,' said Debbie at once.

'Oh, dear,' said Tilda, sighing in her turn as she set down the tray.

The following week found Tabitha Ridd in her kitchen with Angela, preparing to cook sea bass in salt. The Slandered Pig had reported a modest success with the first attempt, but not yet good enough for sale: 'timing a little out, most likely, though all et up without complaint and enjoyed for the family supper'. Word was passed to the crew of M.V. *Priscilla Ornedge* that the next specimen of appropriate size should be offered first to the Anchor.

The Anchor prided itself on good, wholesome, not-too-exotic English food, and Tabitha wondered at first if fish cooked in a salt crust might be a bit… foreign. Angela reassured her by saying the taste and texture achieved by this method were excellent and, if Good Plain Pub Grub was what was wanted, the menu needn't describe the method of cooking although – Angela's eyes sparkled – if they could only find a way of making their own salt, what an advertisement that would be!

'We could ask Mike Binns,' she enthused. 'He's the man for gadgets. Some sort of evaporator – I think I once read something about piles of driftwood branches soaked in seawater, and goodness knows we've an unlimited supply of that.' She'd lived long enough in Tollbridge not to bother taking out her mobile phone to ask the internet. 'I'll check on my computer at home, shall I? What a pity my mother's working on a new book! I daren't disturb her now, but I bet she'd remember straight off.'

Susan Jones was a born researcher, a speed reader and, when reading, an enthusiastic snapper-up of unconsidered trifles. As she said, you never knew when an idle fact might not have its part to play in Milicent Dalrymple's latest offering; almost nothing need be wasted, once you found the right place to use it. Tollbridge wits liked to hint at Susan's hitherto unrecognised kinship with Barnaby Christmas, whose firm and frequently expressed opinion was that all stock was profit if you waited long enough.

'Take a while, I reckon.' Tabitha was thinking. 'You'd heat it in shallow pans, would you, much the same like making clotted cream?'

'Well, you certainly know how to do *that*.' Another sparkle danced in Angela's eyes. 'I mean, think how much cream you use just for the lobster sauce.'

Tabitha Ridd (born Evans) guarded her family's recipe for the famous sauce just as her cousin Evan guarded his for gingerbread, or as Lucia protected from the prowling Miss Mapp her celebrated Lobster *à la Riseholme*. If Angela discovered it for herself, Tabitha would be neither surprised, nor worried: all she would need do would be swear her part-time assistant to secrecy, as had Evan with the gingerbread – about which Angela had never breathed a word, not even to Evan's own cousin.

'And then, the expense to buying new pans!' Tabitha's doubts returned. 'I'd never use my good scalding pans to boil seawater. I'd not be able to persuade myself the taste wouldn carry back over to the cream – and where, more-and-so, could we find room to keep more pans?' The Anchor's kitchen had ample storage space, but all that space was filled. 'No harm in asking Mike Binns – he'll be looking to some new idea, now he and Gabriel have had their fun racing that spider thing of his around the harbour – only, when there's catering packs of salt to be had at very reasonable price…'

'Okay,' said Angela. 'It was just an idea.' She glanced at the kitchen clock. 'I'll leave you to it now. It's time I went to see if Jan needs any help.'

Jan Ridd wasn't, when she checked, in the bar but Gabriel Hockaday and Mike Binns, their brief squabble long forgotten, informed her in chorus that the landlord had slipped out to settle a parking dispute.

'The usual,' said Mike.

'Oh?' prompted Angela. The chorus had hinted strongly at generous tips already earned, and now being enjoyed. She wondered how much – and for which particular story – the visitors had paid; and whether they'd had their money's worth. The old gentlemen were very clearly having theirs.

'Headland or harbour,' explained Gabriel.

'Both free, as you know,' added Mike.

'But a question,' said Gabriel, 'of take the walk, or do the climb? Up and down Coastguard Steps, or over the chezell where it's bin flattened?' Once the mysteries of the Scrambler Tank had been discovered, Gabriel unearthed an ancient stopwatch from the bottom of a might-come-in-useful box and the two friends, reconciled, played happily for days.

'They can use the slipway and walk back along Harbour Path,' said Angela.

'They might – ha, ha – slip.' Mike raised his double-handled cider mug and nodded to her over the rim. He drank deeply.

'Or be washed away by the tide.' Gabriel followed his brother-in-law's example.

Mike laughed again. 'Or a tidal wave!'

So this time it had been the Tsunami of 1607, with no doubt for afters the Great Storm of 1703, as written up by Daniel Defoe and enhanced for local consumption by Susan Jones under the name of Lorinda Doone. Was this not Lorna's own country? Combe Ploverton whispered that Plovers Barrows, home of Blackmore's Girt Jan Ridd, was on certain nights 'when the parish lantern shines straight down the chimley' clearly visible to those who believed; and Susan's skilful pen made it easy to believe in this magical moon.

'Tidal waves.' Susan's daughter sighed. 'If you two aren't careful, you'll be scaring people away rather than encouraging them to visit. Where would you and your stories be then? Or the museum, with no money to pay for the rethatching? What about my mother, taking time out from her own writing to revise the tourist leaflets – or Jane, with her sketches – or Chris Hockaday's wonderful photos?'

Chris Hockaday's grandfather looked solemn. 'True. Between 'em all they've done a grand job – and Sam Farley printing them, too. Yes, 'tis only right you should remind us of the fact. Your very good health, midear – and theirs!'

'Likewise,' agreed Mike Binns, even more solemn.

Angela shook her head and left them to their cider, as Jan Ridd came in.

'Can you keep an eye on things for us, Angela? I'm asked across to the shop and help sorting out a delivery set down in the wrong place and too heavy for Debbie or Tilda to move by theirselves – another new driver, so it seems.'

Angela held up a mischievous hand. 'Fingers firmly crossed this one doesn't knock the chimney down like his predecessor!'

'Ah,' said Jan, 'you'll be pleased, midear, for tidn a man – only, being new to the job, the young lady says she wadn given details of exactly where it all should go and unloaded to the front of the shop, 'stead of going round to the back. Did the paperwork signing and then took off, saying she'd a timetable to keep and was confident they'd find someone to help – which o'course, they did. Shouldn take me long.' Big Jan Ridd was as strong as his fictional namesake, and equally kind-hearted.

'Always 'cepting they don't have 'ee up on the roof again.' Gabriel's whiskers quivered with quiet hilarity. Mike's beard wagged. They raised their mugs in unison.

Jan ignored them. 'I've bin advising a couple where to park,' he told Angela, 'and once they've settled on exactly where they'll be along for a bite to eat, they said.' He lowered his voice, though the drinkers were paying him little attention. 'Best keep an eye open, after the Pig. A touch of bickerment's only natural, but I couldn tell – it might be play-acting, or it might not. Moreover, the car's a hired one.' The former policeman had automatically noted the logo in the rear window. 'I've kept the number, but by far the wisest course is to stop it happening in the first place.'

Angela nodded. 'Leave it with me.'

'And Tabitha. I've let her know too – more-and-so, I should be back before long.'

It seemed the bickering twosome weren't as troubled by the threat of tidal waves in the Bristol Channel as the eloquence of Gabriel and Mike could have expected. When, a few minutes later, the couple entered the Anchor they were still mid-argument.

'You know what the doctor said about exercise, you lazy whatsit,' the lady was saying. 'If we'd left the car up on the headland like I wanted, there'd have been all those steps to climb on the way back, not just ambling down the seafront and straight inside the car.'

'Steps to climb?' The lazy whatsit was horrified. 'With indigestion? Or cramp, or even a heart attack? I thought you worried about me, Nicky. I never knew you didn't really care. Everyone knows you're not meant to take exercise right after eating. You trying to kill me off for the insurance?'

'Chance would be a fine thing.' Nicky rolled her eyes. 'It's far too late for anything like that. What insurance company would look twice at you these days, you great lump?' She swung round to poke him in the middle. 'Terry of the Two Spare Tyres, they should call you. Just look at that tum!' She poked again, then swung back to address Angela as she drew near.

'If there's salad on your menu, ducks, my hubby will have double helps and plain water to drink, thank you – less calories – oh, and no pudding, either.'

'Nicky!' Terry's protest was weak. His wife laughed.

'Poor old Tez! Okay, hon, as we're on holiday if you're good then maybe one scoop – just one – of low-fat ice cream, if you can get muck like that around here?' She winked at Angela, who entered warily into the spirit of the squabble.

'Well, not easily. Round here it's clotted cream with everything possible, and it's good though I say it myself. We make our own, and I can recommend it.'

'Sold,' said Terry, 'when the time comes, but first things first. Fish and chips, Nick?'

'Yes, please,' to Angela. 'Is there clotted cream in your tartare sauce, too?'

Terry and Nicky dined with enthusiasm. They had cider to accompany their fish and chips, choosing the best, most expensive brand on the Anchor's list. They sprinkled cider vinegar ('D'you make this, too?') with a lavish hand, and asked for extra chips: Nicky ate rather more than half. Terry grumbled that she'd also had a larger helping of peas. Angela offered to bring more peas. Nicky said no, thanks; Terry said yes, please, and talked about legumes, and improved cholesterol levels.

'Oh, yeah?' Nicky rummaged at once for her mobile phone. 'Any excuse to be greedy, that's what.' She tapped and fiddled with the screen in her hand. 'Dammit, no signal. Can't be my phone, surely – I'll try over there.'

Angela whipped out her own mobile, ostensibly for demonstration purposes. 'Sorry, but we don't get a signal in this pub – in this village, actually, not unless you go to the end of the pier at certain times of day, or – sorry again,' with a sideways look at Terry, 'if you climb Coastguard Steps to the headland. It's far too hilly and the cliffs are too high.' She pointed. 'Somebody once tried leaning up that chimney to get a signal, and fell in the fire and was pretty badly burned. Skin grafts, and months of pain.'

'Poor cow,' said Nicky. Terry shuddered.

'But you can take photos well enough,' Angela went on. 'Smile, please!' And with relief she took several shots of the pair she'd been dithering about since they first came in: were they – was their behaviour – suspicious, or not?

Terry spent a long time pondering the puddings. Nicky muttered bitterly to Angela.

'I know we're on holiday and I said he could, but I wish he wouldn't. The doctor wasn't joking – at least, I don't think so, but he won't listen. Always thinks he knows best. Men!'

Angela might be anti-man, and the customer might be always right, but she didn't want to get involved. 'If you can't make up your mind I can always bring two half-size portions,' she offered. 'Same plate, same price as one. Would that help?'

Terry patted his tummy. 'Everything looks so good. I don't suppose... three?'

'Two-Tyres Tez,' mocked Nicky. She laughed. 'Hey, might as well make it four, ducks. Much easier to measure out.'

'I'm not a pig.' Terry scowled. 'And what about you?'

In the end, though it wasn't on the official menu, Angela assembled a tasting plate and brought two spoons. Jan Ridd, back from the shop, nodded approval in the distance. He'd spotted Angela's camera stratagem, and approved her quick thinking. He still wasn't sure about Terry and Nicky: when the time came to pay, he would be watching.

At the end of the meal Nicky vanished, ostensibly to powder her nose. Tabitha arrived to clear empty coffee-cups and Angela brought the bill, explaining that it must be settled on the machine at the bar. At the bar, Jan leaned slightly to one side, his eye on the toilet door.

Terry's card didn't work.

Terry swore under his breath, and punched in the number again. Jan and Angela exchanged looks.

'It does play up sometimes,' apologised Angela, now very much on the alert when for the second time – third time – the screen stayed blank. 'We do take cash, of course.'

'She likes to keep cash for shopping,' said Terry. 'A great one for little bits and pieces, my Nicky.' He brightened as his wife emerged, smiling, from the loo. 'Hey, Nick, we got ourselves a problem!'

'Not me I haven't.' She strolled over to them. 'Everything very nice, thanks.' She smiled at everyone except her husband. 'So – what's he done wrong now?'

'Not me, their card machine.'

'Your card, you mean.' Nicky's smile faded. 'I told you it was filling up, the way you've splashed the cash wherever we've gone.' A sigh. 'So I've got to pay, I suppose.'

'I didn't do it on purpose—'

'You never do.' Again she rolled her eyes. 'What did I say about men? Okay, sunshine – but listen, you owe me!'

'Slap-up meal tonight,' he promised, 'once I've sorted the bank.'

She was rummaging in her bag. 'I'll hold you to that – and I'm sorry,' to Angela and the watchful Jan. 'It's not the first time. What he'd do if he didn't have me to bail him out all the time I don't know.'

'Sink,' Terry almost chirped, as after an uncomfortable hesitation Nicky's card was accepted. 'I'm sorry too,' to Angela, 'because she's right, it's not the first time. I'm out of cash, hon, but can you find something extra and make it a decent tip?'

'See what I mean? How he'd cope without me…' Nicky bit back the rest of what she'd been about to say, rolled her eyes, and rummaged again inside her bag. The Anchor staff were duly grateful – and relieved as Terry and Nicky, with a fresh reason to squabble, went on their way in as discordant a mood as they'd arrived, seeming ready to bicker for the rest of the day if their breath, and their tempers, held out.

Jan Ridd gazed after them, and laughed. 'Well, and so we were wrong about they two, but you can't never be careful enough,' he told his wife.

'That you can't,' Tabitha agreed. 'And tidn by no means my idea of a peaceful wedded life, though it seems to suit them. Takes all sorts, don't it?'

Angela, thinking briefly of Paul, smiled for her lucky escape and pulled out her mobile phone. 'It certainly does – but I don't think I'll delete their photos just yet.' She glanced at Jan. 'Not for a few days. Okay?'

He nodded. 'Not yet,' he agreed. 'You never can tell. Not yet.'

'Just in case,' said Tabitha.

And all three nodded, gravely.

Chapter Five

Miriam Evans and her apprentice left the post office, pleased with their morning's work. The latest batch of handwoven scarves, blankets and throws from Tiffler & Thrums, as Miriam had named her small business, was on its way. Each item had been folded to size, competently, by Miriam and secured neatly with fine satin ribbon in bundles to be turned into postworthy parcels – by Angela, with strong brown paper and sticky tape. Angela (once a librarian, now a museum curator, always able to organise) had watched in horror as her new friend prepared a delivery for one of the London stores she supplied. Horror could brook no argument. Angela snatched the scissors and tape from Miriam's hands with an anguished 'No! Let me!' rather than suffer any longer.

At first she had supposed Miriam must be joking when she struggled to stop the tape folding back on itself, twisting flat, or tangling round her fingers. Work was a serious business: perhaps her new boss was for some strange reason trying to put her at her ease. The eventual realisation that Miriam couldn't help herself came as a nasty shock.

'But you never tangle the ribbon!' protested Angela.

Miriam agreed this was a fact.

'And you never fumble that what-d'you-call-it figure-of-eight knot that slips round and stops you wasting even an inch more ribbon than you need—'

'A packer's knot, midear.'

'And you can fold any size of cloth into the right shape just by – by looking at it!'

Miriam sighed. 'Folding idn... sticky.'

'I guess it was all okay before the post office wanted sticky tape instead of string?'

'Oh, yes. Never any trouble with a cardboard box and string. But now...'

On the occasion of Angela's next weaving session she carried with her a tape dispenser borrowed from the post office. Debbie Tucker had grinned as she agreed the loan 'just to try out, midear?' The grin widened when Angela returned the dispenser with brief thanks, and no explanation.

'We didn think 'twould work,' Debbie said, 'but we didn want to make you no determent, just in case 'twas a different outcome for you to try. We've all tried, midear. In the end she took to bringing all her parcels straight here for one of us to sticky on her behoof. A downright puzzle, Miriam being otherwise so handy, but there's no explaining it. Her's glad to have you help her now, I'm sure – as are we. Why, most times she'd have a queue forming up behind her and at least half the shop made to wait!'

Today Angela had applied tape to the packages but permitted Miriam, as the founder and focus of Tiffler & Thrums, to apply the peel-off labels printed for this burgeoning cottage industry by Sam Farley, as designed by Jane Merton. Labels, once peeled, might be sticky but they weren't large enough to tangle round anyone's fingers, although in the early days one had somehow found itself stuck to Miriam's hair.

'A good job, well done,' gloated Angela, as Miriam tucked the receipt in her pocket. 'I'm on duty at the Anchor in half an hour – we've got a family booking. Come with me and I'll buy you a drink before they arrive.'

'Thanks, but now that lot's done and dusted I've the loom to warp up for the tapestry.' Miriam had woven a delightful picture for her goddaughter Jane's wedding and, after several years, with Jane and her husband now living so close, had become inspired with the design for a companion piece.

'Is it for a particular date – birthday, wedding anniversary, special occasion?'

'No, but now I've the image in my head...'

'Fair enough. I know what mother's like when she's got an idea – that first, wild rush – and talking of my mother, have you spoken to her recently?'

Miriam shook her head, and smiled. 'Guess who else has bin asking that very same question, as if you'd any need.'

Angela hadn't. 'Mickey Binns. He's asked me, too. I told him, at the moment the only news of her I get is from one or other of the Farleys when she collects her groceries, and they told him the same and he was a bit bothered because – well, *you* know how she is, if anyone in Tollbridge does –' Miriam was Susan's closest friend locally – 'and when she's preoccupied with *thinking* like this and doesn't want to use her car, she'll take a taxi over to Minehead or Ilfracombe...'

Miriam nodded. 'Mickey would liefer by far he drove your mother than let anyone else do it, but the Hockadays say they've not bin asked neither. He's worried he've upset her in some way.'

Angela shook her head. 'She's got a completely new idea, she did tell me that much. You remember when I arranged that sort-out morning at the museum?'

'I do! I'd no notion you could be so hard a taskmaster, midear.'

Angela laughed. 'It was wonderful to have so many people wanting to help. We were able to get so much more done with everyone knowing just what we were looking at. I can catalogue books and papers okay, but only think of those pole heads, for instance. I had no idea what they were, but Gabriel could tell me tons about the local Friendly Society and the parades and the club meetings.'

'Upalong to the Pig there's one room still bears the club sign, I think. The Anchor was never so large to warrant keeping the space apart. Have the Tuckers not shown you?'

'No. I'll ask, next time I see Dora – but it was finding so much Friendly Society stuff that seems to have set mother off in this new direction. When we unearthed the club daybook, diary, whatever it's called she was straight into it, and when she finally surfaced she asked if she could take it home.'

'I seem to recollect,' said Miriam with a twinkle, 'how you wouldn give consent until she'd a-gid her solemn promise to set the cover and the loose pages to rights.'

'Fair's fair. I know my mother! It was obvious we wouldn't get another minute's tidying out of her once she'd found something to read. Besides, if it's to help her work I can't really complain, and she seemed so – so fired up, if you get me, I hadn't the heart to say no.'

'Mickey made that joke about Sherlock Holmes,' said Miriam slowly. 'No, 'twas Gabriel spoke of him first, talking of clues unearthed and the mysteries of the past…'

'And Mickey quoted that bit about Irene Adler always being *the woman* for him – for Holmes, I mean.'

'And looked at Susan silly-like and languishing, and she didn pay him no heed, so he turned it into a joke – and that was pretty much the last time they exchanged words.'

'I believe it was. But I'm sure she wasn't annoyed with him. She realised she had an idea on the way and – she simply didn't notice. Not very flattering to Mickey, perhaps, but that's how she is when she's working. I told him, she's not speaking to me either. It's nothing personal.'

'Don't I know it, midear. Nor idn she speaking to me, as I've told Mickey.'

'Oh, well.' Angela glanced at her watch. 'Sure you won't pop into the Anchor for a few minutes? Okay. Have fun with the warping.'

She was about to cross to the pub when Miriam, turning to acknowledge her goodbye, grabbed her arm. The two had been so busy chatting that neither heard the approach of a large and powerful car driving from Stickle Street into Harbour Path. 'Careful, now,' warned Miriam. 'Seems likely here come another bang on the Trendle Cottage wall.'

'Thank you!' said Angela. 'Yes, that's quite a monster for these roads – ah.' Rather than carry on along Harbour Path to the cliff, the cottage, and the turning circle, the stranger had pulled in towards the Anchor. 'It might be them. I'd better go,' said Angela, part-time waitress, washer-up, cook and barmaid. 'Like I said, have fun!'

While there isn't much space outside the Anchor, there is enough for a carefully parked car to wait with only half its body blocking the public highway as it disgorges drinkers, diners, and/or luggage before the driver goes elsewhere.

'Are you lost?' enquired Angela. 'Can I help you?'

'I don't really think we can park here,' began the driver.

'No, not on this corner, but…' She gave crisp directions to the breakwater slipway.

'You mean we have to park on the beach?' The rear passenger window slid open; a sleek, dark-haired woman of around Angela's age looked out. She wasn't pleased. 'Surely there's somewhere closer!'

'You can see it from here—' began the driver, but was interrupted by a second voice from the rear.

'I want to go on the beach!' it squealed. It was a young, self-assured voice; and penetrating. As she tried to identify the source Angela felt, rather than directly saw, the front passenger wince.

'Later,' said the driver.

'But you promised!' cried the squeal.

'I know, Seffy darling—' soothed the dark-haired woman.

'I said later,' broke in the driver. 'We'll check in first, if it's not too early, and make sure everything's comfortable for

Gramps before any of us go anywhere. All right.' He wasn't asking, he was telling.

Angela made swift deductions. The booking was in the name of Tolliday, so – grandfather, son, daughter-in-law (presumably: a daughter by blood would show more concern for an elderly relative) and – she peered in the back of the car – granddaughter. Seffy (Saffy? Saffron?) was as sleek as her mother, though her locks were a rich honey-blonde rather than brunette, which could explain her name. She wore a sparkly top in toothpaste pink, and huge purple velvet hair bows on diamante clips. The saffron crocus was purple, wasn't it? Probably an only child. Angela looked back on her own solitary childhood. *Evidently a damsight more spoiled than I was. Thank goodness for a sensible mother!*

'No, it's not too early to check in,' said Angela, introducing herself before going on to tell the driver that, if Mrs Tolliday had concerns about leaving their car on the chezell, there was alternative parking up on the headland. She pointed. 'Tollbridge isn't really designed for modern traffic, you see.' She said nothing of the Anchor's tiny round-the-back car park. The Ridds used their judgement when telling guests of its existence, and had warned Angela she must learn to use hers. The Tollidays had a large car.

'I remember,' came the unexpected voice of grandfather from the other front seat. 'I've been here before. On a motorbike,' he added, with a dry, creaking chuckle, 'not by car. It was all I could afford, as a student – and I certainly couldn't afford to stay in the pub. I had a tent in the woods, and a sleeping bag!'

'I don't want a sleeping bag,' announced Saffron. 'I want a proper bed.'

'Seffy,' warned her father.

'And you shall have a proper bed. We all will,' promised her mother.

'Not until you've checked in,' said Angela. The sooner the car moved away from the corner, the better for Tollbridge traffic. 'Would you like any help with your luggage?' She had to smile, thinking of the assortment of parcels she and Miriam had recently taken to the post. Bags with proper handles would be far easier to carry.

'You're laughing at us,' came Seffy's accusing voice as she scrambled out of the car. 'Why are you laughing?'

'Persephone!' snapped her father as he made to open the boot.

'Why not?' countered Angela, mentally bidding farewell to Saffron. 'Beats crying or making a fuss, any day.' She grabbed a suitcase bigger than common sense advised, but she was too annoyed to care.

The younger Tolliday, one eye on his father, didn't stop her and his father took a long time to emerge from the front seat. Tolliday Senior stretched, rubbed his back, and stood breathing deeply as his daughter-in-law put an arm about the child's shoulders to give her a very gentle shake, and led her towards the Anchor's front door.

'Wonderful sea air,' said the older Tolliday, happily. Persephone whirled round.

'Where's the sea? I want to swim my unicorn.'

'Later,' said her father.

'But where's the sea? I want to see it.' She started jigging from one foot to another. 'I want to see the sea! I want to see the sea!'

'Over there, if I remember,' said Gramps Tolliday. 'Maybe you're not quite tall enough to look over the sea wall, but if you go round the side of the pub…?'

'You remember okay.' Angela smiled again in response to his questioning tone.

'I *am so* tall enough!' protested the child. Being stuck with a name like Persephone she couldn't (Angela supposed) be entirely to blame for her behaviour. Her mother seemed very much the sort of person who would change her own dull Diana or

Daphne to the more exotic Demeter... 'I am! I'm as tall as – as tall as the sky! I can see for miles!'

'Don't shout, darling.' Diana-Demeter cuddled her daughter again, looking towards her husband. 'She's over-tired, aren't you, darling, and her little legs are fidgety after so long in the car. Shall we go for a walk to find the sea while Daddy sorts everything out?'

At least they weren't first-name parents. It could have been worse. Angela was smiling again as, brushing off grandfather's belated efforts to wrest the suitcase from her, she led the way into the Anchor.

Jan Ridd was there to check the Tollidays in. He took the case from Angela, saying that he thought Tabitha might need her in the kitchen and he himself would show the visitors to their rooms. His shrewd gaze ran over Gramps Tolliday's weary face. 'Reckon you could do with a pot of tea,' he suggested. 'On the house, midear. Up in your room, or down here once you've unpacked? Come far, have 'ee?'

'Not as far as you might think, but far enough,' said the weary man's son, addressed by his father as Eddie. 'My wife isn't used to these narrow lanes of yours and kept worrying about how long the trip would take, and saying we should leave plenty of time – especially once we realised the satnav assumes there are never any farm vehicles to slow you down, or wandering sheep, or –' he looked sideways at his father, and grinned – 'or goats.'

Gramps Tolliday grinned back. 'Yes, I've never forgotten those goats. Some things don't change – like this pub, I'm glad to see.'

Jan laughed. 'The plumbing could well be better'n you remember – all depending on how long ago you were here!'

Gramps followed him cautiously up the stairs, using the handrail. Without being too obvious, Jan moderated his giant stride along the corridor. He ushered Gramps to his room, saw him safely inside, and turned to Eddie with a quizzical expression.

'He's not so good,' said Eddie. 'It's his heart. Thanks for being tactful. He doesn't like to have a fuss made because we haven't told my daughter yet. She's sharp enough to start asking awkward questions, and he wanted a – a last, peaceful time together before...' His voice broke. 'Sorry. You've been very kind – and thank you, downstairs would be fine. We can keep an eye out for the girls coming back.'

When the girls came back, Eddie and his father were discussing a pot of tea and a plate of chudleighs with jam and clotted cream. This treat was another local speciality from Widdowson's Bakery that Gramps said he recalled from his previous visit, but hadn't been able to afford on a student grant.

'On a professor's pension you can afford it.' His son looked pleased as almost a whole chudleigh was layered with cream and devoured with a generous spread of jam. Eddie had made the mistake of calling these small, light-gold buns dusted with icing sugar *scones* and been set right by Tabitha, who brought out the tray.

'In other places they're splits,' she told him, 'or they could be tuffs, but to us hereabouts they're chudleighs, and highly regarded. Evan Evans – that's the baker – he uses butter still, as do I, where other folk will cheapen them with marge.'

'I can taste the butter,' said the professor, his eyes bright. 'Very tasty – and well worth a wait of more than fifty years.'

He renewed the compliments just as Persephone and her mother reappeared.

'Why did you wait fifty years?' demanded Persephone. 'Wasn't it so tasty then?'

'Very tasty,' said her grandfather, 'but I was very young – though older than you,' seeing a question hover on her lips, 'and I've already explained I didn't have much money.'

'Have you got much money now?'

'Enough, thank you. Would you like to try one? Just a taste?'

'It looks very rich,' said his daughter-in-law, watching Tabitha top up with boiling water. 'Full-fat butter? And all the sugar! You can't call it a balanced diet for a growing child.'

'I want to try one,' said Persephone at once.

'Just a taste,' repeated Professor Tolliday, 'as your mother's not keen.' He cut a neat slice from his own snack, and put it on a side plate. 'Here you are – and do remember, Lucinda, it's a holiday. At the seaside. Good grief, you'll be saying next the child can't even have an ice cream.'

'Why can't I have an ice cream?' came the whiplash return, through a spray of crumbs. Lucinda shot an anguished look at her father-in-law; Eddie rolled his eyes.

The professor rose to the occasion. 'It would curdle your insides to eat it straight on top of jam. Perhaps we'll find an ice cream for you later, when we go exploring.'

'We already went exploring.' The child dropped her empty plate back on the table. 'And there's nothing here! No proper shops, no funfair or candyfloss or paddling pool – no proper beach, just stones, and the water's all horrid and dirty. Mummy says I can't swim my unicorn – and she promised!'

Lucinda shook her head. 'You know I never promised candyfloss, darling. It isn't good for you – and I'm sorry about the unicorn, but you really mustn't paddle in contaminated water.' She turned to Tabitha, still hovering in case anything else was required. 'There should be notices up. Health and safety. Don't people in this place –' *subtext: you ignorant peasants* – 'understand how dangerous it is to be exposed to raw sewage?'

Three voices spoke as one.

'Look here, Lucy,' protested Eddie.

'Really, Lucinda!' from his father.

'Yes,' said Tabitha, 'we do.' Years of pub landladying had given her voice authority. The others fell silent. 'Only, seeing as how tidn raw sewage in the river but iron, and – and similar mineral content, all washed down from Exmoor by the rain, we've no need for health and safety signs because tidn unhealthy. Nor dangerous.'

'That's true,' interposed the professor hurriedly. 'When I was here before, camping up in the woods by the other river – I forget the name – but that was running dark brown, too, and people told me then it came from Exmoor, after heavy rain.'

'The Rindan,' supplied Tabitha. 'Empties into the harbour near the breakwater.'

His thin, pale face brightened. 'Rindan, that's it! Thank you. I remembered the Chole, but the Rindan's too small to have a name on our road atlas.'

'Ordnance Survey map,' suggested Tabitha. 'Farley's shop sells the local ones – if you'd care to go local shopping. Tide tables, likewise, for parking your car on the chezell, though we've tide tables here too, o'course.'

'That's a good idea,' said Eddie quickly. 'Thank you, we will.'

'Both,' said his father. 'Maps from the shop, tide tables from the pub.' He smiled again at Tabitha. 'And might there be leaflets we could buy, describing places of interest, things to see? Have you anything like that?'

Tabitha smiled back. 'We have, though perhaps a touch old-fashioned these days and we'm in the way of updating them – but it takes time. We've a proper published author living local, Susan Jones, and between her own work she's to rewrite all our tourist books for us, with proper illustrations. Photographs, too, showing what may remain of the old stories you can go and see for yourselves.'

'There isn't anything to see for ourselves,' objected Persephone. The male members of the party shushed her. Tabitha ignored her.

Lucinda shook her head. 'It's not polite to contradict, darling – but, really, there isn't much here, for a child.'

'You said,' said the child, 'I could swim my unicorn—'

'And so you shall!' Lucinda shot a triumphant look at her husband. 'Daddy and I will take you to the *proper* seaside tomorrow, with sand and – and shops and everything, while Gramps has a little wander down memory lane all by himself. How would that do?'

'And where would we go?' asked Eddie, as Persephone considered this new option.

'Minehead,' suggested Tabitha, 'or maybe Combe Martin—'

'Where's memory lane? Is it far? Why can't Gramps come wandering with us instead?'

Two seconds of silence was broken by a burst of adult laughter. Young Persephone's lip began to quiver. The professor reached out to pat her hand.

'No, not far. Only fifty years. It can wait another day. I'll come with you tomorrow.'

The tantrum was averted. 'Come with me now.' She wore a triumphant grin as she tugged at his hand. 'Come and buy an ice cream from the shop!'

'If they sell them, yes.' The professor cocked an enquiring eye at Tabitha, who nodded. Lucinda, relieved to have won at least part of the battle, said nothing.

Eddie said: 'An Ordnance Survey map of the area, too, now we know they stock them. We'll all go.' He was watching his father, without seeming to. 'We'll have a stroll round the harbour, perhaps go to see where Gramps pitched his tent, then an early supper and, while we're digesting, we can think about where to go and what to do tomorrow.'

Lucinda unbent. 'We'll buy some of your tourist booklets, too.' She smiled at Tabitha. 'I'm sure there's plenty to do in the area if – if we only read everything up and ask sensible questions.' She laughed, lightly. 'We've already tried googling Combe Tollbridge, and the signal here is non-existent! We met an old man who said we ought to try climbing to the top of the headland, but somebody's legs are rather too short for those steep steps.'

'No they're not,' said Persephone at once. 'I can climb steps as good as anyone!'

'*You* might be able to,' said her father, glancing at his own, 'but we certainly can't. And as we're down here, where we can't get a signal, I think we'll stick to the good old-fashioned technology of printed paper that never goes wrong.'

'Unless there's a power cut at midnight.' The professor winked at Persephone. 'What *I* think is, we'd better get along to that ice cream shop quickly, in case the freezer stops working.'

Tabitha watched the little family party set out. She cleared the remains of the tea-and-chudleigh snack away to the kitchen, and thought of distraction dining…

And wondered.

Chapter Six

The Tollidays returned from their expedition, the child bouncing with ice cream and excitement, the professor looking tired, his face a little grey. 'I think I'll have a quiet half-hour in my room before we eat,' he murmured.

Eddie accompanied him up the stairs, one cautious step to the rear. Lucinda saw Jan Ridd's thoughtful gaze follow the pair and put a hurried finger to her lips, glancing across to her daughter, who was standing on tiptoe trying to see into a display case on the wall.

'Your husband did explain,' said Jan quietly, likewise watching Persephone. The display case had a lot of glass. 'You've no need to worry, midear, there'll be nothing said in front of her, but, so long as – anyone – might need help, you've only to ask.'

He raised his voice as he walked over to join the child. 'You interested in the cannon-bullet, midear? A piece of history, that is. Ever heard of a lady called Lorna Doone?'

'No,' said Persephone. 'Who's she?'

'Well, now. You a great reader?'

'Not if it's lessons. You said history. That's lessons, and I don't do lessons on holiday.'

Lucinda, flushing, smiled an apology to Jan. He winked, but abandoned any idea of giving the child a leaflet: she might find the pictures of interest, but she was still very young. 'Lorna Doone is in a story, a famous story, written taking place among true history, one part being the Battle of Sedgemoor. Tidn so far from here, Sedgemoor, as the crow flies.'

'What crow? There's only seagulls. One flew at me and tried to steal my ice cream and I dropped it and Gramps bought me another.'

'Yes, gulls can be somewhat troublesome at times; crows, likewise. Known for flying in straight lines, the crow – same as a bee. Or,' he dropped his voice to a thrilling whisper, 'a bullet. That-there bullet you see before you, was dug up on the very same moor where the battle took place, four hundred years past.'

'Did they dig up any bones with it?'

'Seffy, darling!'

Jan laughed. 'No bones, no armour, not so much as a bullet from a gun. After such a great battle they'd have tidied everything away –' he could see her about to argue – 'if they could find it, bodies and all. But this bullet having bin fired from a cannon, not a gun, being a far larger weapon it went far deeper into the ground, and was lost. And many, many years passed before upheavals in the soil, wind and weather and farmland ploughing, could bring it back again to the light of modern day.'

Lucinda had drifted over to stand with her daughter peering in the display case, with its neatly-typed explanatory notice at the wrong angle for a child to make out. 'I haven't read *Lorna Doone*,' she admitted. 'What's the connection with this battle of yours?'

Jan looked down. 'Know what a highwayman is, young lady?'

'Dick Turpin.' Persephone lifted her hands, fingers in pistol pose. 'Stand and deliver! Your money or your life!'

'That's right. You know the name of Dick Turpin's horse?'

She hesitated; her mother whispered 'Black Bess'. She scowled. 'I knew it was Black Bess. Don't rush me! I'm not a cheat!'

'And nobody said you were.' Jan smiled. 'Howsumdever, Black Bess idn the only horse that belonged to a well-known gentleman of the road. This Lorna Doone, in the book of which I spoke, she married a man whose cousin was Tom Faggus, a highwayman notorious in these parts, his horse being Winnie. So when poor Tom got caught up in the battle, clever Winnie went a-looking and searching for him all over the moor, while the battle still raged about her – and this very cannon-bullet is written in the book as going between that brave Winnie's feet and burying itself in the ground. And now, there it lies!'

Mother and daughter gazed at a battered bronze sphere, rather smaller than a tennis ball. Lucinda looked enquiringly at Jan. He nodded. 'Yes, 'twas an uncle of my grandfather, or maybe *his* father, who dug it from a blocked drain. And who's to say, after so long, whether or no a cannon-bullet's the true identity for the thing? But there's no doubting it came from Sedgemoor. None at all.'

'My father-in-law would enjoy that story,' said Lucinda. 'And listening might encourage him to sit and rest rather than tire himself out,' she added in a murmur. Jan nodded.

'And you, midear, how did 'ee care for the tale?'

Persephone looked at her mother. 'If it's a story, that means it's not true. And if it's not true, how do people know it's the same bullet in the book?'

Jan was shocked. 'Why, how can 'ee think it's not? It's bin found by my own gramfernuncle in the middle of Sedgemoor, my name being Ridd same as his – heavy enough to blow man or horse or mule to kingdom come should they be directly hit – you tell me how many other cannon-bullets have 'ee ever known such as this!'

'Well…'

'Care to hold it? I'll fetch the key, but be sure not to let'n fall. Tidn no featherweight, I have to warn 'ee.'

Lucinda had doubts. 'She can't damage it, can she?'

'Course not,' flashed Persephone.

'Never,' said Jan, laughing again. 'Solid brass, is that ball – bullet,' he amended, 'as the book says, I forget which chapter, but as to damaging *herself*... well, drop that on your toes, midear, and you'll be walking hoppety-kick for the rest of your days!'

When Eddie came back there was much to tell him, and he agreed that Gramps would like to hear about clever Winnie and the cannon-bullet that so narrowly missed her questing feet. 'Will you let him hold it, too?' enquired Persephone of Jan Ridd, by whose narrative she'd been more impressed than she liked to admit. Jan said it was a privilege he afforded to only *special* people, and he'd have to give the matter some consideration. Persephone started to preen herself. Eddie shook a quietly warning head.

Lucinda, forgetting that Tollbridge was an internet not-spot, tried unsuccessfully to find the text of *Lorna Doone* to check for herself the chapter on Sedgemoor. Jan said Susan had said they did really ought to keep a copy of the book with the bullet, and Susan's daughter Angela, who'd be working later behind the bar, had found them one and brought it in – only, for the life of him he couldn't rightly say just where it had gone.

'Happens, in a busy pub,' he said philosophically. 'Best ask Angela. Very knowledgeable about books, having bin a librarian.'

There was no hurry to order the evening meal. Gramps was resting, Eddie explained when his daughter began to fidget. Would she like another fizzy water?

'Rocky petrol water!' corrected Persephone, with a giggle. When she'd first given her order she was thrilled when a small hand-pump, attached to a springy hose, appeared from under the bar to be squirted neatly by Angela into a tall green tumbler. 'On the rocks,' had enquired Angela as she squirted, 'or as it comes?'

'Rocky petrol water coming up,' said Angela now. 'Not a bad name.' She wouldn't encourage the child by saying it might be useful. How would it look on the bar list? Would a blue tumbler be better than green?

'Ah, here's my father,' said Eddie. Angela brought menus.

'It's all fish,' announced Persephone after a quick scan of the card.

Lucinda looked at Angela. 'Isn't there a children's menu?'

'Sausage and chips, egg and chips, chicken nuggets, baked beans,' chanted Angela. 'Smaller plates, smaller cutlery, and tomato sauce by the gallon.' She tried not to wince.

'For my birthday,' Persephone informed everyone, 'we went to a proper restaurant and I had 'nduja on an individual pizza. Why can't I have pizza?'

'Pizza needs a special oven,' said her grandfather quickly. 'I don't suppose there's room for one. There wasn't the last time I was here.'

'Still isn't.' Angela smiled at him before addressing Persephone. 'And this isn't a restaurant, it's a pub, where people eat pub food. A seaside pub, which is why there's lots of fish on the menu: most of it has been caught –' she waved towards the Bristol Channel – 'out there. In the Severn Sea.'

'I'm so sorry,' began Lucinda. 'Seffy, darling, your birthday was weeks ago.'

'When visiting Rome,' said her husband, frowning his daughter down, 'you do as the Romans do. In Italy the Romans eat pizza. In Tollbridge the visitors eat fish.'

Persephone hesitated between tantrum and tears. Angela gazed at her, then relented.

'No, *I'm* sorry. I forgot that today we have scampi, too.' She was annoyed by her forgetfulness, and directed some of this annoyance towards Persephone in a slow, warning look. 'Would you like scampi, or would you prefer proper fish and chips?'

'Also caught locally, I gather,' said the professor pacifically as the child, faced with a direct choice, subsided in order to think.

Angela nodded. 'So much of the daily menu depends on what's been caught and, as you'd expect, that's affected by the weather. We freeze what we can, of course, but sometimes…'

The warning look had worked. Persephone abandoned her other options and asked – politely – for scampi.

'Good choice.' Angela made further amends. If the adults of the family were right, this holiday was for them a stressful, rather than a restful, break. The child was bound to have picked up on the tension, without understanding it. At home, safe on her own ground, she was probably far less the spoiled brat that she now seemed. 'Wriggly chips, or straight? Peas or broccoli or sweetcorn, or how about all three?'

With food safely ordered, it was time for drinks. Eddie opted for a pint of cider, Lucinda for a half. 'When in Rome,' said Eddie.

'Take care,' warned his father. 'Make it last, both of you – if it's anything like what I tried all those years ago, it's potent stuff. Don't even think about the other half.' He smiled at Angela. 'I'll take a leaf out of Seffy's book and have a glass of "petrol water" please.'

As they finished their meal the bar began to fill with regulars. Mike Binns set up court with his son and their friends at a nicely-judged distance from the visitors: close enough to be heard, without being intrusive. Local accents were instinctively modified to attract without the need for subtitles. Jokes were told at a slightly higher volume, and a good time was clearly being had by all.

'Well, now, if tidn the man himself!' Mike brandished his cider mug to welcome Gabriel Hockaday. 'Speak of the Old Scratch, and in he comes.'

'A good thing's worth the wait.' Gabriel, seeing strangers, dragged out a chair and sat down, ready to play his part. 'Drop of the usual, please, Jan, in my usual penny dish.' The terminology might be antique but it was almost genuine, being one of the more fanciful usages unearthed for her friends' entertainment by Susan Jones in the course of research. The smaller halfpenny 'dish' or mug had a single, not a double, handle.

From the Tolliday table wide, wondering young eyes fastened on Gabriel. Persephone's mouth dropped open, and the spoon clattered on her pudding plate.

'You said Father Christmas wasn't true!' she burst out. 'But I told you he was – I told you, and you didn't believe me, and there he is! It's Father Christmas!'

'Seffy, darling—'

Then the child grew quiet. 'But this is summer. Why is he here *now*? Is – is he really only pretend, like you said?' Her mouth puckered, and her eyes began to brim.

Gabriel knew what to do. As Jan brought cider in an impressive two-handled mug he left his chair and, smiling broadly, came across to the little girl. 'See now, midear, there's no cause for you to fret yourself. Even Father Christmas has to get away for a holiday in the summer, as I should know, for while 'tis true I'm not the man himself, there's a strong family likeness on account of him being a cousin of mine.' He turned to his cronies. 'Idn that right, all? I've a Christmas for my cousin? Jan Ridd, you tell the child!'

He spoke confidentially. 'Jan, here, his job used to be a policeman, and as such he's duty-bound and sworn to keep the law and always tell the truth. Idn that so, Jan?'

'It is,' said the former policeman, gravely. 'You've a Cousin Christmas, Gabriel, I'll take my Bible oath on that.'

Mike Binns, Mickey and the others loudly confirmed these reassuring words. Persephone's father saw her smile, and offered to pay for Gabriel's drink. The cousin of the absent Barney Christmas was charmed to accept and, looking smug, returned to his cider. The laughter and jokes began again, welcoming the visitors into the group. Gabriel casually let fall that his famous cousin had once dropped by 'upalong to Ploverton' in search of reindeer fodder 'being as they beasts eat much the same as goats.' None of the company voiced the uncomfortable truth that, whatever reindeer might eat, goats aren't noted for their gourmet habits. The youthful audience at whom Gabriel's words were directed watched and listened, breathless, the rest of her pudding forgotten.

Persephone's parents consulted their watches, and wondered about licensing laws.

'No cause for anxiety.' As ever, Jan missed nothing. 'True, you've finished your meal, but even in a general way she can bide here till eight, so long as you'm with her – only, on account of being residential the rules don't apply the same way in any case.'

'Perhaps she'd rather be out in the fresh air,' suggested Gramps, with a wary eye on the table where the conversation of Gabriel and his friends seemed to be taking a livelier turn. Children these days weren't the innocents they'd been at that age when he was a child, but this was a child who still believed in Father Christmas.

'If you like,' he told his son, 'you two can stay here while the two of us take a little walk before bedtime. We'll go as far as the breakwater again to check on the car, and we can see how the sunset's coming along.'

All his granddaughter's bounce had returned. 'We can go and look for where you saw the goats.' She looked towards Gabriel, laughing with his friends. 'Father Christmas might be there again! You said you were too tired before, but you're not tired now you've had something to eat, are you? Protein is good for you.'

The professor forced a smile. 'At my age I need time to digest my protein properly before I go exploring, child. That little valley is pretty steep these days for a poor old man like me. If I'm coming with you tomorrow, I don't want to wear out my legs before we start, do I? The harbour walk is nice and flat. Come along.'

He held out his hand. After a quick look at her parents, she accepted his escort.

'And we can go and look at the other river, the big one, now we know it's not dirty.' She shot a saucy look at her mother. 'I could go paddling, couldn't I?'

Jan saw Lucinda's look of horror. 'Oh dear me, no,' he said quickly. 'That water have come a long, cold way down from the moor – so very long and cold it's like to freezing even as it meets the sea. You go a-paddling there and Jack Sharp would nip your toes clean off, so sure as that cannon-bullet would have squatted 'em flat had you dropped it!'

'Oh,' said Persephone, doubtfully. It was the sort of thing grown-ups always said to stop you doing what you wanted because it wasn't what *they* wanted. They'd wanted her not to hold the cannon-bullet in case she dropped it, but of course she hadn't. They'd said she was all wrong about Father Christmas, and she'd been right – *right!* Hadn't his very own cousin told her so – *and* all his friends?

But this man called Jan, which was a girl's name but nobody laughed, was a policeman, and they said he always told the truth. It was all very puzzling.

'Oh,' she said again, clutching her grandfather's hand. Gramps was someone she could always trust. 'But we can just go and look, can't we? Let's go and look!'

Together, they went; they looked; and on their return, both were ready for bed.

Though assured it would be less than an hour's drive, the family were keen to set off next morning for Minehead and the 'proper sandy beach' where Persephone could at last give her unicorn its promised swim. This bright pink inflatable toy boasted a mane and tail of electric blue, a silver-grey horn, and googly green eyes with feathery black lashes painted to an improbable length. Lucinda shuddered each time she saw it, but Persephone loved the thing. Having made her father inflate it she refused to let the air out again, even when packing. 'If you make him go flat you'll have killed him, and he'll be dead!' she wailed. For the sake of peace inside the car on a long, tiring journey her parents yielded, though many times during the trip her grandfather longed for a penknife, or even an un-safety pin.

Jane Merton, toiling for much of the day over photos and sketches, finally pinned them at arm's length for consideration through coloured glass filters. Okay, she'd never get it just as she wanted it, but perhaps the result of her labours... wasn't so bad, as an experiment. The chocolate brown and whipped creamy foam of the tumbling river, the grey-blue-pewter of the Severn Sea – yesterday's sunset, tipping the waves with fire... under the influence of different colours the little series of paintings looked quaintly, pleasingly surreal – and nothing at all like anything she'd ever created before.

'Business cards,' said Jasper at once, when at last he was allowed to see how she'd been spending her time. The work surprised but intrigued him.

Jane contemplated the paintings. 'For me? It's hardly representative of my usual stuff. I've no idea what happened, or where it came from. I was just trying something out for a bit of fun, and I think it worked – probably because it *was* just for fun – but I wouldn't want to mislead people into thinking it's – well, the way I want to go.'

'We applaud Jane Merton's versatility,' intoned Jasper, using an exaggerated Trendy Critic voice. 'This promising young artist challenges us far beyond our comfort zone each time she presents her latest masterpiece. Who knows what further bold, dramatic and daring steps she might not take on her creative journey? We look forward to travelling – not at her side, for this would be to presume too much – but certainly close behind as she leads the way far into her visionary future—'

'Idiot.' Then she frowned. 'Expect the unexpected, you mean? But I don't think I want to be unexpected. I'd far rather be... reliable. It's more comfortable for *me*, never mind for anyone who might want to commission my work. We moved away from London in the first place to live a more comfortable life, didn't we? Less pressure? And we love it! At least, I do.' She sometimes wondered if she'd pushed him into moving just because, from a child, she had loved the idea of living in Clammer Cottage and, when the opportunity came, it had seemed too good to miss. But had he begun to regret agreeing with her childhood's dream? Was he now only humouring her?

'I love it here,' she repeated. 'Don't – don't you?'

He stared. 'Of course I do, even if the longer we *are* here the farther away seems my plan to grow vegetables in the old hemp garden!' He chuckled. 'One day, perhaps – just as one day you will establish the Tollbridge School, and wipe the floor with all those has-been artistic movements like the Newlyn School, or St Ives, or—'

'Double idiot,' said Jane, much relieved.

'Idiot yourself.' He took up a painting. 'And no, I didn't mean business cards for you. Anyone who knows you can tell this is just you playing around – and why not? I really like it. Catches the eye. Something new – but I meant cards for me, though I shouldn't have said "business", I should have said "post". Postcards, for compliment slips.'

'For Packlemerton's Publicity? What's wrong with the ones you've got now?'

'You sum it up in one word, my bold and daring visionary: *now*. It ought to be the day after tomorrow. In advertising you need to be seriously ahead of the game, not so much up-to-date as in the next century. When it's always the same old same old, if you don't take care, familiarity can breed whatsit and then you'll sink without trace.'

'You mean I'm wrong to want to settle for being comfortable?'

'Look, you know what works for you, you do it, it sells, you're happy. Why change anything when you don't want to? If the time ever comes when you *do* want to, I'll be cheering you on. Only – yes, I love living here, but maybe I do fancy a slight change of direction for myself. Try something new for fun – like you.' He waved the painting to make the point.

Jane regarded him with suspicion. 'You were pretty thick with Barnaby Christmas the other night in the Anchor,' she said. 'Is he the one who's been giving you ideas?'

Her husband gazed at the ceiling, his face deliberately blank though his lips twitched.

'Jasper, what's that old rascal trying to talk you into now?'

'He's no more of a rascal than Mike Binns, and Gabriel, and—'

'Don't change the subject. Barney's taken a shine to you because you're not in the least bothered that he made a small fortune – or perhaps an enormous fortune, nobody knows – when he left here all those years ago, and you don't make jokes about it now he's back. You treat him as an equal, and he likes it. Fair enough. But until now you've been happy enough with your Packlemerton designs, or if you weren't you never told me – and you've been working so much harder than I like, and getting tired. You didn't even join in when the others were –' she hesitated – 'were amusing the parents of that Tolliday child, while she was safely out of the way.'

'And having drinks bought for them, the more they got into their stride.' He laughed. 'Talk about telling the tale! Expert isn't the word, but of course they've had years of practice at amusing the innocent tourist, never mind the way Susan encourages them with all the new stuff she keeps digging out.'

'They don't need much encouragement.' Jane herself had been surprised at how Gabriel Hockaday managed to add ever more gloss to the story of the Shipwrecked Dog and the Two Drowned Welshmen. He said her drawings had inspired him.

'If it didn't work, they wouldn't do it.' Jasper grinned. 'They enjoy themselves, and it does seem to be what other people enjoy too – and they do understand where to draw the line, as well as the longbow! You really can't say that story about running the squire's son out of town is suitable for a kid her age. I mean – look how long you yourself had to wait to find out, when how many times was it your mother brought you down to camp on Miriam's floor, or squeeze you into a tent beside the chickens?'

Jane made the logical deduction. 'So Barney wants you to handle the publicity for his holiday lets.'

He shrugged. 'Could be. I'm saying nothing. It's early days – we've both got plenty to explore – but he told me it was something I said weeks ago that got him thinking, and he'd like me to be involved from the start because it might really take off, if handled properly, and he pays his debts, he said.'

'I hope he isn't asking you to add to yours. Does he – good heavens, does he want you to put in any money?'

'Don't worry! At first it'll just be payment in kind. I'm giving him some of my time, my expertise, my contacts in due course – but like I said, it's still early days. I'll tell you when – if – anything's decided.'

His tone suggested this was, for now, his final word on the subject. Jane returned to contemplation of her paintings. 'Compliment-slip postcards – yes, I can see they'd work for that. The same as before? My design on one side, your details on the other.'

'Even if almost everything happens electronically these days, you must admit it's been a good gimmick to send *physical* receipts at close of business. The ones that don't go straight in the recycling or stuck away in a file make handy bookmarks, shopping lists, gift tags if you cut them up – and if people actually send them through the post the way we intended, that spreads the word even better. I should think every postman in the country must read every single card as he sorts the day's delivery, to find out what's going on before they land on people's doormats.'

'We need to have another word with Sam Farley. He did such a good job with your last batch. You'd never know they were printed by a different company.'

'Not unless you check the small print! Don't forget, it pays the printer to advertise, too.' He sighed. 'Oh, it's too good an afternoon for wasting the whole day indoors working. What d'you say we head up to Sam's in half an hour or so? Give us both time to tie up our most urgent loose ends and still get plenty of sunshine.'

'And time to phone to make sure he's in. I don't mind the walk—'

'The climb, you mean.'

'The exercise,' she compromised, 'or the fresh sea breezes, and certainly not the sunshine, but it's been a hot day and I don't want to carry anything more with me than I need.'

'Camera, sketchpad, pencils, phone, keys…' He counted on ostentatious fingers.

'Today, just my keys, unless there's a very good reason for anything else. I've been working all day and this will be down-time.'

'Me, too.' He smiled. 'Half an hour, okay? I'll phone the Coastguard Printery to check and then – we synchronise watches!'

Chapter Seven

As they turned into the drangway – a narrow alley between two cottages – in Boatshed Row, Jane and Jasper saw Captain Longstone ahead of them, climbing the Coastguard Steps with no need to pause on the halfway corner where so many other climbers had to admire the view for rather longer than they'd intended.

'He may be pushing fifty, and spent most of his working life in submarines, but that man is fit,' said the admiring Jasper. 'On a day like this, though…' The Mertons, having debated the risks of heatstroke and dehydration, were not hurrying.

Jane giggled. 'He knows it's hot, and he's taking precautions. He's not wearing his albatross hat!'

Rodney Longstone's everyday headgear was a quiet tweed affair, a modest spray of feathers tucked in the band. Tollbridge liked to suppose they came from the albatross he'd once shot, a stirring episode recounted in fancy verse by some old poet or other.

'I hadn't noticed,' said Jasper, 'but you're right. It's a panama. Bet you anything he rolls it up and keeps it in a tube when he wears the other one.'

'We'll ask Angela. She doesn't say much, and he certainly doesn't, but they do seem to get along pretty well when you see them together, which admittedly isn't that often. I think,' said Jane, with a fond look at her husband, 'they're both rather lonely.'

'The way to a man's heart, remember?'

'If you married me for my cooking you were out of luck.'

Jasper swung the tote bag he carried on her behalf. 'Let's hear it for ready meals, the deep-freeze and the microwave oven. Released from domestic slavery by modern technology, we're free to concentrate on our work – and on each other,' he added hastily. 'Just in case you thought I'd got my priorities wrong.'

The captain reached the top of the Steps to head off at a resolute though not excessive pace in the direction of the Watchfield car park.

'Once right round, and then back down,' said Jane, quoting Angela. 'Every day!'

Jasper shuddered. 'Rain or shine – I know. So, well done the captain and anyone else who's mad enough, but I still think moderation in all things is the only way.'

'Any excuse to stop halfway up the Steps!'

They slowed their pace, but didn't pause on the little viewing platform. Since leaving London, they had found that the hills and clifftop walks of their new home kept them in excellent trim. How much fitter than basically fit did anyone need to be?

Sam Farley leaned on the gate of the old coastguard lookout as they approached, gazing out to sea. The windows of his printery, like the door, were flung wide. Sam's former premises, in the steep valley of Meazel Cleeve, had never been so open to the outside air in hot weather. He was making up for lost time. After an uncertain start he'd come to terms with indoor turbulence by applying to wayward sheets of paper old socks begged from family and friends, weighted with handfuls of Tollbridge chezell.

'A grand day,' he greeted his visitors, 'and a busy one.' He waved towards the dull, distant glitter of the pewter canvas on which vessels of varying size and purpose made their way up and down the Bristol Channel. Here on the headland there was no sound except the ruffle of grass, the shriek of a gull; the indistinguishable shapes on the faraway water were so far away they seemed motionless. The only noticeable movement was the whirl of seabirds over the wake of any likely-looking fishing boat.

'I wish I'd brought my sketchbook after all,' said Jane. 'Or my camera.'

Jasper shook the bag that held her small portfolio. 'First things first. It's not why we're here. Take a good long look and remember the view for when we're home again.'

'Yonder's the *Priscilla* headed for home,' said Sam, picking up on the final words and pointing to a small, dark shape with a curious wake. 'Mickey and Mike with the latest party after that giant conger, as I recall. Certainly taking their time over it.'

When they'd first arrived in Tollbridge Jane, and especially Jasper, had wondered how even the landlubber locals could tell one plodding silhouette at sea from another, without taking time to think it over. Both Mertons knew now that, with the sea in everyone's blood from birth, natural instinct couldn't be denied.

'I bet that eel's tired of having its photo taken every time it's caught,' said Jasper.

'In and out of the water, on and off the scales – by now I should think the poor thing must be dizzy,' said Jane.

'Old enough to know better, but can't never resist a tasty bait,' finished Sam, with a chuckle. 'But never mind what's happening out there, come you along in and show me what you've got, and how you might like me to treat it.'

Mike Binns was at the wheel, changing course yet again to achieve yet another hopeful drift across what was normally a productive fishing area. Once more he stopped the engines of the *Priscilla Ornedge* and once more Simon adjusted the hook, line and sinker attached to the rod that leaned, dejected and solitary, against the ship's rail. The other (successful) rods were long ago packed away with the rest of their owners' gear, and everyone except the owner of the solitary rod felt very guilty.

He, however – assuring them that, honestly, he didn't mind, he'd had a great day anyway – sat back down on his upturned box and continued (he said) to think positive as he watched the end of his rod for any hint of bending. Everyone else tried to look the other way as the little fishing boat followed her slow and erratic course to harbour.

And yet the day had begun so well for the positive-thinking Simon. He'd slept in a comfortable bed in the Slandered Pig's best room, and risen early. He'd enjoyed a hearty breakfast, laughed with his fellow early risers as he read his birthday cards, and been collected by the Hockaday minibus to drive in celebratory state to Tollbridge, in good time to board the *Priscilla* at the right stage of the tide.

The preliminaries once completed, Mickey had begun his act. He might not be the showman his father was but he did his best, glancing over to Mike, who gave a quick nod.

'First thing,' announced Mickey, gathering the young men about him, 'you eight will draw lots for where to sit—'

'No, they won't,' broke in his father on cue. 'That's to say – not ezackly.'

'We thought, as it's Simon's birthday—' someone ventured, but Mike Binns had his performance by heart, and spoke right over him.

'My son can be a bit forgetful on occasion.' He turned to Mickey in mock indignation. 'So what about my Scrambler Sorter? Arter all my trouble and sacrifice, what's more!'

'There now, if "forgetful" idn the very word.' Mickey stroked his dark beard, and sighed. 'Sorry, Dad – sorry, all. So, as to this Scrambler. Now my father, being a man of original and inventive mind and skilled with his hands –' Mike bowed – 'he thought it poor sport for folk like you, coming out with us for the fishing, just to put bits of paper with numbers in an old cap and shake them. He said anyone could do that.' He gazed round the little group. 'I'm sure you'll be in agreement with him that you've done such a thing many times yourselves? Seemed to him you might just as well be buying a raffle ticket, or – or playing tombola. Nothing out-of-the-way special.'

A chorus of the anticipated agreement came from eight obedient throats.

'So he had this idea,' Mickey went on, 'and, it being the birthday of young Simon here, he shall do the honours – which, speaking of birthdays, is how it all came about. My dad wanted a drone, but from one cause or another I gave him a Scrambler Tank—'

'Money,' interposed Mike. 'Sometimes that boy of mine can be a regular pinch-fart.' This term for a miser was another research gem from Susan Jones, and he'd been longing to deploy it: but in all-male company only. Mike Binns had the instincts of a gentleman.

'—and so,' Mickey shook his head at his father, 'to settle accounts with me, what must he do but reinvent the thing just to choose numbers—'

'And it does!' Proudly, Mike produced from a nearby locker an elaborate pipework frame of green and yellow, to the centre of which he had fixed his dramatically modified Scrambler Tank. The tracks had been removed and combined to make one long drive-belt. Round the midriff of what remained, a metal band (green) fastened it to the main pipe (yellow). There were clockwork wheels, cogs and gears of assorted size in various places; in front of the whole stood a miniature lobster pot, woven with thin silvery wire. From a pocket Mike produced a drawstring bag. He shook it; it rattled. He tipped out the contents on the palm of his hand. The young men drew close and saw eight small wooden spheres, painted in different colours. Mike tipped seven of the little balls back in the bag.

'You each pick one,' he instructed. 'Our birthday boy has this red one, meaning first choice, but the rest of you must take what comes.'

They did as they were told. Mike nodded. 'Hold fast, all.' He produced another drawstring bag, repeated his shake-and-tip performance, and displayed on his palm eight wooden cubes, each numbered in sequence with a different colour; red was Number One. He passed this to Simon, returned the others to the bag and handed this also to the birthday boy. 'Into the pot with the magnificent seven, young man.'

The cubes were shaken carefully through the mouth of the silver lobster pot. Simon tried to hand the empty bag back to Mike, but the old man stopped him. 'You'll have need of it shortly, midear. Just wait.' He turned to his son. 'Show him, Mickey.'

'You pull this handle,' said Mickey, 'and stand back a bit, and when anything falls be ready to catch it in the bag.'

As Mike stood and supervised, Simon pulled the handle. Gears clunked, wheels turned, the caterpillar-track belt squeaked as it moved. The arms of the Scrambler waved at random, opening and shutting their claws; then one arm shot down into the lobster pot and groped inside. At last it pulled out a cube, straightened, and stopped in mid-air.

'Quick,' said Mike and Mickey in unison. Simon held the mouth of the drawstring bag under the cube. The claws loosened their grip. Simon caught the cube neatly, emptied the bag, and announced that the fourth choice of fishing station was allotted to the holder of the peacock blue ball.

'There, now!' Mike bowed repeatedly and smiled, acknowledging the applause.

'Oh, yes,' he went on, as general interest and admiration were expressed. 'Took a fair while to work it out and build it, but tidn at all a bad job, though I say so myself.'

'Far better than bits of paper in a hat,' everyone agreed, as Simon prepared to pull the handle for the next station choice. While his friends had already decided that Simon's first choice was no more than his birthday due, they couldn't deny that the Binns Scrambler experience was an unforgettable (and fun) contrast to merely picking out a piece of paper at random, or simply being told (boring) that of course he should choose first.

His birthday had indeed begun well.

The phrase 'downhill all the way' can't apply at sea, but perhaps it should. Mickey and Mike stopped the *Priscilla* long before she arrived at her mid-channel fishing ground, for lines to be cast for bait; Simon watched the rest of the company land mackerel after mackerel, while he caught nothing. He attached fresh spinners; he begged feathers from his friends; he still caught nothing. After some thought and much teasing he considered a change of station – did indeed change – and still caught nothing. After further thought (and somewhat muted teasing) he swapped to the other side of the deck. Nothing, yet again.

There were thunderous cheers when at last he hooked a ray. The huge flat body wriggled and the great wings flapped as he reeled it in – a renewed roar of thunder – and then, as the muscular tail thrashed clear of the water, the absence of any obvious tip to it prompted an outburst of groans, jeers and laughter.

Simon laughed with them: what else was there to do? 'Put it back,' he said. 'Put it back! I won't risk getting anywhere near the thing – no, not even for a photo,' as protests erupted from every side. 'With today's luck, what are the chances it'll be the only de-stung stingray in angling history where they didn't do it right? Blood poisoning will only be the start of my troubles!'

In the circumstances it was hard for anyone to disagree.

A party of eight young men is a party in high spirits, especially towards the end of an invigorating and sociable summer's day.

No alcohol was permitted on board the *Priscilla Ornedge* but none was really needed: friendship and fun were enough. Even Simon, whose birthday hadn't gone at all as expected, felt no particular need to drown his sorrows as the *Priscilla Ornedge* began to zigzag slowly on her homeward way.

Simon looked around the chattering, laughing group of his friends and tugged at the sleeve of his fishing jacket to check his watch. He made up his mind. 'Right, enough's enough!' They all stared at him. He shrugged, rose a little stiffly from the upturned box, and stretched. 'Captain Binns! Thanks for trying, but let's call it a day and head for port, and hope for better luck next year—'

'—or sooner than that,' said someone who'd had many photos taken, including several with the celebrated conger.

'Hear, hear!' shouted someone else who'd been almost as successful.

'Give Simon a chance at that eel!' cried another, amid catcalls and loud whistling.

Mike Binns asked if he was sure. Simon said he was. Mike duly set a new course and all eyes, apart from those of the helmsman, were on Simon as he began to dismantle his rig from the stern rail. Mickey was below, ministering to the engine. Mike was glad to be at last steering directly for home.

Simon turned with one hand theatrically raised and his mouth open, about to suggest that his photo should now be taken as he made to hurl the unlucky rod into the sea – when he shook his head, and blinked.

He shook his head again. 'Hey, what's with all the commotion on top of the cliff? Talk about summer lightning!'

In the Coastguard Printery up on the headland Sam, Jane and Jasper were busy with a colour chart, holding samples under different lights to see which had the most striking effect, when they heard the shouts. They'd been so engrossed in comparison that at first the noise seemed no more than the scream of gulls in an even greater frenzy than usual.

'Fish-guts over the stern,' suggested Sam. 'Tidn like to be that conger, but the cries do suggest Mickey's folk may intend a fish supper tonight.'

The shouts became shrieks.

The three turned to stare at the open window.

There was a bang at the open door as Captain Longstone rushed in. He didn't bother with preliminaries.

'A shaving mirror, quick,' he said to the startled Sam.

'A – what?'

'Mirror, man. You must have one – you've no beard – or a smooth metal plate – anything you've got that will reflect the sun. And hurry!'

So urgent was his tone that Jasper was thankful the captain hadn't demanded a shaving mirror of him. To minimise clutter in their new home the Mertons had positioned the bathroom cabinets with care, and Jasper shaved each day with the help of a mirrored door. He could see himself tearing the door from its hinges – or even the larger, wardrobe door – in response to that voice of command.

Sam reacted as Jasper would have done, leaping almost to attention before sprinting from the room, to return not fifteen seconds later with a shaving mirror on a monopod stand.

'Thanks.' Captain Longstone seized it and went back outside.

Sam, Jane and Jasper followed in silence. The shouts and cries grew louder.

The captain hurried almost to the cliff edge and stared out to sea. He looked up at the sun, down at the sea, changed his position slightly and raised the mirror between his hands. He began to move it to and fro, muttering under his breath. Clearly, whatever he had hoped would be happening, wasn't.

Jane looked warily over the cliff towards the harbour far below. There was the pewter sea, stained with its dark fan of chill Exmoor rainwater dragged from the shore by a strong outgoing tide. There were... two people running along the short stone pier waving, shouting, screaming at—

At a very small, very pink dot floating in the middle of the dark and freezing fan being dragged out to sea by the tide. The second-highest tide in the world.

'Ah,' said Sam. 'Someone in trouble.'

'It – it must be that little girl,' said Jane. 'She kept talking about taking her unicorn for a swim – they told her it was too cold here – too dangerous—'

'That age,' said Sam, 'there's nobody ever credits their parents with talking sense. That age they think there's no rules apply to them.'

'But they were going to Minehead—'

'Seems they've come back,' said Sam.

'There's always the lifebelt at the end of the pier,' said a hopeful Jasper.

Sam judged the distance with a knowledgeable eye. ''Twouldn never reach so far, and she'd miss catching the thing even if it did. Then she'd lose her hold and fall off – if she's not lost it already and slipped, with panicking.'

'Oh, no!' Jane wrung her hands. 'I can swim – why can't her parents? Oh, why am I up here and not down there? There's nothing anyone can do!'

'Nonsense,' snapped the captain, still busy manoeuvring the mirror. 'If the man at the *Priscilla*'s helm will only look this way there's plenty he can do, if the child keeps her head.'

Jane gulped. 'She's – she's only just seven.'

'Old enough to keep her – ah!' The whistle of M.V. *Priscilla Ornedge* erupted in a series of toots. 'Good,' said the captain. 'He's seen my signal. Now, then!'

Mike, at Simon's talk of summer lightning, looked up. Simon's friends had likewise heard, and tried to follow his gaze, but the early start they'd had to their day was finally catching up with them. Eyes blinked – were rubbed – and were rubbed again.

'Mickey!' roared his father.

Mickey wasn't slow. That roar had been urgent. 'What's up, Dad?'

'Signal from the Watchfield.' Mike gripped the wheel. 'My code's a touch rusty, but I reckon – I think O, O, O means...'

'Means "man overboard",' said Mickey after the briefest of pauses. 'Signal them we've seen. I'll get the book.' As he rummaged in a wheelhouse drawer, his father rocked a switch to and fro, firing a quick salvo of toots in reply to the clifftop flashes.

'GW,' read Mike aloud. 'GW – followed by MC, I think. GW, MC – that right?'

'Yes,' came the unexpected and confident response from one of the anglers.

As Mickey unearthed the code book and stood up, everyone else stared at the confident responder, who blushed. 'No idea what it means, but it's Morse all right. I was in the Scouts when I was a kid. Some things kind of stick with you. When I was a kid,' he repeated firmly. 'But then I found out about girls.'

As his friends drowned this confession in more catcalls and whistles Mickey leafed his way to the appropriate pages of the *International Code of Signals*. 'GW – "Man overboard. Please take action to pick him up." Dad—' But Mike was already adjusting the controls. The engine hummed. Mickey continued leafing.

'MC, MC,' he muttered. 'Ah! MC – "There is an uncharted obstruction in the fairway. You should proceed with caution." Everyone to the rails and start looking! Whoever's out there must be adrift with the tide, or maybe caught by one of the river outflows – we've no way of knowing whether he's got a boat or a paddleboard or a rubber duck – so, all eyes peeled for whatever might be coming our way!'

Until the alarm was raised all eight anglers had been in tearingly high spirits, even Simon the Unlucky effervescent with sunshine and good company: but now sixteen eyes focused calm and keenly as the young men, four to port and four to starboard, crowded against the rails and concentrated on the grey-brown waters of the Severn Sea. Mickey left his father at the wheel to busy himself assembling boathook, lifebelt and first aid kit before he joined the watchers.

Being the youngest on board did not mean having the sharpest eyes.

'Pink!' yelled Mike Binns, spinning the ship's wheel. 'Something pink afloat, fine on the port bow!' As a wartime evacuee Mike had learned his boating lore and lingo from old Ralph Ornedge; eighty years on, and like the rest of Combe Tollbridge Mike saw no urgent need to pander to modern ways. Mickey would know at once what his father meant, and right now it was Mickey who mattered.

'Over there,' translated Mickey, pointing as he hurried away. The four on the starboard side rushed to join their fellows to port, found no room, and scrambled towards the bow.

Mickey emerged from the wheelhouse with a pair of binoculars. He positioned himself with care, peering through the bins. He saw – he started – he let out a quick yelp of laughter, and from sheer surprise reverted to childhood utterance.

'By Jobs, if tidn the Tolliday child! So her's a-tookt herself and that unicorn for the very swim her ma promised, arter all!'

'By Goramighty, so she have!' Mike was shocked at Persephone's daring, and horrified by the risks she didn't know she ran. 'The daft young osebird! And when they all went over to Minehead with her special, just today morning – and the water here so cold, and her such a liddle snippet of a thing...'

Throughout this lament the old gentleman shook his head in disbelief, but M.V. *Priscilla Ornedge* did not deviate from her new and urgent course. As questions burst from eight uncomprehending throats, Mickey left his father to concentrate on steering while himself giving a quick update. Still holding the binoculars, he was able to reassure everyone that the child's arms seemed to be fast around the neck of her unicorn float, and so far she showed no immediate signs of falling off – or the float any sign of losing buoyancy.

'Talk about a miracle,' muttered somebody hanging half over the port rail, crowded by his fellows and standing on tiptoe.

'So far,' said someone else, who couldn't really see the little figure in the water.

'Don't wave!' roared Mickey, who could. His fingers clenched suddenly white about the binoculars as he stared ahead. 'Keep still, you little fool! Hold tight!' His voice shook as he turned to the others. 'She sees us coming, and the blamed young lollipot's let go the float to – to wave at us, and she's laughing!'

'And very soon like to laugh on the other side of her face,' said his father grimly. 'Let me once get my hands on her—'

'Let's hope we do,' said Mickey. 'And sooner than very soon. You lot, stop this minute with your shouts and waving! She thinks you'm egging her on. She thinks it's a joke!'

'Thinks she's done something clever, damn her.' Simon sounded anxious. He was a bachelor but knew much of small girls, having some half-dozen years earlier been presented by his sister with a niece of rather too similar character to the enterprising imp floating now in the unicorn's embrace. 'Don't encourage the kid to show off, you others. You'll only make things worse. Shut up and leave everything to the experts!'

He tried to follow his own advice, but it was hard to look on and do nothing as Mickey flung open a midships locker to remove a heavy coil of rope with wooden slats, knotted skilfully into an emergency ladder which he hooked over the side, ready to let fall. The others, finding it impossible to keep quiet as instructed, rushed up and down giving advice to the child in the water, to Mike at the wheel: but there came no more laughter from Persephone, while the older Binns studiously ignored everyone as he concentrated. Simon ran to join Mickey in checking that the ladder was secure. Mickey then double-checked Simon's checking, and frowned as the younger man took up a position by the rail and the *Priscilla*, at last, began the long, slow, curving sweep that should directly cross the river-water path down which the unicorn was drifting.

'He's coming round to make a lee,' said Mickey, as voices clamoured to know why Mike seemed to be steering in the wrong direction. 'The wind is of a temperamental nature today. We'll get in position, then the current ought to bring her right up against our side.' His gaze swept the agitated deck. With his father the only other person staying calm, how far could he rely on any help from these young men?

'Now listen, all. An adult in such a fix and we'd drop a lifebelt, but a youngster – she'll be more chilled than she thinks, and her hands numb, never mind she's frightened, so you –' he pointed – 'and you, for extra precaution take a lifebelt each – one of the horseshoes from this locker, not the rings – and when I give the word, drop 'em fore and aft of her.'

He glanced at his father. 'Better not use the winch.'

Mike nodded. They both knew that, with so many excited landsmen eager to help, they would never manage to keep the deck safely clear.

'So,' said Mickey, 'I'll be getting down there –' he indicated the ladder – 'ready to grab her, while the rest of you—'

'No,' said Simon, thinking of his niece, blocking the path of Mickey Binns and catching him by the arm. 'No, *I'll* do the grabbing and you organise my friends into a – a chain gang, to pull us both up once I've got her safe.'

'I'm insured,' said Mickey. He looked round at the agitated young men; at Simon, in particular; at Mike. 'And I reckon maybe we should risk the winch, if—'

'No! I'm thirty years younger than you,' broke in the birthday boy. 'I can swim — you could give me a lifebelt — and I lift weights at the gym three times a week.'

'He does,' someone said, as Simon began removing his boots.

'And he is,' said someone else. 'Or maybe forty years.'

'Any advance on forty?' said a third. There was some sniggering; one or two outright chortles, quickly stifled. Perhaps it wasn't so funny, after all.

Mike continued steering, slowed, and prepared to stop engines at his son's command.

Mickey looked at Simon. 'We're insured,' he said again, 'and this boat's belonged to my family since building. Saving that child's our responsibility, not yours.'

'That she is,' said Mike. 'More-and-so we're known to her. You're not.'

Simon opened his mouth to argue. Mickey raised a hand. 'We'll see,' he temporised, and ordered the two lifebelt-holders to their posts. As the silent *Persephone* floated closer, he waited for the right moment.

'Stop engines!'

Simon thrust him aside, hurled the rope ladder into the water and swung himself through the rail, bumping his toes on the planking in a frantic rung-by-rung descent.

He needn't have hurried. Mickey knew that two people on one ladder added up to danger. He uttered a single scorching oath, dared with his eye any of Simon's friends to interfere, and grimly picked up the boathook. Whether he used it to rescue the would-be rescuer or to brain him once rescued was a decision he would leave for later.

The sea slapped in hearty lumps against the *Priscilla*'s planking. With no way upon her, she rocked as she waited in the unicorn's path, thrown to and fro by the waves and the wind together. Simon let out a yell as his stockinged feet smashed into the boat's side.

Instinct curled him almost double with the pain. His forehead struck the planking. He yelled again – lost his grip – and tumbled – arms and legs flailing, mouth wide open – backwards into the sea.

Chapter Eight

Mickey Binns abandoned the boathook, kicked off his boots, and shoved aside the horrified spectators to unhook the railing chain.

'Drop the lifebelts now!' He pinched his nose – locked his grip with the other hand – and jumped.

Mike saw him go. It was fortunate that few in his audience understood even half of what he then said. The repeatable part was to the effect that if they didn't all stand by to start hauling on the ladder the instant Mickey gave the signal, they would regret it to their dying day, which if Mike Binns had anything to do with it wouldn't be long in coming.

'But first, you lifebelt pair to the ladder-head – and then *every man* to keep watch. I'm starting the engine, and if there's anyone let drift *anywhere near the propeller* I'll not be answerable for my actions to nobody. Understand?'

They understood. They watched. They waited.

A cry came from the water. Two words only, but enough: 'Got her!'

The fishermen cheered. Eager hands that had dropped lifebelts now seized upon the ladder that hung near the gap through which Mickey had jumped. With the *Priscilla* back under control the movement of the deck had steadied a little.

Those at the ladder-head waited to start hauling on command, while their friends stood by to join in as required. In the wheelhouse Mike kept the engine ticking over. He did not speak.

Sounds of splashing and shrill argument rose from below.

'So far, so good,' whispered someone. 'She's alive, at least.'

People held their breath.

The argument resumed, more urgent in tone. Mickey's voice prevailed. 'Haul away!' came a roar, less definite than before. Were his vocal cords strained – or was he bodily exhausted? 'Haul away now!'

'You heard,' said Mike through the wheelhouse window, after the briefest of pauses: but the hauling was already begun, hand over hand over hand.

'You –' Mike pointed – 'and you get ready to take the child when the time comes – and *you* and *you*, look out for my son!' He sounded almost cheerful now.

At last the grizzled black head of Mickey Binns appeared, bent protectively over something that, with further hauling, proved to be a small bundle of white and dripping misery in a strong, one-armed clasp. With his other hand Mickey gripped the rope. His feet were balanced at a precarious angle on one of the ladder's lower rungs; he was trying his best to protect the dripping bundle by keeping as much of his body as he could towards the wooden planks, rather than rise sideways or facing them, which might hurt her.

'Steady,' called Mike from the wheelhouse. 'Steady!' He knew Mickey wouldn't waste breath or energy giving further instructions.

'And – welcome aboard,' in a voice that shook only a little. Mickey coughed, and held Persephone out to waiting arms; he was seized by enthusiastic hands and helped to safety.

He grinned at his father. 'Got her, Dad.'

'So you did.' Mike assumed full command. 'You lads, drop that ladder again for the birthday boy. Be mindful of his head – and tell him he idn to climb, just hold on. Safer to be pulled up than climb, you hear? Mickey, put a drop of water on for boiling – and you, go with him to help. Bumps and bruises we'll look to later. But first – the state of the child?'

As Mickey, having retrieved his boots, squelched towards the tiny galley with his escort, all eyes turned to the young man who had first taken Persephone from Mickey and borne her out of everyone's way.

'Watch that ladder!' The wheel shook in Mike's hands. 'You want to see your friend drownded afore your very eyes when you blamed young fools have turned your backs on him? Keep a proper watch, I say!'

The blamed young fools ignored the dodgy logic, accepted the rebuke, and turned to their allotted tasks. Persephone's chief protector had seated her gently on a convenient hatch cover and now, with his arm about her, murmured reassurance, wishing she would do more than shiver and sniff. Unlike Simon, he hadn't even a niece for reference. How pale should a child's face be? How cold and blue her hands? Would she become hysterical if he let go of her to remove his jacket?

Captain Binns was glad to see that she was conscious, and could sit up without falling. Nobody had mentioned blood; the first aid box might not be needed after all. He pointed. 'Emergency locker! There's foil blankets, and make sure you wrap her well.' He saw Persephone's face turn slowly towards him, recognising – he thought – his voice. Or perhaps – as her eyes widened, and she weakly smiled – his beard.

'You wrap that child with just the same care you would your Christmas turkey!' He was pleased to see the smile broaden.

Then the deck was all confusion as Simon, having retrieved a lifebelt and squirmed within its sheltering horseshoe, dog-paddled to the foot of the ladder with so many people shouting that he could make no sense of what he heard; and he heard almost nothing above the chug of the engine, the slap of the waves.

When his friends realised this they shouted even harder and, as efforts at communication redoubled, so did the confusion. Mike, focusing on young Persephone and her attendants, had little time to worry over a full-grown and proudly fit young man who had chosen of his own free will, against all advice, to behave with some courage – and with great folly.

As Persephone's shaking hand crept from under the blanket to tug the foil more tightly round her neck, Mickey reappeared. Mike relaxed. The younger Binns, soaked but not shivering, ordered everyone to stop shouting and himself leaned over the rail, to see how things were going with Simon.

'You all right down there?' he called through the megaphone of his hands.

Simon waved. 'Doing fine – just fine! I've caught something at last!'

Mickey was speechless. With one hand, Simon waved merrily at his would-be rescuer. With the other he clutched – not the lifebelt intended to keep him safe, not a rope, not a rung of the ladder – but the battered silver-grey horn of Persephone's unicorn float.

'The catch of the day!' crowed Simon, then yelped as a slop of seawater forced his head under the waves. People gasped.

The splutter as Simon resurfaced loosened a thankful Mickey's tongue. 'You [censored] young fool, forget that [heavily censored] pink horror and take hold of the ladder!' The roar was back to full strength. He'd spent an age coaxing the dazed and dumbstruck Persephone into releasing her clutch on the unicorn so that he might carry her. He hadn't liked to frighten her, but in the end he'd had to lose his temper to make her let go – and now, this!

'Leave that damned thing and take proper hold! Set it adrift!' In a fury he turned to Simon's friends, who retreated in alarm. 'He some kind of idiot?'

'He – he's got a niece about the same age,' someone ventured.

'He adores the kid,' offered someone else, 'even if she's kind of spoiled.' A quick nod indicated the hatch cover where, between her two protectors, a pale and still silent Persephone shivered in her blanket. 'He – might be trying to avoid even more trouble?'

Mickey snarled something unprintable and turned back to Simon. 'No more words, just take hold – and *don't try to climb*. We're pulling you up dreckly minute!'

Seizing the top of the ladder he glared so hard about him there was a general rush to take position by the ropes. There wasn't room for everyone, but the fastest found their places in double-quick time and not even the outliers dared to speak. Mike from the wheelhouse nodded in grim approval.

'On a count of three,' Mickey megaphoned to Simon, 'whether ready or no, we pull up this ladder! One – two – and now!'

Ah. The young fool might not be so foolish, after all. It seemed he must have learned from his toes-to-the-planks descent, or perhaps from watching Mickey rise with Persephone in his arms; possibly, from both. As the hauling crew pulled and the ladder began its bumping upward journey, Mickey let out a shout. Simon, though hampered by the lifebelt, had positioned himself on the rungs as well as he could with the unicorn float, still defiantly in his free hand, being manoeuvred as far to his personal stern as possible.

'A blow-up bum-shield!' cried Mickey, while hauling continued and Simon's ascent, clumsy but steady, advanced. Watching the unicorn contortions suddenly made Mickey laugh so much that he lost his grip on the ladder. Perhaps this exuberance stemmed from the realisation that what might have been disaster was turning into comedy, if not farce; perhaps it was simply shock.

As Simon's head drew level with the deck, Mickey sobered. 'Clear a space all round, saving the first three or four of you.

He'll need room for manoeuvre to be safely on board – and *I'll* take hold of the lifebelt.'

'Would this help?' The fifth, no-longer-on-duty member of the team had retrieved the boathook and now brandished it with more enthusiasm than skill.

'Put that down! You aiming to crown the lad?'

But the thrill of witnessing an apparently successful conclusion to the watery adventure overcame all common sense. As Mickey reached for the lifebelt's grab-rope and other hands prepared to help Simon achieve the safety of the deck, the end of the boathook swung in a wild sweep so close above the cluster of bodies – and heads – that everyone instinctively ducked…

Everyone except Simon who, giddy with relief, had at last felt able to relieve the unicorn of its backside-shielding duties, and was poised to throw his prize to safety before allowing himself to join it on deck.

A cheap inflatable toy, further weakened by circumstance.

A working boathook, in the charge of an exuberant amateur.

There was an immediate and inevitable Convergence of the Twain.

There was a pop – a hiss – a slow, sad deflation.

Whereupon the shivering, shocked, and still silent Persephone let out a horrified shriek – and then exploded in the welcome relief of tears.

With all three impromptu bathers dripping safely on deck, Mike Binns tootled in triumph on the ship's horn: dot-dot-dot dash, dot-dot-dot dash. It wasn't correct international code, but with Persephone's family waiting for news they would know what he meant. *V for Victory. We've got her: she's safe.* Steering for the harbour he wondered if it had been Captain Longstone who signalled that first, correct warning. Captain Binns of the *Priscilla* felt sure his fellow captain would pardon his own inaccuracy.

Mickey Binns, professional fisherman, so close to home scorned a foil blanket, but insisted that Simon should follow Persephone's example and be treated like a Christmas turkey. Persephone, hearing her name, emerged from her shining cocoon to lament that her unicorn was dead, killed by the naughty man and he was a horrid, cruel murderer.

Mickey looked at Mike. A silent exchange flashed between them. The child had survived her unorthodox voyage in better shape than her naughtiness deserved. 'Tea for all,' decreed the captain of the *Priscilla*, 'meaning you too, my son.'

'Aye, aye, cap'n.' Mickey's boot-heels squelched in an obedient click and he saluted with exaggerated respect. As his hand came down a mug was thrust towards him by those members of the party who'd been busy in the galley. Simon was offered another mug, and the third was handed to Persephone.

She sipped, choked, and made a face. 'I'm not allowed sugar! This is nasty!'

'You're a shipwrecked mariner, rescued from a watery grave,' Mickey told her. 'Hot sweet tea's the standard treatment. If you were a grown-up there'd be a tot of rum besides, but as rum's not to my taste we'll both of us stick with sugar. Right?'

He fixed the rescued mariner with a stern eye, and pointed to Simon. 'There's sugar in his mug too, but he makes no complaint – do you, birthday boy?'

'Certainly not. Hot sweet tea's going down just fine, right to the tips of my toes.' Simon swallowed a heroic mouthful. 'I can see why it's the traditional cure.'

'The sea's a great place for tradition,' said Mickey, still with that stern look, 'and at sea, my child, is where you are. Drink that up and let's have no argument.'

There was something in his tone that made the unexpected passenger do as he told her, though between mouthfuls she muttered that she wasn't his child and she was glad, because he was a bully and when her mummy and daddy heard how he'd shouted at her, they would shout at him.

'I would hope,' replied Mickey, 'they would first have the good manners to thank us all for saving your life – and especially young Simon here, for trying his best even if it didn't go quite the way he planned.'

Simon started a laugh that turned into a sneeze. 'Pity about that rum,' he said once he'd finished coughing. 'I've probably caught pneumonia.'

'Soon be on dry land, ready for the doctor. You're all –' Mickey's gaze swept the deck – 'staying upalong in the Pig, aren't you? Someone down here will phone ahead and let 'em know, then whoever's driving the minibus can take you straight there. My cousin Jerry or my uncle, most likely.'

'Oh, it was only a wetting. Just a drop in the ocean!' Simon could laugh now, as the *Priscilla* passed the breakwater beacon and chugged on towards the pier. 'Honest, I feel fine – and it's certainly a birthday to remember. I've never caught so much as a mermaid before, let alone a unicorn. Like I said, the catch of the day!'

'It's *my* unicorn, and he's dead!' Persephone saw too much attention being directed away from her own all-important self. 'My birthday present!'

'Ah, my precious!' With great solemnity Mickey toasted the child over his mug of sugared tea, hoping to delay any full-throttle tantrum until her parents had her safe again in the aftermath of what had been a very close thing.

Simon guessed his intention. 'Gollum, Gollum, Gollum,' he returned, making everyone laugh; which made Persephone forget further tears in a scowl.

To general relief the scowls and sulks lasted until M.V. *Priscilla Ornedge* came to rest alongside the pier. Only when Persephone saw her parents in the forefront of the small crowd waiting on the quayside did the little girl's tears return; and Mummy was quite as tearful as her daughter. Even father

Eddie could barely speak for the shock of seeing his child safe and resplendent in silver wrap when he'd been afraid his next sight of her would be cold and silent in a shroud.

As Mike stopped engines the Tollidays were rushing to Persephone, both trying to catch her in their arms at the same time. Maternal ferocity won. 'Seffy, darling!' Lucinda could say no more, her voice stressed by emotion and screams. Her daughter's reply was a sobbing jumble of naughty men, cold water, dead unicorns, and nasty things to drink. Lucinda soothed and cuddled, Eddie patted and stroked even as they shuddered at what might have happened had the *Priscilla* not been in the right place at the right time.

Captain Binns tapped Eddie on the shoulder, and drew him to one side. 'That's a very lucky little girl, and all's well as ends well – but don't you let her think she've done something clever, grown men jumping in the water to save her life. Now, my son Mickey's used to water, more so than this lad here – who did his best, and got it wrong, but the intention was willing and he's every bit so brave as Mickey – and no less chilled and wet as the child! Best have 'em straight to the Ploverton doctor, and save scolding for tomorrow.'

'I can't thank you enough,' said Eddie. 'Both of you – all of you – not to mention whoever first raised the alarm.' His eyes looked a question.

Mike shrugged. 'We saw flashes from the old coastguard station up on the headland, but as yet we've no idea who it could've bin. Someone with knowledge of codes, is all I'll say.' He had spotted Captain Longstone among the quayside crowd, and seen him nod his approval before beating a quick and modest retreat. Captain Binns could guess who first raised the alarm, but he would say nothing. All Tollbridge knew how Rodney Longstone disliked being in the spotlight. 'No doubt,' Mike went on, 'sooner or later we'll find out who 'twas, then you can thank him privately as he deserves.'

'I certainly will – we both will, once the shock's worn off. Just now Lucinda isn't thinking straight. She's… upset. You see, we left Persephone with my father – they both seemed worn out after Minehead – we thought she'd fall asleep while we went looking for my father's old campsite in the woods. She told us she was tired, and we believed her…'

'The artful little dodger!' Mike bit back the rest of what he might have said. 'Well, she's the age for it, venturesome without the needful common sense. She'll grow out of it, I hope. Now you get her upalong to Ploverton, and let the doctor see her.'

'Thank you, we will. And then will we see you in the Anchor? The least we can do is buy everyone a drink – a dozen drinks!' Eddie looked at his wife, still on her knees with her arms round her daughter. 'You're absolutely right. Once the doctor has given the all clear, Persephone's going to get the lecture of a lifetime – but as I know I'll be the one to deliver it, I'll need plenty of Dutch courage!'

Chapter Nine

During the day the angling party had taken many photos, and thought nothing of it. While the *Priscilla* was plodding along her mid-Channel beat they had also used their phones to call friends who'd missed this particular trip, sharing the joke of birthday Simon's lack of success. Mike and Mickey looked on, listened, smiled, but kept quiet.

They were unsurprised by the party's indignation when, once past the breakwater, all offers to phone ahead for the doctor were declined. With his father at the helm it was left to the younger Captain Binns to explain that, because the cliffs loomed so close and so high, mobile signals just didn't happen in Tollbridge.

'Out at sea, yes – but here, no. You can try if you want, but I'll wager you'll get nothing that's worth the effort.' Thumbs were already poised for action before it dawned on everyone that nobody knew the doctor's name or number. This wasn't, happily, a situation demanding the emergency nine-nine-nine.

'But we were able to phone from Combe Ploverton,' someone had objected.

'A thousand feet above us on the edge of the moor,' said Mickey. 'A different part of the world, Ploverton. In Tollbridge the nearest working public phone's in a box on the far side of the harbour –' he pointed – 'between Farley's shop and the Anchor.'

'Not forgetting Barney Christmas in Boatshed Row,' called Mike from the wheelhouse.

'Well, yes, Barney for emergencies – which thankfully idn how we're situated now. Of course we would have phoned ahead, or used the boat's radio, had things looked like ending badly, but 'twas clear soon enough there was no need. More to the point now, with Barney there's never any telling if he'll be home at this hour.' Then Mickey frowned. 'Can't make out what's happened to Jerry. That minibus I'm sure was booked to meet your party, so either him or Gabriel should have bin waiting there by the quay. I wonder.'

The *Priscilla* had nestled softly against her fenders, the Tollidays had rushed to claim their wet and wayward offspring, and the anglers began to talk of going ashore. Until the minibus arrived, however, there seemed little point in abandoning what might remain of a possible thrill. With a more appreciative audience, would the child succumb to hysterics? Would there be room in the minibus for everyone? If not, who must surrender their seats to young Persephone and her parents?

Chatter and speculation abounded as everyone relived the events of an exciting day that had started so quietly. Mickey looked again for the minibus. Accustomed as he was to cold water, even he began to feel in need of warm, dry clothes and his own mug of hot tea with something special added. He didn't mean sugar.

Mike understood his son's feelings. He glanced at the wheelhouse clock, then decided to order Mickey to get along home sharpish and leave the rest to him; but before he could say anything he stopped, cocking his head to one side.

'I hear him now!' Mike, for once quicker than his son, was proud of it. 'Coming this way, but with echoes and voices all about I couldn say ezackly when – aha!'

The crimson minibus purred into view down Boatshed Row. As it approached, the V-for-Victory rhythm sounded on the horn until the driver executed a skilful three-point-turn, and came to a silent halt.

The passenger door opened. A man jumped out, and turned to drag after him a bulky yellow bag. He was of medium height, plump, red-faced and with a shock of white hair that bristled above a pair of startling jet-black eyebrows.

'The doctor!' cried Mickey Binns as Galahad Potter-Carey, M.D. strode purposefully towards the *Priscilla*. 'Well done, Jerry!'

Leaping on board, the doctor shook his head. 'No: well done, Rodney Longstone. He made sure nobody was seriously hurt and then went to phone from the shop – no point in wasting time trying Barney Christmas – but before he was halfway there he spotted Jerry heading this way. Flagged him down, told him to turn back and fetch me from Ploverton – called me at the surgery – and here I am.'

Dr Potter-Carey had a pleasant, unexaggerated West Country accent and a confident manner to reassure even Lucinda, whose instinct was to mistrust advice from any non-London professional who didn't wear a well-cut suit. Sending the Tollidays, with detailed instructions, to await him below in the *Priscilla*'s small cabin, Galahad took a brisk approach to his adult patients. A quick chat with Mickey and a more rigorous exchange with Simon soon released these gentlemen from Gally's nominal care. Knowing Mickey would probably ignore him, he nevertheless prescribed warm baths, hot drinks, dry clothes and an early night for both. Simon was staying at the Slandered Pig? He himself would have a word with Tom Tucker regarding as late a start as possible for tomorrow's homeward journey.

He took more care with Persephone, neither making light of her escapade nor dwelling overmuch on what might have happened. The little girl had been stripped by her mother to her underwear and vigorously rubbed with a towel supplied by Mike Binns, who produced another foil blanket and took the wet one away to dry.

Gally put appropriate medical questions to Lucinda, and nodded. He turned to her daughter, listening with interest to the child's narrative as he tapped her knees with a little hammer and surreptitiously checked various other physical responses.

'A pink unicorn? Not many of them in these parts. Pink elephants, yes, or so I'm told by some of our more enthusiastic cider drinkers, but a unicorn – oh, he's dead? Let me tell you, young lady, you're damned lucky you aren't dead too. Not a nice way to go, being drowned. A birthday present? Swimming at Minehead – wasn't Minehead enough for the pair of you? Why not? Oh, your mummy said...'

He glanced at Lucinda. 'A warning to parents to be careful what they promise, Mrs Tolliday. At this age children have a curious logic of their own. But you've a fine healthy specimen here, I'd say.' His smile invited the silent Eddie to share the compliment. 'Lasting effects unlikely, I imagine, except maybe a brief sense of her own mortality. Get her back to the Anchor for a change into something dry after a warm bath and...' He pondered. 'Hot chocolate, I think, possibly with marshmallow sprinkles—'

'I don't like marshmallows,' he was informed.

'—or a dusting of cinnamon. Have they never told you it's rude to interrupt?'

Persephone opened her mouth, caught the twinkle in his eye and, with a faint twinkle of her own, meekly subsided.

He nodded. 'Doctor's orders, though I'll let you off the marshmallows. A hot drink, but as long as it's hot and rehydrating she can have – oh, ginger tea, if she likes. Ask Tabitha Ridd for a mug of her famous cold-cure. Tabitha was born an Evans, and in that family they swear by their ginger and aniseed; and live to a ripe old age, what's more. Do the child no harm at all, ginger tea. But no ice cream. Then an early night after a light supper, and –' he looked at Eddie – 'a stern lecture tomorrow morning before the matter's closed for ever.' He winked at Persephone. 'No horsewhips or spanking, of course.'

'She'll get the lecture,' Eddie promised. Lucinda tried to argue, but with her voice still in shock it wasn't hard to talk over her. 'She doesn't need to go to hospital? You're sure?'

Dr Potter-Carey snorted. 'You seriously suggest cluttering up Accident and Emergency with a tough little tyke like her? Three of you on three separate chairs? Talk about a waste of space!' This time he winked at Persephone's father.

'I'm not a waste of space,' said Persephone.

'You're a waste of my time, young lady.' Gally returned various bits and pieces to his bulky yellow bag. 'I've far more important people than you to look after now – people who are ill. Get back to the pub with your parents and enjoy the rest of your holiday. If I see you again, it must be for a broken leg at least.'

He tugged the drying wisps of her hair and patted her on the head, twisting his features in a comical grimace. He handed a slip of paper to Lucinda.

'I've prescribed a mild sedative, but I doubt if she'll need it.' He grinned. 'You might, of course! But I said she was a tough little tyke.' Persephone preened herself, and he tugged again at her hair before bidding them a general farewell.

Lucinda studied the prescription. 'A sedative? Well, I must say—'

'Just pipe down for now,' said her husband. 'Please.'

'I like that doctor,' announced Persephone. 'He made me laugh inside, and feel warm all over.'

'That's good,' said Eddie. 'I liked him too.'

Lucinda managed a smile.

That evening Persephone slept upstairs with her tummy comfortably full, as her father read a book in the next room.

In the bar Professor Tolliday bought drinks for the captain and crew of M.V. *Priscilla Ornedge,* wishing he could have done as much for Simon. He knew he really should take a taxi up to the Slandered Pig to thank the young man in person; he had phoned the landlord with a heartfelt message to pass on, giving his credit card number for Simon's room, board and any extras; but he didn't care to leave Lucinda, who had needed much persuasion to allow even her husband to keep discreet watch over their child once she had fallen asleep. Lucinda would never consent to leaving the perceived shelter of the Anchor to drive even the short distance to the Pig.

Anchor regulars were agreed the man was right not to abandon 'his poor daughter-law, just a shadow of herself after yesterday, and small wonder, with the child so close to drowning and only saved by the nearest of chances'.

'Captain Longstone?' The puzzled professor looked at the latest speaker, Sam Farley, and turned to Mike Binns. 'But I thought—'

'The cap'n idn a great one for company,' Sam explained, 'unlike Mike here, and Mickey when he'm in the mood. Cap'n Longstone prefers his own company, in a general way –' he saw Angela watching, and dared name no exceptions – 'though he's friendly enough when you meet him out walking—'

'—which is how he sighted your youngster, and was able to send us the news,' put in Mickey Binns. 'Flashed "Man overboard" from the headland and my dad spotted the flashes and – well, we were in just the right place to help, so we did.'

'And we can't thank you enough,' said Charles Tolliday. At his side Lucinda could only nod, and sip a silent toast in the drink she'd at last been willing to accept. For the light supper as prescribed by Dr Potter-Carey, Angela and Tabitha had rustled up the most tempting of menu choices but, while Persephone asked for second helpings, her mother had barely picked at her food. Angela wondered if alcohol was such a good idea on an almost-empty stomach, but the professor said that his daughter-in-law was suffering from delayed reaction, and he would keep a careful eye on her.

'You've thanked us just fine.' Deliberately, as Sam beat a strategic retreat, Mickey raised his mug. The child was safe, the family grateful, the point made – and the embarrassment growing acute. He wasn't as comfortable as his father at being centre-stage. At least Mike had been agreeable to steering the Tollidays to a quiet corner, away from those who would otherwise be pulling Mickey's leg for weeks if they heard even half of what had been said in his praise.

'You've thanked us just fine,' Mickey insisted. 'We'll be blushing like a couple of brides if you keep on this way. There's no need to go overboard!'

'True, my son, I'll agree there idn now.' Mike chuckled, and drank deep.

Mickey stared, realised what he'd said, and laughed. 'Well caught, Dad: no need to go overboard now – and for my part, that's the last word on the subject. We'll talk of something else.' He turned to Charles Tolliday. 'You'm a professor, I recall from last night: but what discipline? I'm a mining engineer. Took my degree at Cardiff, over the water –' he waved a vague hand – 'but a long time ago. I grew weary of treasure-hunting, as Dad likes to call it, all round the world with no more than moderate success, so I've bin home working alongside this old rascal for I couldn say how many years now.' He stroked his beard. 'You know, people warn about settling into a family business, but while I can't speak for Cap'n Binns here I'll say for myself that things might have turned out a damsight worse than they have –' he winked – 'so far! Michael Ornedge Binns, Bachelor of Science and still 'prentice fisherman, according to the captain here – that's me.'

He bowed ironically. His clumsy but resolute change of subject had the desired effect. Professor Tolliday took the hint and began to speak of botany, bryology and modern ecological studies, telling Mickey that his previous visit to Tollbridge had been as an undergraduate on a field trip, researching for his thesis.

'I was first attracted by the coincidence of the names – Tolliday, Combe Tollbridge – but my supervisor told me this is one of the few remaining areas of temperate rainforest in the country, noted for its rare ferns and mosses – and various hybrid trees of the whitebeam family.' The professor smiled. 'Bottle gardens were all the rage back then, and I was a lazy student. I thought ferns and mosses would be easier than trees to study at home – but then I saw the height of the cliffs I'd have to explore for the best specimens, and gave up. I'm no Tollbridge goat: not even halfway athletic. Riding a motorbike is one thing. Abseiling over a cliff is quite another, especially with a river at the bottom.'

Mickey nodded. 'The Chole and the Rindan flow fast and deep even at normal times. But when there's bin heavy rain on the moor it can bring down soil, stones, rocks – oh, all sorts, to scour the river-beds still deeper.'

'I thought it was sewage.' Lucinda cleared her throat. 'Effluent, I should have said.' The others stared. She'd kept so quiet they had almost forgotten her presence; they hadn't noticed the now empty glass whose contents had evidently relaxed her vocal cords along with the rest of her. 'When I first saw that dark water spreading across the harbour, I mean. But the landlady told me it was… iron, I think she said – and it was flowing very fast.' Her voice quavered as she gazed at Mickey. 'Very fast – and that's why poor darling Seffy had that ghastly experience, and –' she gulped – 'if it hadn't been for—'

'Ironpan,' Mickey interrupted firmly, to deflect another emotional scene. 'We've some complex geology on Exmoor, midear, which in part explains how the flooding can get so bad. There's patches of the stuff here and there all over, and—'

He saw the professor's questioning look, and reverted without thinking to his student days. 'Ironpan? A hard layer below the top surface of the ground, formed by the percolation of water through rock, precipitating iron salts as it goes.'

'Oh, he's a clever boy,' observed his father. 'Sometimes,' he added quickly.

Mickey grinned. 'So, the iron that's bin dissolved by the rain soaks just so far down and then – well, it sets, like a metal raincoat under the soil. Result: poor drainage. Now, millions of years backalong the moor was covered in trees. They rotted as they fell, and mixed with other material – result: these days when it rains, the streams run brown.'

'Let me top you up,' invited the professor as Mickey, exhausted by his efforts, without thinking finished his drink. 'Decayed vegetation, I suppose.'

'Maybe later, thanks.' Mickey moved his mug to one side, and suddenly chuckled. 'Wait! Now it comes back to me. We used to say he'd make mincemeat of James Bond.' His eyes narrowed, and his voice thrilled. He adopted a foreign accent. 'The spy with the ruthless brain – Stagnos Podzolitch, the man you hope never to meet!'

'Stagnos – oh, very good. Stagnopodzolic soil, of course,' said Professor Tolliday. Both men burst out laughing. Mike Binns beamed happily at a joke he didn't understand.

Lucinda could only glare. 'What's so funny? What have Russian spies to do with poor little Persephone? My innocent child is – is swept out to sea by a dangerous river, with not one notice anywhere in sight to warn of the dangers – and her own grandfather seems to think he can make a joke of it!' She subsided, breathless.

'Nonsense,' snapped Mickey. 'Water's a potential danger at any time. You can drown in half an inch, if circumstance allows. Anyone as don't know that shouldn be out alone.' Too late he recalled that Charles Tolliday's son and daughter-in-law had only gone exploring in the belief that their child was safe in her grandfather's charge, resting quietly back at the Anchor after the Minehead excursion. The man was in poor health: he'd fallen asleep believing the little girl to be as tired as himself, and had no idea she'd been pretending – or, giving her the benefit of the doubt, perhaps she hadn't been pretending but had woken up, and not cared to disturb him. Either way, unless he'd had eyes in the back of his head and full use of his wits he could have had no idea what she might be doing as he slept on.

'Accidents will happen,' said Mickey. 'She was lucky, and you won't let her do it again, but maybe a notice would help – or maybe not,' he had to add. 'People don't always read what's right under their noses, never mind up on a pole or a wall or a railing they might not walk past at just the right time.'

'Or a tree,' put in the professor. 'As you'll recall, Lucinda.'

'Tree? What am I supposed to – oh, yes!' Lucinda blinked at her father-in-law, then at Mickey. 'No parking,' she told him. A giggle escaped her as she repeated the words. 'No parking! He said, if an idea's a good one it's worth using again – didn't you?' She turned to the professor, who confirmed her words with a nod.

Angela appeared at the table, a tray in her hands. She'd kept half an eye on young Mrs Tolliday for some time. 'Tea and biscuits,' she announced, 'with the compliments of the house. Mickey, you can pour.' She judged Mike too relaxed after so much free cider to be safe near boiling water.

Charles Tolliday looked at her, with a smile of gratitude. 'She's overwrought, and no wonder,' he murmured, as Mickey made jokes about being mother, and his father's liking for short-bread as baked by Tabitha Ridd.

'Well, I made these,' said Angela, 'so they'll have to do. Enjoy!'

'About this tree,' prompted Mickey, as everyone accepted cups, and the biscuit plate passed round. 'Or – about the parking?'

The professor watched as Lucinda pushed aside her glass to drink tea, and nibble at shortbread. 'Yes, that was something else I got from my supervisor. When the ferns and mosses were a non-starter, I decided the whitebeam might make a better topic for research. I already knew that the genus *Sorbus* –' he glanced from Mickey to Mike – 'that's to say, this particular botanical family, which includes the service tree and the mountain ash, or rowan – the *Sorbus* can present with many subtle differences in leaves and fruits such as colour, size and indeed shape that mean an individual tree might be the only one of its kind in the world. What we could call a micro-species, often found in a particular micro-climate – one of your deep local valleys protected from any extremes of your local weather. Which is partly why the rainforest is called temperate. Nothing too extreme.'

Mickey looked genuinely, and Mike owlishly, interested. The professor warmed to his theme. 'The area has a rich variety of whitebeam, many of which are classified as rare.' He smiled. 'One of these rarities is *Sorbus admonitor*, otherwise known as the No Parking tree. The lucky chap who identified that one spotted it at the roadside near a lay-by in the Watersmeet area, with a notice fixed on the trunk saying – well, give you three guesses.'

'No smoking,' said Mickey. 'No littering.' He laughed. 'Warnings, each one!'

'Exactly. A stern admonition to behave yourself. It seemed a nice little bit of dog-Latin wordplay I could adapt for my own discovery, if I made one.' Again the professor smiled. There was a hint of pride in his voice as he went on: 'Which I did, and by coincidence not too far from where I made my camp in the woods at the top of Meazel Cleeve. I was –' he glanced at Lucinda, who wasn't really listening to a tale she'd heard before – 'I was answering a call of nature after a – a friendly evening in this very pub.'

He gestured round the bar, and suddenly seemed a little embarrassed. 'Things were slightly out of focus, you understand,

and then all at once they weren't and I could see that the very tree I – well, the very tree…' He grimaced, and fell silent.

Mickey Binns, B.Sc., forced his memory back many years. He roared with laughter. 'Never tell me you named your micro-species *Sorbus urinator*, for I'll not believe it!'

Professor Tolliday laughed, too. 'No, I wouldn't have dared even make the suggestion. My supervisor was a real stickler for correct procedure. No, I thought the name should commemorate the location of my whitebeam hybrid – the woods at the top of Meazel Cleeve – so I looked up "measles" in a Latin dictionary.' He laughed again. 'My find was recorded as *Sorbus morbilli*, and so it appears in the literature to this day.'

There was a pause.

'Prof, let *me* buy *you* a drink,' said Mickey Binns.

Chapter Ten

Signalling to Angela, Mickey saw his father nod. 'And the same here, son!' cried Mike. 'There's only so much tea a man can swallow when there could be another tip of cider – though the shortbread's very good.' He smiled at Lucinda, who returned the smile. She was no longer pale; her eyes weren't hazy. Like Angela, Mike had kept a kindly eye on her as she pulled herself together in the aftermath of her daughter's adventure.

Thoughtfully, Captain Binns rocked his mug from side to side. 'My son, I reckon you might perhaps tell the man what Susan told us t'other week. Can't do so much harm after – how long? Fifty years?' He looked at the professor. 'Idn that right? Honesty's the best policy, truth will out, and so forth.'

Charles Tolliday moved uneasily on his chair. Lucinda blinked. 'Susan? Who's she? Have we met her?' She gazed at her father-in-law. 'What does she know – what can she have told them about you that's dishonest?'

The professor looked from Mike to Mickey. 'I don't – that is, surely you can't—'

'Susan? Why, she's—'

'Dad,' warned Mickey.

'Susan Jones,' said Mike hurriedly, 'the world knows as Milicent Dalrymple. You've maybe heard of her, midear?'

Lucinda, after a moment's thought, shook her head. Professor Tolliday likewise indicated ignorance. Mike sighed. 'Oh, well. Very proud of Susan we all are in these parts – right, Mickey?'

'Right.' Mickey spoke firmly. 'All of us. Sells a deal of books and no bragging about it. Nice woman, Susan Jones.'

Mike knew his teasing had gone far enough. 'Clever, too. Finds things out on her computer, with writing so many books set at different times and places, and needs any number of interesting facts different for each book – and writes special little books about them here, too.' He lifted the mug Angela had silently refilled. 'Leaflets, telling all the local tales – and, like I say, any number of interesting facts!'

The professor took a deep breath. 'About – mugs, you mean?'

'Mugs?' Mike for a moment looked blank, and then laughed. 'Oh, yes. Well, they called the likes of this-here a penny dish in olden days, or so Susan told us, on account of how much it cost to buy.' He winked. 'You'd pay a sight more'n a penny for one such as mine now, of course, being as it is an antique.'

Lucinda sat up. 'A dish of tea! That's what they used to say, in the old days. I read it – somewhere.' Mickey hid a smile as she waved a would-be careless hand. Was the elegant Mrs Tolliday a closet fan of Milicent Dalrymple and her sisters? 'Your friend Susan must have read it somewhere, too.'

'Reads all sorts, does Susan. Knows a lot.' Mickey paid tribute as his father toasted the antiquity of his personal penny dish. 'She told us a ha'penny dish for the smaller sort, holding a pint. O'course, at the time they were cheap and cheerful, being merely cloamen – that is, made from clay – but crockery's all too soon broken, and there's not many left. I remember it happened to my uncle Gabriel – your little girl's Father Christmas – but the family all put together to have a new one fashioned for his birthday. A very handsome gift you might ask him to show you, should you be interested.'

'A very handsome gift,' echoed Mike, in wistful accents.

Mickey laughed. 'You old fraud! You know you wouldn drink from a mug of solid gold, should I have one made for you – which I've no plans to do at any time.' He tried to explain. 'Dad's mug, here, he wouldn dream of changing for another, belonging as it did backalong to Ralph Ornedge, and I believe to Ralph's father before him, but as he didn have his name glazed on as some did, we can't be sure.' He smiled. 'Talk about a family inheritance! No doubt the mug will become mine in the years ahead, with me being named for old Ralph, as I think I've mentioned—'

'Many years ahead! Don't 'ee get your hopes up too soon, Michael Ornedge Binns.'

'I'm in no hurry.' Mickey regarded his father with wry affection. 'Pay no heed to him, Prof. When there's a drop or two of drink in him and his friends, they can talk a deal of nonsense that would drive a sensible man to distraction.'

'About this Susan Jones?' persisted the puzzled Lucinda. Her father-in-law was more than bewildered.

Mickey caught his father's eye, and took a deep breath. 'Prof, maybe we should have said nothing from the start, but it's too late and can't be unsaid and need surely make no difference to your discovery.' The professor stared. Mickey floundered on.

'It's only – well, I believe there was a big change of Latin naming for plants a while back, which might accommodate the problem – if you see it as a problem, and maybe it don't matter, save for accuracy, which as a former scientist I know you'd want – though I reckon there's no particular need to tell the world the truth of it unless you feel you must…'

The professor continued to stare. Mickey hesitated. He'd seen the older man's colour come and go, his general unease; he could almost wish that Susan had said nothing, except that research should never be wasted. All she'd done was confirm from online documents what Tollbridge had always believed: what had been written up as fact by Sam Farley's father, in the tourist leaflets that hadn't appeared until after the prof's previous visit. Only... what right had they to spoil a good story when, for all he knew, the man's whole career might have been founded on the discovery he'd made fifty years ago when camping in the woods above Meazel Cleeve, beside the Meazel's Leap?

But although he now specialised in ferns – or was it moss? – a tree remained a tree, a rare hybrid a rarity, a discovery a discovery whatever name you gave it.

'Forget childhood illness,' said Mickey bluntly. '*Meazel* is a mediaeval word for *leper* – and that's the story Susan looked into, for next time she's able to write one of her updated leaflets – which at present she's too busy to do, so we can't show you the truth, but...'

He shrugged, helplessly. Charles Tolliday said nothing. Lucinda wavered between voicing sympathy for a fifty-year-old error, and annoyance that the Binns family should have drawn this error to the notice of her ailing father-in-law.

'My supervisor,' said the professor at last, 'advised me to check before committing to the name. So I did. When I found that "measles" is also used for tapeworm in pigs, the term seemed sufficiently vague for me to get away with it as a rather foolish joke – as it seems I did!' He smiled. 'Someone mentioned the legend of Ploverton's Slandered Pig. I'd like to think the original slander may have been saying that the pig was measly.'

Mickey, much relieved, smiled back. 'Might well have bin, might well – though o'course we can never know for sure.' The smile became a grin. 'And, so far back in time, there was no *Whiffle on the Care of the Pig* to be consulted, neither.'

Charles Tolliday, equally relieved, likewise grinned. 'And no George Cyril Wellbeloved to do the caring, drunk or sober. Pig hooey, indeed!' But before they could enjoy a happy celebration of P.G. Wodehouse, there were serious matters to be discussed.

'Now,' he said to Mickey, 'I know you personally don't want further thanks, but we feel there must be something we could do to thank the village for the great kindness we've been shown – and our gratitude for the happy outcome of my naughty little granddaughter's... unfortunate voyage.'

'Naughty?' Lucinda bristled. 'Unfortunate?' She could hardly nag her ailing father-in-law publicly, but she had to let her feelings out. 'If the sea – the rivers – are as dangerous as these people insist, then the very least they can do is have notices put up to warn everyone – and what they ought to have more than anything else is a lifeboat!'

'You never spoke a truer word, midear.' Gabriel Hockaday, having caught above the laughter of his friends his name across the bar, had materialised at the Tolliday table in time to catch Lucinda's complaint. In his hand he carried the handsome cider mug so admired by Mike and Mickey. 'A sad day for Tollbridge, when they took away the lifeboat. Oh, with the telephone there's Minehead and Ilfracombe –' he gestured to either side – 'to call upon as needful – and no argument, they come when called – but a boat of some sort right on the spot would save time.' He patted Lucinda's shoulder. 'And could have spared your young one breaking her heart for a dead unicorn!' He set his mug on the table; commandeered a nearby chair, and sat down.

'She was certainly upset, but –' Lucinda glanced at her father-in-law – 'I'm not sure that's altogether a bad thing, if it diverts her mind from what might have happened—'

'She won't find it so diverting tomorrow.' Charles Tolliday was stern. 'She'll have the talking-to of her young life, I hope. And anyone who even thinks of buying her a replacement for that hideous object will have me to reckon with. Until the child can demonstrate at least a modicum of common sense, and prove she can be trusted – *and* that she can swim – she shouldn't be allowed anywhere near the water unsupervised, not even to paddle.'

At the end of this speech he sat back, grey in the face where the casual onlooker might have been expecting him to turn red.

His hand, as it reached for his drink, shook. Lucinda, who had opened her mouth at his first words, straightway closed it and now, restraining herself with an effort, still said nothing.

Gabriel, Father Christmas lookalike, tried to evoke the season of goodwill.

'O'course, you not being party to recent events in Tollbridge, which indeed there's no reason you should be, you'd have no knowledge of the serious consideration being given to this very subject, namely, a return to the village of some sort of lifeboat, for when the incident may be considered local, as happened with your youngster. A small RIB working close to shore for emergencies – not as a regular service, and leaving all mid-channel activities to the big boys – oh, given time we could raise the money to buy such, only... tidn just a matter of *buying* a Rigid Inflatable Boat, midear.'

He paused for cider. Mike picked up where his brother-in-law left off. 'You see, the boat once bought there'd be shelter needed, against weather and tide, damage and theft – for RIBs don't come cheap, and even in these parts there can be rascals. You just ask upalong at the Pig and they'll tell you – but tidn dishonesty Gabriel means. A lifeboat, and storage: yes, there's empty sheds by the harbour for a boat... but the people to crew it, that's another matter. These days in Tollbridge we've not so many with understanding of the sea as at one time there were.' He stroked his suspiciously auburn beard, nodded apologetically to his schoolmate, and braced himself for the great confession.

'Gabriel here's like the rest of us... more experienced citizens.' The impromptu phrase pleased him: anything rather than *elderly*! 'We don't care to own it – but there idn one of us that's growing any younger.' He shook his head. 'Lifeboat rescue is work for the strong and hearty. At sea, far more than everyday life on land, you'll cause greater trouble to others with trying to achieve something when the strength idn there, than if you'd been wise enough to admit you'm not able and leave matters safe alone from the start.'

Reluctantly, Gabriel nodded, directing a rueful grin towards Lucinda and the professor. 'Tidn often I find myself in agreement with this old osebird, but for once he've the right of it. Tollbridge idn what you'd call a thriving place. There's a lack of young blood sufficient for the enterprise to flourish without overmuch reliance on us... what did 'ee say, midear? Us *more experienced citizens*.' He hesitated. 'We'm a dying breed, in short, our skills and knowledge dying with us and few coming along to be taught. Which is what must deter us from immediate pursuit of such a scheme, desirable though it may be.' His gaze embraced not only the family members near him, but also the rest of the room. 'Why, even my nephew here idn so far distant from entitlement to his pension—'

'Such as it is,' Mickey broke in. The two old gentlemen were talking sense, but it was of little comfort to the Tollidays. 'Best leave politics out of this, though. What we *could* do, and soon, is find space for the sort of notice you feel might be of assistance – just so long as you can come up with acceptable wording, and the best place to put it.'

This gentle turning of the tables gave the professor and his daughter-in-law food for thought. As they began to ponder, the others exchanged swift glances. Gabriel, feeling the atmosphere ease around him, said a thankful goodbye, collected his now-empty mug, and returned to the bar for a refill.

Mickey saw the lines on Charles Tolliday's pale face. The man looked both tired, and unwell. 'You might like to talk the matter over with her dad,' Mickey said, 'before settling to anything final. That river has run through Tollbridge from the moor these million years past. A few more days won't make much difference. And I'll tell you what,' as inspiration dawned, 'Prof, you want it impressed upon the little girl how fast-running rivers and the sea are no safe combination. I'd suggest at her age she's still too young for full understanding of the problem, but I reckon if you could demonstrate it, so to speak, in real life the message would have a far better chance of sinking in.'

'If that recent demonstration didn't send out the right message, I despair of the child,' muttered Persephone's grandfather. Lucinda frowned.

So did Mickey, hushing them both. 'Mrs Tolliday, your husband will be talking to her tomorrow, I know, and an excellent idea, in moderation; only, remembering from my own young days – sorry, Dad – how a child will often switch off listening far too soon to get the benefit of even the most sensible advice... well, I wonder.'

Mike spluttered at this, but the professor achieved a weary chuckle. Lucinda, after a pause, curved her features in something like a smile.

Mickey smiled back. 'Yes, give her a scold, but not too long, and then why not take her for a trip to Lynmouth? Tidn so very far down the coast, and there she could witness – could experience the full power of water at first hand, with no danger to anyone.'

Mike sat up. 'My son, despite of you ignoring me when young, seems I did learn you some sense after all!' He rose to his feet. 'I'll have a look-see for you dreckly minute.'

'Thanks.' As the puzzled Tollidays watched the old gentleman amble across the bar, Mickey hurried to reassure them. 'He'll not be long – he's trying to help, is all. Never mind our Tollbridge booklets rewritten by Susan Jones; the Ridds keep a selection for other places in the neighbourhood, too. Lynton and Lynmouth are like Tollbridge and Ploverton, but bigger on account of having for over a hundred years what we never could afford: namely, a railway up the cliff making travel betwix the two far easier than to climb a winding road that can be so steep you can't see it for the bonnet of the car blocking the windscreen.'

The academic in Charles Tolliday had doubts. 'But we've been told the terrain in these parts is unsuitable for a railway, and I certainly remember in my student days being limited as to where I could go because it was often hard, on a fully-loaded motorbike with a dodgy engine, to get from one camping place to another. This whole area is nothing but gradients far too steep for a railway.'

'All depends on the railway.' Mike reappeared with leaflets in his hand, delighted at his clever son's ability to set this posh professor to rights.

'Lynton idn the usual loco-pulling railway,' Mickey explained. 'You're right, this whole area's unsuitable for such, but Lynton has no worries about slipping on the rails with loss of friction. It's a funicular, guided up and down the cliff by cables, and powered by water.' He glanced at Lucinda. 'Everything's water, even the hydraulics — about as green and carbon neutral as could be. Built when Victoria was queen, bin running ever since. No need for buying fuel of any kind, apart from a splash or two of oil for lubrication; and the water's returned to the river after use to carry on flowing to the sea.'

Mike handed a leaflet to Lucinda. 'She'll be sure to enjoy this, midear.' He gave the other to the professor. 'Seems you missed out, fifty years ago — but better late than never.' He resumed his seat.

Charles Tolliday hesitated before unfolding the little brochure. 'Indeed, yes. Thank you. I was... very young at the time. A student on holiday, with a hint of study thrown in.'

Mickey nodded. 'More interested in trees than engineering, anyway. And as Dad says, better late than never. But I'd suggest driving to Lynmouth by the main road, for all that the back way's through Watersmeet, where you might yet find the No Parking tree you talked of. For one thing it's single track and your car — well, tidn that small.'

'It isn't.' The professor grimaced. 'Even on a motorbike those hairpin bends were terrifying. I wouldn't have dared stop anywhere looking for any kind of *Sorbus,* even with a – a Nobel Prize for biology at stake, never mind an undergraduate thesis!' He smiled. 'And by then I'd discovered my own *Sorbus morbilli.* My interest in the other tree was just for historical completeness – it was discovered in the 1930s – rather than using it as a footnote to my study of the Measles Whitebeam. There was enough information already written up and published about the other for me to consult and reference it easily.'

Mickey nodded. 'So, take the road direct to Lynmouth and park down in the harbour, then take the child along to stand by the railway entrance and watch the power of the water emptying on the track – and hear it, too. She'll get a far greater understanding if she's seen it happen a time or two before entering the car to be pulled five hundred feet up the cliff to Lynton.' He stroked his dark beard. 'She's fond of animals, no doubt. You tell her, in the old days almost all but the basics had to come by sea – food, clothes, building materials, visitors – and the packhorses had the hardest time and a very short life of it, struggling to carry what Lynton needed up that steep hill from Lynmouth harbour. Which was one argument for building the railway: kindness to animals.'

Lucinda beamed at him from her quick perusal of the leaflet. 'You're right, she'll love it. And the Jack Russell terrier, too – I wonder if it's true? I do hope so.'

Mike Binns could never resist the chance for a tall story, and he remembered Persephone's belief in Father Christmas. 'Tell her, while there's never bin a sighting of the ghost of the old man beside the track, there's times – rare, but she might be lucky – times when that little terrier can still be seen at the self-same place he always waited with his master for the driver to halt the car and let them aboard for a trip down to the sea and back. Tell her, if the driver skitters the controls anywhere near the old halt, could well be on account of he's spotted the little dog waiting and wondered about stopping to pick him up—'

'Dad,' broke in Mickey. 'He's partial to a good tale about a dog,' he apologised to Lucinda, observing her father-in-law apparently oblivious to the chatter as he continued to read – no. As he *pretended* to read, Mickey realised; and wondered why.

'Not so partial to pigs, though,' he went on; and saw the professor's smile, and knew his guess had been correct.

And was intrigued.

Chapter Eleven

Over breakfast next day Jasper Merton, for no immediately obvious reason, proposed egg and bacon flan for lunch. In response to Jane's query he said he had just checked the fridge, and the cupboard she liked to call the pantry, and – he coughed – they did seem to be short of some essentials. As he was expecting a business call, how would she feel about going down to the shop without him?

'Aha,' said Jane. The reason was now obvious. 'You coward.'

'Who, me? The forecast says, another sunny day. The sooner the shopping's done the sooner the cooking can follow – and then, the better the chance for the house to cool down for us both to be able to work.'

'You mean, catch up on the work we missed yesterday for… various reasons?'

'You got it. Besides, you're so much better at this kind of thing than me, being sort-of local and all – and I really do expect that call—'

'Okay! Once in a while I don't mind an early start, and I accept that one or other of us has to face the music. But when lunchtime comes we'll have it cold, with salad – and no mayo, because of cholesterol – and if you pull faces like that I might just check for myself before I go, to see how short of the essentials we really are.'

'Sadist! But my heroine, too. Tell you what. While I await your safe return from the inquisition I can do the dishes, hoick stuff out of cupboards, generally behave like the downtrodden scullery boy every kitchen needs – oh!' He clicked his fingers. 'Lightbulb! If only we had a dog, we could train him to turn a spit inside a chimney and spare me one of my more humble tasks – if only we had a spit, that is.'

'Idiot,' said Jane. 'And, like I said, coward. I'll write a list of jobs – oh yes, and a shopping list for me. Adding verisimilitude to whatever-it-is the Mikado or whoever says.'

'I'm sure you'll cope just fine. After all, it was your idea in the first place to move here and become part of the community.'

'Two parts of the community,' she said quickly. 'You and me. Both of us.'

'Both of us. I suppose we really should have dropped into the Anchor last night, but coming back to all those frantic emails and messages—'

'Don't worry! You catch up on work – *after* you've completed those humble tasks of yours – and leave me to face the inquisition alone.' She laughed. 'It's not so bad if you take it in the right spirit. Almost fun, sometimes. I shouldn't be long, though I can't promise.'

'I wouldn't expect you to. Right, have your fun – and good luck!'

Jane knew that the moment the doorbell rang in Farley's General Stores she would be pounced on by all present, as indeed she was. The shop was busy, and she couldn't identify everybody, but she saw enough smiles, and returned enough greetings, to guess they'd all had to linger far too long over imaginary errands as they waited for someone in the know to arrive and satisfy their curiosity about yesterday's excitement.

Nobody said as much in so many words, of course: it wasn't the Tollbridge way. Sam Farley at the Printery, knowing how Aunt Louise Hockaday would try to wrest every detail from her Binns in-laws in an attempt to score over Cousin Olive, had phoned the elderly postmistress as soon as the uproar died down to tell her what he could remember. The twins, sharing the one telephone extension, put eager questions of their own and made copious mental notes of everything Sam said.

More was gleaned later from bar-room chat in the Anchor, to be disseminated and distorted even later in comfort, at home. One or two enterprising persons phoned contacts of varying degree upalong to Ploverton – for everyone to be thwarted by Tom Tucker at the Pig, who told all enquirers that Doctor Gally had said young Simon was to be left in peace to get over the shock, and he would put no one through to the lad's room and disturb him, not if it was his own mother! The doc had said what he needed was resting for the night, and rest he should. No, it was of no use asking to speak with Dora. Gally Potter-Carey's orders were that they should both keep quiet – Simon, likewise – and the doc, as all knew, was not a man to ignore. Goodbye.

With the names of Simon's fishing friends unknown, the most promising source of information was lost and Tollbridge couldn't decide on who should next be approached. Too few locals had known of the business in time to get down to the harbour and watch the end of it. Witnesses there certainly had been, but insufficient to the purpose. Mike and Mickey Binns last night had done little more than exchange general greetings before withdrawing to a quiet corner with the Tollidays: understandable, but frustrating. Sam Farley had repeated what he knew of the start of the child's adventure; when the shop opened next day the twins passed on what they could, but this still made it no better than second-hand for most of the village. Tollbridge reluctantly settled for repetition and rehash of hearsay, surmise and speculation until one of those who'd actually been up at the old coastguard station could be induced to spill some genuinely first-hand beans.

Eyes brightened as Jane came in. Earlier than usual, she was still a most promising sight, when it might have been Captain Longstone for his peppermints and newspaper. After Mickey Binns the captain was, of course, the hero of yesterday's adventure, but he was also notorious for saying little beyond a general *Good day* and passing a comment or two on the weather.

'Jane, hello!'

'And a very good morning to our Mrs Merton!'

'How are 'ee today, midear?'

Jane returned the greetings promptly. 'Isn't it another lovely day!' Her smile included everyone, whether they were on first-name chatting terms or mere *Good morning* walk-past acquaintances. 'Do excuse me, but I really must hurry through my shopping so that I can have it back in the fridge before the sun gets too hot.' She consulted the list she didn't need. 'Let's see, fresh cream – a pint of milk...'

'Eggs?' Her godmother and cousin, Miriam Evans, emerged from the far side of some display shelves with a half-dozen box in her hand. 'Always useful, eggs, and these of mine guaranteed fresh and like to keep well, seeing as I brought them in only yesterday.'

Did that last word hold a slight emphasis? Jane wasn't sure.

'Or,' persisted Miriam, with something of a glint in her eye, 'perhaps you'd soonder have the plain variety? If so, midear, then you need asking one of the twins. Sadly, I'm not so well informed... about them.'

Jane noted the glint, and felt there had been definite emphasis in a final sentence that could be taken in more ways than one.

Miriam's hens enjoyed their greenstuff as did any domestic fowl, but some years ago, after an exceptional storm battered the harbour and hurled seaweed from the depths into gardens on shore, the tiny Evans flock, trapped and waiting for the ground to dry, developed an unexpected appetite for kelp: which local seaweed gave a robust salty tang to eggs, as Miriam found when she boiled two for breakfast. Tollbridge doesn't readily abandon the habits learned from previous generations: the wartime maxim of Waste Not, Want Not still holds. Miriam knew she must use the eggs, so she did.

She found she rather enjoyed the taste, and wondered if others might do likewise.

Evan Evans at the bakery experimented on his cousin's behalf. Before long he swore her to secrecy regarding certain spiced cakes and biscuits that became best-sellers. Locals, of course, didn't take long to guess the secret, but nobody grudged Miriam her good fortune – deemed a fair exchange for the havoc caused by the storm – and the village wished her well. When she discovered and shared the knowledge that meat from her fowls had a most palatable flavour, she found a ready neighbourhood market for boiler hens, selling any surplus to the Ridds at the Anchor or the Tuckers in the Slandered Pig. One of the Pig's holiday diners with gourmet aspirations referred, cider-merrily, to his meal as Saltmarsh Chicken, and the inaccurate nomenclature caught on.

But salty eggs weren't always appropriate. Where a recipe calls for *a pinch of salt* the wise cook must take pains to pinch, sprinkle or teaspoon with care when making certain puddings, cakes, or sweet pastries. Miriam's 'saltmarsh eggs' as supplied to Farley's General Stores were packed in boxes of a different colour, clearly labelled, but shoppers in a hurry could still sometimes be caught out.

'Eggs – yes, thanks,' said Jane. 'How clever of you to guess! Jasper fancies ham and cheese flan for later, but I'm doing the shopping because he's so busy right now. He says there's a ton of catching-up to do, after –' the faintest of hesitations – 'such a lot happening yesterday.' A collective sigh and rustle as people moved closer, ears flapping.

'You wouldn't believe,' Jane chattered on, 'how many messages arrived from America while we were at Sam Farley's place, and – and because of the time difference—'

She couldn't keep this up, and burst out laughing. So did Miriam. Reproachful looks were duly directed at both Jane and her godmother, who sobered first. 'Jane, as a child you were one of the most exasperating I've known – and I went to school with Mickey Binns!' She winked at her young cousin so quickly Jane wasn't sure she'd seen. 'Strange how some folk can change as they grow older, and others never do.'

After which the conversation became a cheerful free-for-all of questions, answers, and further questions.

'A pity they took the lifeboat away,' was the general opinion. 'As more than one can bear witness.' Old Mrs Beacon gestured discreetly towards Tilda Jenkyns in her back-of-the-shop post office section. The twins' mother Olive might be official postmistress, but today was one of her less mobile mornings. She had temporarily surrendered authority to Debbie and Tilda, whose father – like Tilda's husband, and so many others from Combe Tollbridge – had been a fisherman, washed overboard in a storm: but the body of Olive Farley's husband had been borne by the kindly waves to shore, and the comfort of decent burial. Tilda's lost spouse – again, like so many others down the years – knew no grave but the sea.

Debbie had joined Jane's conversational free-for-all as keenly as any but, curiosity partly satisfied, prompted by half-heard whispers of conscience, she now moved with resolution to the counter and prepared to ring up groceries on the till. Debbie had cartons and boxes to unpack, empty shelves to be restocked. She needed room for manoeuvre, which must mean clearing out of her way all those who'd done nothing but get under her feet diddle-daddling round the shop since the door was unlocked – without once opening their purses – while hinting that she could no doubt tell rather more than whatever Sam Farley might have told them, if she chose, having once been married to Tom Tucker's own second cousin's son. The connection with 'them at the Pig' still being acknowledged, the

Tuckers might be expected to tell Debbie anything of interest locally and, in present circumstances, it would be most surprising if they didn't.

Distant-cousin-in-law Debbie Tucker had to concede Dora Tucker was one of the newsiest chatter-bags in the two villages, but it was unlikely even Dora would have disputed an order from Dr Potter-Carey. 'And when I asked to speak with her myself,' Debbie had confessed, 'on the chance she might risk it, Tom told me straight he wouldn'have me talk to her, no more than he'd let anyone else! So that was that.'

With Jane's arrival and subsequent bean-spilling, the diddle-daddlers ceased to dither over imaginary purchases and became genuine customers. A short queue formed as Debbie rang up Jane's shopping, wrapped a few items in paper bags and watched as they were stowed away in what could be recognised as another of Angela Lilley's learn-on-the-job woven tote bags. Debbie's next remark followed a logical train of thought.

'Yes, that little girl was uncommon lucky Cap'n Longstone was there to warn the *Priscilla* she was drifting into their path.' She shook her head. 'Now, if we had our own lifeboat I reckon he'd be one of them chosen to take charge, or at least helping organise it all. I suppose,' with a thoughtful look for Jane, 'he said nothing yesterday of the matter?'

Jane hesitated. 'Not exactly.' A pause. 'Not about a lifeboat – but I do know he thinks Prue Budd's legacy might be better employed in funding something less... ambitious—' she hesitated again – 'and less expensive – but,' as a murmur arose, 'but in many ways just as useful – practical, I mean.'

'Expense was what they said before, when they took our boat away,' said Debbie.

'How ezackly, practical?' Miriam frowned at her goddaughter. 'Practical's what they talked about back then, too. Best spending it on bigger, faster boats at Ilfracombe, they said – and Minehead, and across the channel to Porthcawl – and indeed, there they are, putting out to sea as necessary and doing a grand job, only, we all know Prue wouldn want her money to go anywhere but Combe Tollbridge, as her will made plain. Does Captain Longstone so easily forget what the vicar said at the funeral?'

'He wadn in church that day, remember,' said old Hilda Beacon. 'Out patrolling a near-empty village in case of burglars, wadn he.'

Everyone remembered that he was. 'But he've had time enough since then to hear us all discussing the case and come up with thoughts of his own, surely?'

'He's never bin one to put himself forrard,' said somebody else. 'Not unless asked direct, which nobody so far's we know have done on this topic, for all he did such a fine sort-out of the Octopus rota after Mike and Mickey Binns restored that old pump.'

Like many rural areas Tollbridge has a retained fire service, crewed by local volunteers who mostly live in Ploverton: farmers are more likely than fishermen to be at home when the alarm is raised. Electronic pagers these days supplement, but cannot entirely replace, the wartime air raid siren that summons people from home or from work in places where other methods aren't always reliable. When Tollbridge's Jubilee Hall burned down, one of the first mental ticks on the list of essentials was to open the museum and bring out with the ancient siren (for which Louise Hockaday cranked the handle) the Octopus Pump, an ingenious and surprisingly powerful device for drawing water from the river to play on the blaze until the official pump from Ploverton could arrive. Captain Longstone, Gabriel Hockaday and Mike Binns between them organised a bucket chain, too.

'A good man, the cap'n, but quiet,' was the summing-up. This won a further chorus of agreement, Miriam adding that it made it all the more a puzzle that it seemed, from what

Jane was saying, the captain might not favour a new lifeboat for Tollbridge when yesterday's doings must have shown him how useful such a boat would have been. 'Why, if the *Priscilla Ornedge* hadn bin there—'

'But they were,' said Jane, 'and because the captain was on the headland he was able to warn them to look out for the child, which is what gave him the idea.' Once the clifftop watchers had seen everyone safely aboard the *Priscilla* and Mike Binns steering her towards the pier, Rodney Longstone left Jane and Jasper discussing their print order with Sam and hurried down to the quay. Having arranged for Dr Potter-Carey to attend the scene he waited near the foot of Coastguard Steps to intercept the Mertons on their way home, and had asked if he might accompany them for part of the way.

He understood (he said) that Jasper had an excellent internet connection and knew how to use it. He himself chose to live with little more than the essentials of technology, after years spent in submarines perpetually surrounded by beeps, whirrs, clicks and bright lights. 'I moved here for a quiet life, but I understand from our mutual friend Angela that the pair of you are becoming very much involved in village matters. Yes?'

Jasper had confirmed the captain's understanding, and asked what particular topic he wished to have researched. He wondered, but didn't like to ask, why the matter hadn't been put to the indefatigable Susan Jones, or (doubly so) to Angela; but in the early days of their acquaintance with Susan's emotionally-bruised daughter, Jane had delivered a stern lecture about leaving these two quiet people to advance (or not) their relationship (if any) at their own speed. She'd added that the same applied to Susan and Mickey Binns, but had been less emphatic because these two had fewer years ahead of them to waste.

'The captain thinks,' Jane said now, 'that being able to signal to the *Priscilla* was the second most important part of the rescue – the most important being seeing the whole situation develop. His idea is to have, rather than another lifeboat, a – a substitute for the coastguard.' There, she'd said it; and the roof hadn't fallen in. Perhaps the captain's reluctance to interfere in village matters had been taking modesty a bit too far. It was a good idea; and nobody was disagreeing with what she told them.

She continued with growing enthusiasm: 'A regular patrol of coastal watchers up on the headland, he thinks, at critical times – bank holidays, weekends, fine weather, spring tides, you know the sort of thing – with access to a permanent landline rather than trust to mobile phones that don't always work even as high up as the Watchfield area—'

A buzz of enquiry drowned out the rest of what she meant to say, but she saw Miriam's look of approval and was pleased for Rodney Longstone's sake, as well as for the general interest his suggestion had wakened among his fellow-citizens.

'In short,' said Miriam, 'our own coastguard, to keep watch over our own coast!'

'It's still early days,' Jane said quickly. 'Still at the finding-out stage – but he thinks it's do-able. He's asked Jasper to look into how it's all organised, how many people we would need – I believe one similar station started with just three – and how to get a telephone connected to the shed or motor home or, I don't know, caravan that might be our headquarters. He thinks some of old Prue's money could be justified for that kind of stuff. Sam Farley rents the coastguard station from Barney Christmas in good faith, remember. He's got a business to run. We can't expect him to stop work every five minutes at the height of summer to lend his phone because someone's being washed out to sea on a surfboard! We'd need a dedicated phone for calling the official coastguard, or the lifeboats, who have all the latest equipment and training we –' she took a deep breath as she paraphrased the captain – 'we could never seriously afford to keep going as a long-term prospect in such a small place as Tollbridge, if we're honest.'

Miriam couldn't hide her smiles. Before moving from London her goddaughter had said she and Jasper wanted to join in properly with village life. If her words just now didn't prove she'd meant what she said, what else could? Miriam beamed fondly upon Jane as eager questions came from all sides.

Pleading the need for groceries to be refrigerated Jane escaped, but not before suggesting that everyone should consider the Coastal Watch idea among themselves and pass the word around. If they approved the basic concept, they could each come up with their own ideas on how best to get such a project going in the most efficient and – she glanced at Miriam – practical way. She and Jasper were of course keen to help, but they couldn't research much beyond what the captain had asked for: they had no real understanding of likely problems at sea, while a submariner must of course know more about what went on beneath the waves rather than upon them. It was a matter for coastal experts to discuss... a matter for Combe Tollbridge.

The cause of the previous day's commotion arrived at breakfast next morning in the rudest of health, ready for whatever fresh excitements lay ahead. Persephone's bounce was in direct contrast to the sobriety of her adult companions. Before coming down Eddie had braced himself to administer the promised scolding but – warned by his wife of the harm he might do to their daughter's personal development with any excessive demonstration of authority and negative energy output – the scolding was at best a half-hearted effort, leaving Persephone only slightly subdued, and himself exhausted. The thought of driving even the few miles to Lynmouth made him quail. The Binns/Hockaday taxi service held considerable appeal for Persephone's wilting father. Could he really ask his wife to be the driver?

Eddie wanted Lucinda to enjoy what could be this last family holiday before Charles Tolliday's health deteriorated. Lucinda was Eddie's second wife, Persephone his third child.

He couldn't remember getting so much grief about personal development from the first Mrs Tolliday when he'd had to reprove their sons: on rare occasions he'd even spanked them, but they had grown into a couple of friendly, well-balanced youngsters who seemed to bear no grudge against him, even for being divorced from their mother. 'Grown apart – mutual consent – no hard feelings,' both parties had said, which was true, but Eddie didn't want to risk going through even a remotely similar experience again. He buttered toast and drank coffee in silence, while Lucinda sipped orange juice and Persephone chattered of the promised ride up a cliff in a tank of water. How cold would it be? Should she wear a swimsuit under her top and trousers? What about buying an umbrella?

The professor sighed for the child's lack of comprehension – or (rather worse) for his son's inability to explain things – but could say nothing. Charles Tolliday felt considerable guilt for the lapse of concentration that had allowed his granddaughter to find herself in such peril, though she really should be old enough to know better and he wasn't a well man, and could be excused his need for an afternoon nap. But while he might hope others could excuse him, he couldn't excuse himself. He had slept very little last night, and there was no need to exaggerate his weariness. His son and daughter-in-law weren't really surprised when he told them that, even though he'd missed out on the remarkable railway fifty years ago, he just didn't feel up to joining them on today's excursion. He would be far happier staying put, to enjoy coffee and fresh-baked chudleighs with clotted cream when Angela, or Tabitha, or big Jan Ridd told him they were ready.

His secret hope that it would be the landlord who greeted him when he returned to the bar for elevenses was fulfilled.

'Angela's not here today morning,' said Jan, 'this being one of her bakery days; and Tabitha's busy in the kitchen, with her own chudleighs due from the oven dreckly minute. The cream have risen well overnight, and skimmed up lovely for clotted.' He glanced at the discreet rucksack by the professor's feet. Puzzling. Hadn't Tabitha said the old gentleman had told his family he would remain at the Anchor until they all returned from their trip?

'Unless,' probed the ex-policeman, 'you'd thought of going out on your own for some peace and quiet? Understandable, after yesterday. Tabitha mentioned you did no more than pick at your breakfast, and small wonder. I don't doubt you'd enjoy tea and a bun at Widdowson's, for Evan Evans is as good a cook as Angela – if that idn a brave statement to make, me knowing Evan all my life and young Angela barely a minute!'

Professor Tolliday smiled, but didn't cap the little joke or even chuckle. He looked round the empty room and said: 'Is there somewhere we can talk? Without being interrupted?'

'Well, tidn so easy keeping folk out of a public bar – but this time of day we don't see what you'd call any great stampeding to fill the place. We'll sit yonder in the corner and, should any come to interrupt, I'll say I'm telling you what my father told me of the Meazel's Leap, Mike and Mickey Binns having made a poor show of it t'other night, and I can't risk the loss of my story with talk about anything else.'

'I should, indeed, enjoy hearing your version,' said Professor Tolliday. 'But... not until I've told you my own story, and – and made my confession.'

Jan Ridd shot him a curious look, but said nothing as he led the way to a small table in a distant part of the bar. The professor quietly followed him.

As they took their seats, Charles Tolliday gently set his rucksack – it was neither large nor heavy – on the table.

'It goes back a long way,' he began. 'About fifty years, when I was a student with a thesis to write and very little money and... not much head for alcohol, which no young man who believes he's in his prime ever cares to admit.' Jan Ridd – former beat copper, later station sergeant – nodded encouragement. The professor sighed.

'I simply didn't – couldn't – believe what people told me about the cider in this part of the world. All the talk of sheep's heads dissolving in barrels, rats eaten alive by apple acid rather than drowning – I thought it was simply... making fun of the innocent tourist.'

Jan nodded again. 'Kind of tale Mike and Gabriel and a few others would tell 'ee, if they hadn got me to keep an eye on them. So you took a drop too much Tollbridge scrumpy in your young days. Well, you're not the first, and won't be the last.'

'It was like a personal challenge,' said Professor Tolliday, looking deep into the past at the folly of his impoverished but boastful youth. 'One of those two-pint earthenware mugs with a handle each side – they said the other night your writer friend had found a special name for it—'

'A penny dish,' Jan supplied, 'with a ha'penny dish for one handle, one pint.'

'—and they filled it to the brim for the idiot townie to drink. And I did.' He spoke more quickly now, and sat up straight. 'Drained it, as far as I recall. How I got back to my camp in the woods I couldn't tell you, but I'm sure it can't have been with any assistance from my audience because I don't believe they would have let me... would have watched me – allowed me to...'

He gave up, opened the rucksack, and brought out a large bundle swathed in a towel. He unwrapped the towel to reveal a majestic earthenware mug with a handle at each side. He pushed rucksack and towel to the floor, and set the mug in the middle of the table.

'Ah,' was all Jan said, for some moments.

'I don't know how long I've got left,' said Charles Tolliday, 'but I'd like to clear as much from my conscience as I can, before – it's too late. This mug came from this pub. You're the landlord. You must know which local family it belongs to, and how best to give it back to them with my profound apologies…'

His final words were both embarrassed, and plaintive. Jan picked up the mug to study it, turning it in his hands to admire the flowery copperplate in which the original owner's name had been added to one face while the other carried the mass-produced, transfer-printed little verse so popular in Victorian times, as explained by Susan Jones to an admiring audience when Mike Binns displayed the mug he'd inherited from Ralph Ornedge.

'The Farmer's Prayer,' said Jan slowly. 'Very nicely done, too – and the name, as well. A handsome piece.' Then he looked up, and grinned.

'Oh yes, the name's well-known in Tollbridge. And no doubt you'd also wish me to pass on your thanks for the fifty-year lend of this-here liddle cup?'

Chapter Twelve

Seeing the smile in the landlord's eye, Professor Tolliday ventured a smile in return.

'Gwilym Christmas.' Jan put the two-handled mug on the table, the owner's name towards him. 'There's few left of that family now, even upalong to Ploverton, where likely he was born. Our Barney is about the last Christmas to the name in either village, and even Barney's no direct connection, Gwilym leaving but the one son and him, none but daughters. Three generations start to end in one village, idn that what they say?'

'I believe it is, although how accurate the statistic may be—' The professor broke off and apologised. It was hard to abandon the habits of a pedagogic lifetime at even the most embarrassing of moments.

'Accurate? Well, doubtless there's a man with a computer somewhere who could tell 'ee, but I can't.' Jan smiled. 'Another saying is, it's the exception always proves the rule, and certainly we've families in Tollbridge who won't dispute this, being able to count back well past three generations.' He thumped himself on the chest. 'The Ridds, now, to give *Lorna Doone* her due – always supposing me to be a descendant, for we know Girt Jan and his Lorna had children, and as he himself had no brothers I can't ezackly claim descent from the distaff side, now can I?'

'It seems unlikely.' Charles Tolliday didn't mention cousin marriages, but let his eyes flick in the direction of the display case hanging on the wall.

Jan slapped the table. 'Ezackly so! That cannon-bullet in its glass box yonder bears powerful witness to the notion, I would say. Wouldn't you?'

'Oh, definitely.'

The landlord nodded, deliberately grave. 'Howsumdever, that's all theory. Facts, now. With the family long gone it's hard to tell fact from legend, though some of Gwilym's antics are legend enough. But our Susan's found little in what written records she's consulted, so it's memory on which we must relay.' He picked up the mug again. The penny dish could easily hold a quart of cider, but in the big man's hands it didn't look outsize. Charles Tolliday reflected that it would be – indeed, had been – all too easy to drink more than you intended, once your judgement was blurred.

'Gwilym by all accounts was over-fond of what Susan says they called Devonshire wine,' Jan continued. 'And them were the days when folk took a share of their pay in local cider, and heads were more accustomed to the strength of it. He was fond of a wager, too. It's said the man was never slow to accept neither drink, nor a challenge. He'd plank down his money just so quick for disputing two flies crawling up a window-pane as he would over which ferret might first bolt a rabbit from its hole.' Jan, former policeman, sadly shook his head. 'Gambling and drink can be a poor combination.'

'It's not the way to make your fortune,' agreed Charles Tolliday. 'Though I understand it can be an easy way to lose one.'

The landlord warmed to his theme. 'It's said he once took a bet he could down a peck of cider in one tip, meaning, he'd drink two full gallons all at one draught.' Jan saw the professor shudder. 'Sixteen pints – and he did! Laid flat on his back, opened his mouth, and let the liquor do no more than trickle in his throat so as not to overwhelm his insides. Lived to a good age too, they say, but o'course there's no stone above his grave to prove it. He'd drunk or wagered away all the money that should pay for such a thing.'

'You don't surprise me in the least,' said Charles Tolliday.

Jan had been thinking. 'For all you know, you didn so much borrow this-here penny dish as win it fair and square in a similar wager, all those years ago.'

'I might – and it's kind of you to suggest it, but though I honestly can't remember what happened that night, somehow I doubt it. And, as for honesty – I have to admit that it isn't just wanting to ease my conscience that made me bring the mug back to Tollbridge.' He cleared his throat, and sighed. 'I know modern medicine can achieve wonders, but that's the purely physical aspect of my diagnosis. As for the mental... you see, I don't want to be worried by what arguments I may leave behind me – or at least, no more than can be helped.' Jan shifted on his chair, but the professor held up his hand to quieten any protest. 'My will is with my solicitor. Eddie is my only son. It should be fairly straightforward, but – Eddie has been married before. Persephone is my only granddaughter, but I have two grandsons by Eddie's previous marriage.'

'Ah,' breathed Jan, with a sympathetic nod. 'Oh yes, weddings and funerals! Always trouble there. Bridesmaids for one, then the catering, what hymns to choose; the same and more for funerals, o'course, and not least afterwards, reading the will – christenings too, on occasion. I've known a baby's name cause harsh words and sulking with the poor scrap no more than hours old, all on account of no wish to use the grandfather's name for being old-fashioned. Not even for the middle, which might have helped – if only the mother hadn a great dislike for middle names. Or so she said,' he ended with a comical look.

'A mother's privilege.' Charles Tolliday smiled back. 'It was Lucinda who insisted on Persephone. A private joke about pomegranate smoothies, I believe, and to my mind some matters should be kept private. These days perhaps it's not so unusual, but if they had to use the name at all why not, as you say, in the middle? Still, Eddie was happy enough to go along with her, and I naturally kept my views to myself.'

'And you'll have grown to love the child for herself rather than worry over her name, I don't doubt.'

'After six – no, seven years I hardly notice, though strangers sometimes have to hide a smile. Persephone is sensitive to laughter, you may have noticed – and of course you think she is a – a bumptious nuisance – a spoiled brat – a victim of over-indulgence on the part of her parents, but—'

He saw Jan struggle to deny it, and chuckled. 'You'd never make a poker player, Mr Ridd. I agree, Persephone can be all of those things, bless her, but I consider it her way of coping, for which at her age she can hardly be blamed. And it may seem hard to credit, but I promise you she's far past her – well, her brattiest stage, after a healthy dose of exposure to the real world. Eddie put his foot down about that, and insisted on a sensible school. After a slightly rocky start I gather she has several good friends – some with even more outlandish names than hers! There's hope for her yet – or so I myself can hope.' He hesitated, putting out a hand to the earthenware mug. 'No, what worries me now is her mother.'

As Jan wasn't sure how to take this he said nothing, and waited.

'Lucinda is – can be – rather touchy at times, especially when my son's first marriage enters the equation. I really don't know why she should feel this way. The marriage ended some time before they met, and these days it's hard to believe anyone could possibly think a single daughter of less worth than a brace of sons, but I suspect that at the back of her mind, despite every modern ideology, that's how Lucinda feels. Feelings are hard to explain, aren't they? For my part I hope I have the same… fondness for each of my three grandchildren.' Charles Tolliday had never been touchy-feely in public, and wasn't going to start now. 'I'm no King Lear; I don't require them to compete for my affection. When it comes to money it's easy enough to divide it fairly, but something unique…' Again he touched the cider mug, and fell silent.

As the silence continued: 'If you can't decide,' said Jan, 'and they later can't decide between 'em, sell what's under dispute. Let any bid for it that wants, and share out the money equal. So long as there's an independent valuation there shouldn be many complaints.'

'The whole family knows the story – in, let's say, a modified form – of how this "penny dish" came into my possession. You could almost call it the foundation of my academic career – the Measles Tree, the rainforest valley and so forth – and Lucinda looked them up. The Farmer's Prayer mugs, I mean. She knows, as I do, they're not valuable in monetary terms, but the sentimental value is quite another thing.'

He picked up the mug, and read the little verse aloud.

'Let the wealthy and great roll in splendour and state

'I envy them not, I declare it.

'I eat my own lamb, my own chicken and ham

'I shear my own sheep, and I wear it.

'I have lawns, I have bowers, I have fruits, I have flowers

'The lark is my morning alarmer.

'So jolly boys now, here's God speed the plough

'Long life and success to the farmer!'

'I've wondered often,' said Jan, 'if whoever wrote that poem did even a single day of honest farm labour in his life – or hers,' he added, with a grin, 'disguised as a man. But talk with most folk upalong to Ploverton, and I think you'll find our jolly boys and girls not so much speeding the plough as cursing it for being damned hard work. Counting the days before their fair share of all that splendour and state will finally make it worth the trouble!'

'I believe you, but they're surely not alone. Both the farmer and the fisherman must be subject to the vagaries of the weather, but the sea adds a dimension of its own. The life of a fisherman seems quite as hard as any farmer's, from what I hear – and yes, I know how they enjoy telling the tale to us poor townies, but there must be at least a grain of truth in that tale, not to mix my metaphors.' He smiled. 'But of course that's how it happens in Combe Tollbridge.' He turned the mug on the table so that he could study the name of Gwilym Christmas. 'Didn't you tell me he won a bet that he could drink a peck of cider? A peck is surely a dry measure. We all have to eat, as opposed to drink, a peck of dirt before we die – but only in this part of the world do you get double value for the meaning of the word!'

With sudden resolution he pushed the mug across to Jan and sat back on his chair, moving his hands in a gesture of dismissal. 'Please take it, both to ease my conscience and to stop any risk of future squabbling. You said a distant relative of Gwilym Christmas still lives here. Should it be returned to him? I don't know, Mr Ridd – Jan. I leave you to decide where's the best place for it to go.'

Jan Ridd took up the mug by both handles, nodded, and set it down firmly at his side to seal the unspoken bargain. 'Hardly "returned", for while Barney's a Christmas by name, if he's related to Gwilym it's *very* distant. More-and-so, he's well into his eighties with no family, so far as is known. He was the oldest of six, who all got a good start in life through him and then left Tollbridge to better theirselves, with not one thanking him for the sacrifice nor coming back, even to their mother's funeral. Barney stayed on to look after her right through, for all she had him early and illegal out of school – and he was a bright boy – but so soon as she was gone he took off, same like the others. Didn come back for years, not until he'd made his fortune, so they say – and some say that's what he's still about!' He winked. 'Which could well be the reason he idn in the Anchor so often as many of them others you've met – studying his bank-books and ledgers, they say – but for my part I fully understand he's less inclined to be social around those that remember him in his hand-to-mouth days. But he've no children, like I said. I've little doubt, when we ask him his view of the matter, he'll say there's the same problem still, just put off for a few years.'

'I believe I heard some talk of a museum—'

Jan's laughter silenced him. 'One day! As to *which* day – well, I wouldn care to commit myself. That museum is for ever coming to come, same as the old woman's butter! You might try asking young Angela. She has the task of setting the place to rights in what time she can spare from other work, being once a librarian and having an orderly mind – but I've heard her say many a time, it won't be for a while.'

'Or, as you said, a few years.' Professor Tolliday smiled faintly. 'Oh, I know.'

'But if you'd be willing to trust the business to me, or we'll say rather, to the Anchor – then how would you regard something of the same style as the cannon-bullet in its box? With just so much or so little of the tale as you might wish written down? Or all of it written, but about another Anonymous, like the poem. What say you to that idea?'

The professor considered this. 'By your friend Susan Jones? The one who writes for the Tollbridge Tourist Board, when she can spare the time from her own writing?'

'Tourist Board.' Jan chuckled. 'I do like that. Yes, Milicent Dalrymple or whatever new name she invents for herself, writing in a different style and undertaking a life of crime, or so young

Angela warns me. First-hand research material, she said,' said the retired policeman. 'When the time comes.'

'She could start with me,' suggested Charles Tolliday, cheered by the thought. 'Or is my fifty-year-old pilfering a – a misdemeanour, rather than a crime? Or even petty theft? Hmm. Perhaps I wouldn't make such an interesting subject after all.'

'All Raffles did was thieve, but there were short stories wrote about him, and a film or two, not to mention television. You never know. But, being serious, you wouldn object if I asked Susan to get you to tell her in your own words for her to write up for such a display?'

'I'd like to meet her. The only published authors I know write scientific papers or textbooks: necessary, but unexciting. A writer of fiction would make a wonderful change from a person who churns out pages of dry facts with numbered footnotes.'

'For the booklets, she writes as Lorinda Doone – a fiction in itself, for she's no relation but it looks good on paper, she said. Now, here you sit, and with the family out for the day over to Lynton I'd say this might be as good a chance as any for the privacy of an interview, if we could but find the easiest way to break into her concentration. Susan does like to hear a tale in someone's own words – for the right voice, she says. Made Mike Binns and Gabriel tell her twice over their story about the shipwrecked dog before she wrote it down. Have you seen that one?'

The professor nodded. 'The two Welsh sailors buried here during the war.'

'Name of Evans, father and son. No connection to the families in Tollbridge, but they still put flowers on the grave every year on the day of the storm that drowned them. Their little Bran was the one survivor, and Mike the only person small enough to climb the cliff to bring her safe down, careless of the danger – and then he gave her back to Mrs Evans over to Wales, once her proper home was discovered. Ever fond of a dog, Mike Binns.'

'Yes, it's a lovely story. Persephone enjoyed hearing it, though she couldn't settle to reading the booklet.' He smiled. 'Rather too much like school when she's on holiday, I fear. But it was a well-written, lively, moving piece that made the whole adventure very real. If your Susan, or Lorinda, or Miss-New-Name could spare the time to do a similar job on me, I'd be delighted.'

Jan was silent for some moments, thinking. 'When she's like this she keeps strange hours for shopping and going for a breath of fresh air, so... Miriam Evans is the one most like to know if Susan's yet in the mood for interruptions. Angela's presently at work in the bakery. Best left to get on with it, I think; more-and-so, she can go for days without talking to her mother, so she might not know. Nothing personal, just she's always busy – but Miriam would be Susan's closest friend in Tollbridge. If anyone can disturb her and get away with it, she's the one. You bide there while I try to catch her on the phone.'

'Might your Miriam not be out shopping too, at this hour of the day?'

Jan stared. 'If she idn answering her phone I'll call the shop, o'course.' He headed for the telephone, leaving Charles Tolliday to reflect on the benefits of village life where everyone knows almost everything about everybody else, and how very useful that can sometimes be.

The landlord was gone for longer than the professor expected, but when he reappeared he was not alone. A woman in late middle age, with comfortable but not voluptuous curves and a friendly smile, accompanied him.

'Susan,' said Jan Ridd, 'this-here's Professor Tolliday – white-beam expert, bryologist, and a tyrant for drinking scrumpy, in his youth. He wants to meet you. Professor, this is Lorinda Doone! Susan Jones, to her friends.'

Charles Tolliday had pushed back his chair at Susan's approach, and shook hands now in a wary silence broken only by the exchange of greetings. Susan smiled again, motioned the older man to resume his seat, and pulled round a chair to sit beside him.

'I've got to ask, and I'm sure it must happen all the time, so my apologies for being a bore, but – a bryologist? Someone who studies the ocean, as in the briny deep? Or – don't tell me – there are protons and neutrons and electrons, and photons, and pions, and that splendid Higgs boson. I bet there's a bryon, too. A bryologist must be someone who studies yet another esoteric aspect of particle physics – am I right?'

As she'd intended he laughed with her, far more at his ease than when she came in. He applauded her excellent if misguided guess, and explained that in fact his particular area of study these days was moss.

Susan thanked him, committed the term to memory, and smiled. 'You were looking a bit bothered when we arrived. Did Jan give you the idea I'm dangerous when wrestling with a sluggish creativity? I suppose I can sometimes snap at people if they interrupt me – but I never bite their heads off, promise. Not even my daughter's!' This, with a twinkle. 'I gather you're enjoying a little break from your own family at the moment. I'm sure you understand how it goes, and can spare me some fellow-feeling.'

He twinkled back. 'I can spare a little, though naturally I save most of it for myself.'

'Naturally! Well, Jan has promised coffee, chudleighs, and jam with clotted cream in exchange for a good story. Bribery and corruption of Lorinda Doone, I call that – and at just the right moment! You see, for once I felt like taking my morning break bang in the middle of the morning. I was pounced on by this chap in the final stages of my harbour half-circuit – from my place along to Trendle Cottage and back, with a detour to the end of the breakwater – and I bet it was Miriam who tipped you off, Jan. Yes?'

'Yes, it was. Said she'd not long since seen you go past, and waved.'

'And I waved back, not realising it was the preliminary to some deep-laid plot to ambush me and bribe me with food prepared by somebody else, hurrah! And what I say is, bring it on – unless,' with another twinkle for Charles Tolliday, 'you'd prefer our quiet chat to be back at Corner Glim Cottage – my place? I was only out for a walk, so I haven't got my big notebook with me, just this little jotter –' she drew it from a pocket – 'and that's only for the odd flash of inspiration. At some point we'll need to resort to Corner Glim and my full-blown scribbling, but if you'd be happy to give me a spoken first draft, as it were, then the second time round I'll have a better feel for what's important. Get the right balance.'

She made him smile again by admitting her perpetual weakness for hot chocolate dipped with Turkish delight, for chudleighs, and for the carvy-seed cake and gingerbread sold by Widdowson's Bakery 'where my daughter Angela works. Jan tells me you already know the story of Widdowson's, from one of the old leaflets. When I have time to update them, I do hope you'll be able to come back to Tollbridge and buy the next edition.' She hesitated, then went on gently: 'I was so sorry to learn that you're not in the best of health.'

'Thank you. It could be worse – and it's the reason for my being here in the first place, of course. Fifty years ago I thought I was immortal – untouchable...'

'Weren't we all?' She stifled a sigh as she remembered Angela's father, who died far too young, and far too soon. Unlike Andrew Jones, Charles Tolliday had a long, productive and evidently successful lifetime on which to look back.

She pulled herself together. 'So, fifty years ago you came to these parts in order to study the ecology and write a thesis, and you found an unusual tree...'

She made mental notes and showed close, but not pressing, interest in the story she drew from the professor. She admired the mug and laughed over Jan's idea that a woman might have written the anonymous Farmer's Prayer, using a man's name. 'Well, we'll never know – but why not? It worked for the Brontës, didn't it, and for George Eliot? You can't expect me, of all people, to complain if someone uses a good honest pseudonym!'

When the last crumb, lick of cream and sip of coffee had vanished, Susan studied her companion, who had eaten little, but seemed to enjoy it; and drunk more, to ease his throat as he talked. Now he seemed tired but cheerful, after his long narrative. He'd chuckled over the exploits of the goats, and comically exaggerated his fear of heights, cliffs, and strange noises in the wood that might have been the ghosts of long-dead smugglers 'because then I didn't know about the Meazel, poor chap. Now that I do, I think I'd have been even more terrified!' Jan Ridd kept watch from a discreet distance, poised to repel boarders, but nobody came to that corner of the bar and Charles Tolliday reminisced at his own speed.

He sat back, and smiled. Susan was still gentle. 'How do you feel about a walk round to my cottage to go through the story again while I make notes? It would mean going uphill a short way, but it's not very far. In fact you could see Corner Glim from here, if it wasn't for the houses in between.'

'With a ladder and some glasses?' He was delighted to be able to cap her quotation. 'If it doesn't mean walking all the way to Hackney Marshes, you're on.'

He knew the old music hall song! Susan was equally delighted. 'No, I promise you it doesn't, though I can hardly call mine "a werry pretty garden" because the previous owners squeezed a parking spot out of what little space there was. In some ways that's a blessing, but it's impossible to prettify, even with planters. Come along and I'll show you.'

'Thank you. I'd like that – if you're sure I'm not interrupting your work.'

'I'll forgive you for the sake of Gus Elen. Do you know "It's A Great Big Shame"? That was his other smash hit.'

The professor did, and began the chorus in a light baritone. Susan joined him in expressing dismay that a wife of only four-foot-two should so shamefully nag a husband of six-foot-three. 'They hadn't been married not a month nor more / When underneath her thumb goes Jim / Isn't it a pity that the likes of her / Should put upon the likes of him?'

Warbling happily together, the two left the Anchor for Corner Glim Cottage. Jan watched them go. He wondered how Mickey Binns might feel about the obvious rapport that had sprung up between Susan Jones and the quiet scientist she'd managed to bring out of his shell. The landlord couldn't recall if Mickey was working that day in Tollbridge, or out at sea; but he was bound to hear from someone of the morning's encounter, and what it had led to. Susan, when not engrossed in work, was a friendly soul. When he'd told her what he knew of his guest, and how she might be able to help him, it hadn't taken her long to agree to meet the man. Jan glanced at the clock.

He wouldn't be at all surprised if she invited him to stay for lunch.

Chapter Thirteen

Susan, reluctant to offer advice on personal matters, was persuaded to do so by her new friend Charles, after the note-taking was done. She suggested that for peace of mind he might consider asking Jan to keep the Farmer's Prayer mug out of sight until the Tollidays had left Combe Tollbridge. 'Then you'll enjoy the rest of your holiday knowing you can pick your own time to tell the family why you no longer have it. If anyone notices it's gone tell 'em you're afraid of breakages, and are keeping it in a safe place.'

'Location unspecified until later. At my funeral, perhaps.'

'Very much later, I hope!' But Susan too was a realist. 'If you can't face all the fuss, and I for one don't blame you, you could always add a codicil to your will, or write individual letters for your solicitor to give everyone at exactly the same time.'

'The ceremonial Reading of the Will, with variations. I like it.' He smiled, shyly. 'When you're able to send me the final version, I wonder – would it be a breach – illegal – in order for me to make copies to enclose with these letters, or—?'

'Copies? Certainly not! You tell me how many you want and I'll see you get them, hot off the press – but I'd hardly sue you, of all people, for breach of copyright, if that's your concern. It's *your* story, with my embellishment – and I wouldn't dream of taking my friends to court anyway. Only think of the expense.'

'Let's kill all the lawyers?'

'The first thing we do.' It was Susan's turned to cap a quotation. They looked at each other, smiled, and laughed quietly together. He found her company very restful.

Susan couldn't begrudge Charles the time she had already spent (and would yet spend) in the matter of the two-handled mug, but always at the back of her mind her research beckoned. She tried not to let her impatience show. It had been, after all, her choice to accept the disruption of that day's work. When Jan waylaid her she could have said no – but even before he had fully explained the circumstances, her author's antennae told her something of great interest could be within her grasp. Although she would have to abandon her current focus on a different world and time, instinct said she would be foolish not to take advantage of what sounded like a unique opportunity.

The story in itself wasn't unique. On quiet days the news media could often include a brief 'filler' item regarding a souvenir flag, knick-knack or key (often from a hotel, once from a castle) that had been 'borrowed' – usually under the influence of drink – many years before, now being returned with abject apologies and belated thanks. Occasionally the returned object was a long-overdue library book, inherited from a grandparent who'd gone to war/been hit by a bus/run off with a next-door neighbour and forgotten the less important things in life. These returns, however, were usually anonymous. The professor said he didn't much care if the whole story came out once he was gone: it was simply during his lifetime that the fuss would be more than he wanted to face.

'And while I've heard of such happenings elsewhere,' Jan had told her, 'this-here tale is a first for Tollbridge and the Anchor.' He chuckled. 'Not even the Pig, so far as I know!'

Susan had found the challenge offered by Jan attractive, the story irresistible. She enjoyed hearing Charles Tolliday tell it; she looked forward to writing it up and seeing it in print; to sending him a copy – several copies – and making him happy. Given his state of health she knew she must waste little time before starting work on this latest project but, for now, she wanted to resume investigation of the music-hall world that had so unexpectedly inspired her, during Angela's Museum Tidying, with the idea for a very different style of book from those of Milicent Dalrymple. Susan wanted to re-enter the Victorian era, and immerse herself once more in its atmosphere.

When Charles at last said goodbye and left Corner Glim for the Anchor and a late afternoon nap, he took with him Susan's sincere good wishes and an autographed printout of the Legend of Meazel's Leap. It was only a rough draft, he was warned; more work was needed, the illustrations had yet to be discussed; but as he'd already heard the Anchor's version of the story, and had stayed in the exact area (which hadn't really changed in five decades, never mind throughout the eight or nine centuries following the actual event) she hoped he would find it a suitable memento of a very pleasant meeting.

'A delightful, if brief, encounter.' He smiled rather sadly, shaking hands a second time before starting for the pub at a thoughtful pace. Susan watched him to the corner of Three-Square Passage, firmly suppressed the surge of Rachmaninov that flashed upon her inward ear, and with a gentle sigh returned to the yearned-for bliss of solitude, and the peace of what remained of her solitary working day.

The Tollidays checked out of the Anchor next morning. Gramps, Lucinda explained in her most consciously reasonable voice, was very tired, and would like to be taken home. Persephone could have another, more exciting holiday later in the year: perhaps a short break at half term, somewhere fun?

'The railway up the cliff was fun. We can come back here and I can take pictures to show my friends – and a video too!' Whether or not Persephone had absorbed the message that water could be dangerous wasn't clear – in contrast to the shrill annoyance demonstrated in Lynmouth when her phone had died at the critical moment because, on the previous day and for understandable reasons, nobody had thought to charge it. The pink unicorn was again exerting its malign influence on their daughter, for what her parents devoutly hoped would be the last time.

That same day a new guest arrived. While Jan Ridd was busy shifting casks around the cellar, Angela helped Tabitha put the final touches to bedroom rearrangement. Furniture must be moved back to pre-family configuration, carpets must be vacuum-cleaned before and after. The two women were just congratulating themselves on a job well done when they stopped, thinking they'd heard the bell downstairs ping for service, but not quite sure.

As they listened, Tabitha stifled a groan.

Angela glanced at her employer's feet, knew how tired she was, and said she would go herself. 'You'll want to change out of your slippers before you go down, which is a bother, and once you've sorted whatever-it-is – if it's anything – you'll only have to come back up again, which is silly when I know what to do if it's someone wanting a room. If it's anything more complicated then I'll call Jan.'

Tabitha picked up a bright duster-on-a-stick and tapped Angela on the shoulder, as if bestowing a knighthood. 'Bless you, midear, and my thanks. After last night's botheration I can tell you, I'm proper fatigated.'

Angela bobbed a mock curtsey. 'I believe you. When Gabriel and the others are set on teasing anyone it's a real effort to stop them. I'm sure you did your best.'

Had the best been good enough? Angela hoped so. The teasing comments last night, as reported by Tabitha next day, had been muted when the Tollidays were within earshot, but with the professor's sudden wish to curtail the holiday the family, after eating, didn't stay long in the bar. There was Persephone to soothe, luggage to pack, a last walk to take round the harbour – and once they were gone, Gabriel's sense of mischief had kicked in.

'Likeable chap, that professor,' he remarked in a carrying voice to nobody in particular. 'Full of book-learning and interesting facts. The sort of mind that likes to find things out, and tell you all about what he's found like ferns, and moss, and trees.'

'Written a book, they say.' Thus is a B.Sc. thesis granted more deference than its due by those who have never had to write one. Tollbridge is proud of the academic achievements of Mickey Binns, but it's now several decades since they were achieved. 'Just goes to show how some folk will benefit more'n others from a higher education.'

'Not wise to let the habit of thinking lapse. Keeps a man lively in more than his wits.'

'Yes, and a woman. Think of Susan Jones and what she finds out with her computer!'

'And the books she writes! There'd have bin much in common for the two to discuss, I don't doubt, when she invited that man to share her dinner.'

'A widower, I understand – or was it divorced?'

Gabriel caught Mickey's eye. Things had gone far enough. 'They say he's not so long for this world, poor chap. Susan has a good heart, and a com— a kindly nature.' He'd had 'compassionate' on the tip of his tongue, but realised just in time the sort of wordplay his associates were likely to employ if he spoke it aloud. 'It's as well she was able to spare an hour or two from her research to give the man so pleasant an afternoon before going back to London. She'll need leaving in peace now to catch up, o'course, with losing a day's work through her kindness.'

A chorus of agreement brought from Mickey a wry smile, from his father a nod. They both relaxed – a little: they knew the topic of Susan's gracious interruption of her privacy for the sake of a likeable stranger was sure to be resumed, intermittently, through the rest of the evening. They would either have to put up with it, or go home.

As Tabitha described the previous evening Angela felt that in Mickey's place she would have gone home, and let them laugh themselves out where she couldn't hear them – but she hadn't known them all her life, as had the younger Binns, and his father for more than eighty years. Nor, as a single child, had she grown up with such exchanges as normal in a close-knit community. No malice was intended; all victims were equal, chosen as opportunity presented. The next target might be Gabriel himself. Even Barney Christmas, so rich and successful, wasn't immune to such neighbourly barbs as came his way; and could give back, when he chose, quite as good as he got, as did most of those who were Tollbridge born or bred and loved to tease.

Angela had no wish to interfere with Mickey's erratic courtship (if that's what it was) of her mother, nor would she offer advice to a man clearly old enough to be her father; but sometimes she heard the jokes, and sighed. They said Mickey was either too shy to put the question to a world-famous author, or worried he might be thought after her money. Angela wondered if it was Mickey's affection for his father, his wish not to leave Mike alone, that made him hesitate. What cottage in Combe Tollbridge had space for three modern adults with three lifetimes of accumulated clutter? If Mike moved out to make room for Susan, where would he go? Should Angela offer to share The Old Printery with him? She didn't remember her own father; how might she feel about a step-grandfather?

'Nonsense!' said Angela, as she left the bottom stair and made for the reception desk.

The stolid young man with his hand hovering near the bell stepped back, seeming to shrink into himself. Behind heavy, dark-framed glasses he blinked as he gazed at the newcomer. He coughed, and blinked again. 'I b-beg your pardon?'

'Sorry! Talking to myself. Take no notice, please. How can I help you?'

She went to the desk; his first impression of efficient severity remained. He rushed into speech. 'Oh, b-but it's not so much talking to yourself that matters, it's the answers you get. I've had some of my best ideas from listening to my subconscious – at least I th-think they are.' He tapped the breast pocket of his corduroy shirt. 'My notebook. If I don't write it down, I forget.' He straightened. 'Which in my line of work you mustn't do.'

He was trying too hard. Angela didn't know whether to feel sorry for him or be irritated. She managed a smile. 'You're a writer? My mother writes, too—' Then a ghastly thought occurred. 'Genre fiction, not poetry, or plays, or indie film scripts or anything like that. And you?'

He hesitated. 'Oh, dear, nothing so ambitious. You could call me an on-off journalist, not that you'll know my name – it's Peter Twelvetrees, and please don't pretend to recognise it because nobody ever does – but I do sell odd bits and pieces here and there, from time to time. It's kind of erratic but – well, I manage. Even if it isn't mega-bucks, they do always pay for what they publish. Sooner or later.'

Angela doubted this. She'd heard Susan too often discourse on the daydreaming wannabes who knew they could write a bestseller if only they had the time, and a personal introduction to her agent – or who had a really brilliant idea they were prepared to share on a fifty-fifty basis if she could 'just do the writing' and turn it into a book. The film rights alone would be more than worth the effort—

'Nonsense,' said Angela again. 'I mean, good for you. You get paid. You aren't just talking the talk.' Well, possibly. But could he walk the walk: get up and go; go and get the story? What printer would hold the front page when Peter Twelvetrees rushed into a room or yelled down the phone? She couldn't imagine him yelling at anyone. What she'd heard so far gave Angela the impression the man was born to be the founder and life president of Fence-sitters Anonymous, with no particular views on anything. 'So what's a journalist, on or off, doing in this quiet neck of the woods? Business or pleasure?' Perhaps he didn't know that, either. 'I take it you'd like a room? For how many nights?'

'A single, please – but I'm not sure how long I'll be staying.' This didn't surprise her. 'It all depends.' Nor did that.

He coughed again, and grew confidential. 'I'd like to talk to someone called Mickey Binns, and anyone else who saw what happened when the little girl was carried out to sea the other day.'

'Ah, yes.' The non-committal response seemed to encourage him.

'People have posted on social media – there's a video, but it's not very long and very shaky – and there's been nothing in print yet, or picked up by national news. I thought I'd try to get ahead of the game and find out for myself, so of course I had to come. How can I ask questions when I don't know anyone's name except Mickey Binns, and he doesn't use social media?'

'Few people here do. It's too much bother. If you've driven down from the main road you won't have missed the height of the cliffs, and the depth of the valley.' Angela wondered if this was true. The heavy glasses might in theory improve Peter's eyesight, but in practice they gave him a decidedly studious, unobservant air. 'Combe Tollbridge is one of the most negative not-spots in the country. We all use landlines because mobiles just don't work – hence the red telephone box out there.' She pointed through the wall. 'Old, but fully functioning! As for broadband – just how long are you prepared to wait? Most people say swimming through treacle is a serious understatement.'

'Oh.' He considered this. 'I suppose there might be a feature of sorts in that. How do cyber-deprived communities survive being cut off from the twenty-first century in such a competitive world?'

'Deprived?' Angela gave him one of her looks. He blinked. 'We manage very well, thanks. Some of us even find it a pleasant change from living and working in a world where you always have to be on the go in order to keep ahead of the competition.' She watched him think this over, and then relented. 'Look, you might get a feature from that. How the slower pace of life in, yes, a seaside backwater reduces the blood pressure, or something of the sort. Anyway, you said you wanted a room, and to talk to Mickey Binns. The room's fine, though as for Mickey Binns—'

'And whoever else who was there.'

'I wasn't there myself, and I couldn't tell you who was. You'd have to ask around. Of course, at the time everyone got very worked up about it, especially the family – only they've gone home now – and the fishing party who were out with Mickey, but they were staying at the Slandered Pig in Ploverton. It's bigger than the Anchor. You might try asking there – it's only a mile up the valley – but surely it's at least yesterday's news now, isn't it? Or even last week's! Nothing too dreadful happened, and everyone involved is safe. Would people still be interested?'

He seemed downcast. In a way she regretted having voiced her instinctive thought aloud, but to be any good as a journalist he should be able to turn the opening of a jam-jar into a major event. If he could be so easily deflected from pursuit of a story he wasn't going to make it big in Fleet Street – or even medium-sized.

If he was going to make it at all, which she was inclined to doubt. Her smile was almost kindly. 'But of course, I'm no expert. I've no idea what sells.'

'I think, positivity.' For once he sounded almost positive himself. 'Or it *ought* to sell,' he added, spoiling the effect. 'There's far too much doom and gloom put out by the media – all the media. War, plague, politics, cruelty, crime: the list just goes on growing. Nobody has a chance of avoiding the latest fire or flood or famine or – or shotgun massacre, with every gory detail in slow-motion close-up and glorious technicolour to rub it all in. It's horror overload! People need more feel-good stories, as a – a counterbalance. At least, that's what I th-think,' he added, as the breath of inspiration finally ran out, and he shook his head. 'If it can be done, that is.'

'Well, good for you, if you want to try.' Angela again spoke from instinct; she'd been almost impressed. 'You just hold on to that way of thinking, Peter Twelvetrees. A few more like you who think positive, and it could end up as infectious as misery certainly is. Turn good news into a nationwide infection, and who knows what might happen?'

He pushed his glasses back up his nose. 'That's right! We ought to have every day with at least one positive "and finally" piece at the end of the news to give you the reassurance things might not be as bad as they've been telling you for the past half-hour. Such as, two strangers risking their lives to save a helpless child. Two man-in-the-street heroes fighting the power of nature to rescue an innocent from certain death – or, well, something along those lines,' he finished, again deflating as inspiration died.

Angela hesitated. 'To be honest, I'm not sure Mickey Binns would care for the "hero" label. He's not like his father. Mike enjoys being the centre of attention, but Mickey was pretty embarrassed by all the fuss when it happened and he came in for a lot of teasing. Anyway, he's taking the *Priscilla* out again, or maybe he's taken her already, I don't know, but you may well have missed him for today. You might find it easier to check first with the Pig, to see if anyone's still there from the fishing party.'

'They're the ones posting on social media—' He instinctively pulled out his phone, turned it on; stared, fiddled and tapped. 'Oh, right.' He slipped the phone back in his pocket. 'Well, so I can't show you – but it looks like they're all back home now.'

'Let me check you in, then you can go exploring. The shop would be a good place to start, or in the bar this evening – but a word of advice.' She smiled, but spoke with careful emphasis. 'Take everything they tell you with a pinch of salt. Enjoy the performance, they do love to tell the tale – but don't, and this is important, don't have more than one cider. When you do, make it last. If you're thirsty, drink beer.'

His shoulders hunched; his glasses drooped. 'I d-don't drink alcohol. I never have.'

Why did he have to be so apologetic? A cheery *Never touch the stuff, but thanks anyway* would have been fine. The phrase 'total charisma bypass' popped into her head, and she wondered why she had ever felt sorry for him – and immediately felt sorry for him again. Perhaps hers was the common reaction to Peter Twelvetrees, and the secret of his professional success, such as it might be: he made people feel uneasy, and they went automatically into compensation overdrive.

She wondered what Tollbridge would make of him.

'No drink? No problem,' she said. 'There's no obligation!' Thankfully she busied herself with the register, choosing a room and guessing he would need to stay for two nights, if he wanted to interview Mickey Binns. Mickey would oblige, she supposed, but with reluctance, she knew; and she had no idea when. There had indeed been talk of another fishing trip in the *Priscilla*; even a whisper it might be an all-night expedition, with Jerry Hockaday for company and (probably) moral support if anyone else went with them. Mickey wouldn't care to risk more jokes and teasing from his cronies in the Anchor, and he wouldn't relish being interviewed as a Heroic Everyman rescuer of sweet innocence even by the most confident journalist in the world – which Peter Twelvetrees, all too clearly, was not.

She asked where he had parked his car, giving the routine assurance that it would be safe above the high-water mark 'unless there's a tidal wave.' His glasses flashed anxiety. 'Local humour, sorry! There's been nothing like that in these parts for several hundred years. You'll hear about it in the pub tonight – I told you they love to tell the tale – or you could buy one of those leaflets.' She pointed. 'Plenty of local history there. Our bestseller is the tragedy of the lost silver mine, but that was even longer ago.'

'If you don't mind me saying, Combe Tollbridge doesn't seem to do modern very well.' He fumbled at the pocket that held his mobile phone.

'Why should I mind? It's true. And we generally cope okay, but sometimes you just can't – what was it – fight the power of nature, given the way nature shapes the landscape. Topography, geography, whatever – it's bigger than us and we just have to adapt. You get used to it.'

'No internet connection. Just the one road in and out, which seems to be a dead end.'

'It is,' said Angela.

'Suppose it's blocked by a fall of rock – a landslide – a sinkhole?'

'What happened to thinking positive? There's a whole motorway out there in the shape of the Bristol Channel, and vehicles known as boats. Before whoever-it-was invented the internal combustion engine, it was sailing boats and packhorses that kept Combe Tollbridge going. So, packhorses are out of fashion – but we still have boats, with or without sails.'

Recalling the purpose of his visit, he brightened. 'The *Priscilla Ornedge* – does she have sails?'

He stepped back as Angela frowned. 'I've never thought to ask. She's trad built – wooden, I mean, not fibreglass or metal – so there could well be sails for back-up, knowing how temperamental marine engines can be, especially the older ones where it's harder to get spares.' She was surprising herself with knowledge she didn't realise she had acquired from chatting with friends and neighbours. 'Mickey's father Mike inherited her from old Ralph Ornedge, and by all accounts Ralph was a sensible man, so "maybe" is all I can say about sails. Sorry! It's another of the things you'll have to ask around to find out.'

From time to time during the afternoon she wondered how Peter's enquiries were progressing. He had set off from the Anchor with his notebook ready, his phone primed to video any likely subject willing to talk to him, his expectations apparently high that this could be his breakthrough story – but Angela wasn't sure. She had told him her mother was also a writer: the fact had passed without response. No *should I have heard of her?* Or *what name does she write under?* She wasn't so much regretful on Susan's behalf – Milicent Dalrymple, already a bestseller, needed no boosting – as concerned for the on-off journalist's chances of success. His lack of professional curiosity didn't seem to fit the persona he'd tried to introduce. How could he make even the modest living he claimed when his general focus seemed so... blurred? She recalled hearing of a website that reported nothing but good news for a day, and lost over half its readers. Was Peter Twelvetrees capable of finding the right balance between feel-good and disagreeable fact?

Was he even a journalist? Wishful thinking on his part, perhaps. Thoughts of landslides, sinkholes and being cut off had seemed to bother him, but he hadn't even asked how often that sort of thing happened. Wouldn't a career reporter have an enquiring mind for any hint of a likely story?

And the man was teetotal!

He was a reporter in his dreams, Angela decided. She wondered how many others would think the same, and despite herself hoped that people seeing through him wouldn't tease him too much. Tollbridge, and Ploverton too, with the mischief bit between their teeth could sometimes let matters gallop out of hand. Even a phoney must have feelings...

Peter Twelvetrees returned to the Anchor in ambivalent mood. He'd had poor luck at the Slandered Pig. Birthday Simon and his friends were indeed long gone home and it was Tom, not the more effusive Isadora, who confirmed this, politely regretting that he felt unable to tell him more because, so far as he was concerned, there was little to tell. Combe Ploverton was a mile from the sea. Naturally they never saw anything of adventures downalong to Tollbridge. Simon had come back safe and well, but soaked through to the skin. He'd gone early to bed, as advised by the doctor.

'Out on his rounds,' said Tom, when asked how Peter might track down Dr Potter-Carey. 'Could be anywhere. An uncommon busy man, Doctor Gally, with so many patients on his list. Takes his duties very serious; oath of privacy and all.'

He fixed the young man with a quelling eye; waited for a response that didn't dare to come; asked in his best landlord manner if anything else was wanted – and said, well, in that case he himself was likewise a busy man, and must get on.

Peter drove back to Tollbridge, hoping his luck might be on the turn at Farley's. In the absence of customers the twins could give him graphic (if muddled and contradictory) versions of an event they themselves, so busy in the shop, hadn't witnessed – but about which all those who had, had told them in detail, although at one and the same time, so exciting as it had been. If they told different tales – well, that must be no surprise, the general flummox and flusterment being great. Not themselves speaking from first hand they couldn't rightly swear to how accurate a story they told, but they did their best. They watched him make notes, and agreed that Mickey Binns had gone fishing. Mickey wasn't what you'd call retiring, but he certainly didn't care to have a fuss made.

Debbie enjoyed herself in obfuscation but Tilda, less robust, was uneasy. Both, however, did their best. Word had gone round that Mickey couldn't regret what had happened, but he'd be glad to hear no more about it and hoped the tale would soon die down. More-and-so, never mind his own feelings, but if prospective visitors thought the river in Tollbridge was dangerous, how many might be put off visiting? The local economy needed its tourist trade. There must be compromise between treating an individual visitor with courtesy, and the good of the village as a whole – as well as respect for the wishes of a quiet man who was one of their own.

And at least this Twelvetrees chap wasn't asking about Captain Longstone!

From the Pig, cousin-by-marriage Tom had phoned a warning to ex-in-law Debbie, just in case the post office didn't know there was an over-inquisitive stranger on the loose wanting to make a public hero of Mickey Binns. 'Called himself a reporter, but I dunno,' he said. 'And bamfoozled him nicely, I hope!' He told her what he'd done to deflect Peter Twelvetrees; and Debbie accepted the unspoken challenge, warning her twin they should answer the young man's questions as honestly as they could while saying nothing too helpful.

'A lucky little girl, carried out to sea by the river in such a fashion,' said Debbie now. 'Any river can be dangerous, same as a busy road if you don't pay proper heed – and she was too young to pay any heed at all, playing all by herself with that unicorn!'

'Indeed she was,' said Tilda. 'And 'twas rare good fortune the toy should have bin so pink, for it made her easy to see and to rescue.'

'Easy it was,' said Debbie, 'and a happy ending – unlike when the silver mine collapsed.' She launched into her version of the story, Tilda embellishing the narrative at appropriate intervals. They ended by directing Peter to the revolving stand that held the various booklets updated, with illustrations and photos, by Susan Jones.

'If you want a tale of real interest, there it is! And not widely known, for all this part of the world was famous backalong for its silver. These days it's all mined out, even if we do sometimes hear talk of gold and rare metals for use in mobile phones and electronics…'

Peter Twelvetrees – ignoring the possibilities of gold and rare metals but taking a leaflet – returned to the Anchor in ambivalent mood.

Chapter Fourteen

Mickey kept the *Priscilla* out all night. Next morning on the quayside Mike was awaiting their return when Peter Twelvetrees, still apparently hopeful of a scoop, remarked on the legend *Ornedge, Binns and Hockaday* decorating the blue sides of the little green van loaded in the back with crates of ice.

'Another family business?' he enquired.

'O'course. No chain stores in Tollbridge – nor Ploverton, neither, as you'll have seen for yourself yesterday.'

'Like the baker, the post office, the taxi, the bus…' Peter ticked them on his fingers. He'd been told much the previous afternoon, and more in the evening, by a great many very friendly people. His head whirled with the effort of trying to put all the information together. Nobody could write or remember that fast! As a teetotaller he couldn't blame drink for the confusion; it must be everyone talking at once. The confusion wasn't helped by a lingering memory of heavy wooden balls rumbling in the skittle alley his new friends insisted he must see. And play in. And 'doing pretty well, for a beginner! How about another game?'

When Tollbridge wishes to maintain its privacy, the wish isn't hard to achieve. Mickey Binns would cope, but there was more at stake than a modest man's dislike of being feted as a hero. Should Peter Twelvetrees overplay the heroism and exaggerate the dangers of visiting Combe Tollbridge, people might believe the hype and stop coming. Visitors were essential to the economic life of a village whose population was, at best, static. Younger generations no longer chose to remain in the place where they'd been born. Seaside backwaters are, by definition, far out of the mainstream of life.

'And there's Miriam Evans,' said Mike helpfully. 'I reckon you could count her a family business too, inheriting as she did from her grandmother, for all she's worked on her own these many years. But these days her weaving sells so well she's a-tookt young Angela for apprentice – that's Angela who bakes for Miriam's cousin Evan, who's setting the museum to rights in memory of old Prue Budd that was cousin to Barney Christmas – only, you'd not know him on account of him not being present last night – but anyone will tell you most folk here and in Ploverton are kin, one way or another. You might say keeping it in the family comes as second nature to everyone.'

'Does it work? I mean, families d-don't always get along. Don't people say "Never do business with friends or relations"?'

'Elsewhere, maybe: here, never. We pull together as we've always done without dispute, beyond the usual bickerment to be expected of the human race. Like every fishing community we've *had* to pull together – and glad of it, for the sake of all. There's no room in a boat for quarrels or falling-out, no safety in holding a grudge. That way lies danger.' Mike gestured to the harbour entrance, towards which the misty form his proud eyes knew for the *Priscilla* was slowly chugging. 'Here she come. Are they thinking of their catch, do 'ee reckon, or a comfortable bed after being out all night? Not if they've their wits about them! The two most perilous moments at sea are coming into harbour, and leaving it. Thoughts can be distracted and dangers missed, but nobody on board any boat should take safe anchorage for granted until he's alongside the quay and stopped engines. To the very last moment, the sea can surprise you.'

Peter saw his chance. 'Such as someone being washed away by the tide?'

'The Chole's but one of many fast-flowing rivers in this country, and you can be sure it will happen somewhere else before long. This time it was folly on the part of the child for creeping away as she did from her grandfather's watch—' Then Mike recalled the pale face and poor health of Charles Tolliday. 'Or, no, her being so young, rather call it mischief. The foolishness lies with her parents buying such a toy in the first place, and encouraging her to play with it at the water's edge. The place for a pink unicorn is home in a paddling pool, or at a seaside beach with lifeguards and every modern convenience, which we've not got in Tollbridge – not yet, that's to say. With this being still a working harbour, though small, there may be changes in the future.'

'I heard talk last night of a Coastal Watch. It sounds like an excellent idea, but nobody seemed at all d-definite.'

'It's under discussion,' Mike assured him. 'We'll want to get it right.'

The young man thought of the mobile phone he couldn't use except for photos; of how last night he had also heard talk of a village legacy, with perhaps a privately-financed cable to bring faster broadband, or a telephone mast up in Ploverton if a suitable location could be found. One day. When the matter had been thoroughly discussed. One day. 'Nobody seems to hurry very much, in this part of the world.'

'We do when needful – but more haste, less speed. Hurry-skurry can mean careless. We like to get it right.' Mike stroked his splendid whiskers with a slow, deliberate movement. 'With my back how it is I'm not, myself, a hurrying man.' He did his best to look frail. 'But as it seems you may be one who is, let me just say, for now there's no need to rush. You've a good half-hour before the *Priscilla* settles down and Mickey's free to talk.' Without going to extremes, there was no avoiding the encounter.

'See, the work don't just stop –' Mike made to snap his fingers, and winced artistically – 'when the boat does. They've the catch to unload and crate before the ice melts, for one. Can't have our customers forever running the back-door trot on account of poor hygiene! You've time and to spare for a newspaper, should you wish to keep up with the world.' The Anchor's bar is the one room with television, switched on only if someone makes a definite request. When socialising, Combe Tollbridge needs no outside interference. The village can always watch what it wants in the privacy of home.

The newspaper suggestion was so clearly a dismissal from this weary old fisherman in need of a rest that Peter Twelvetrees ignored the evidence of Mike's auburn beard, and the sprightliness he'd shown in the pub the previous night, and headed at once for Farley's. Hurrying along Boatshed Row he passed the bottom of Coastguard Steps, glanced up, and shook his head. He'd been assured that the best, indeed only, spot in Combe Tollbridge capable of receiving even one bar of signal was on top of the headland 'which if you've no wish to climb, you can always drive roundabout and park,' but when he asked for directions he had the distinct feeling that his leg was being pulled. He smiled, murmured polite thanks, and decided against the experiment.

For once Tollbridge was neither teasing nor being deliberately oblique, but spoke only the truth. Had Peter asked Angela, he would have heard that she and her contemporaries, more wedded to their mobile phones than older generations, would use the round trip (on foot) to catch up with world news as well as improving their physical fitness. The round trip by car never occurred to them, but they knew it to be possible; and the Watchfield parking was as free as the breakwater chezell where Peter had left his own elderly vehicle.

He found the Farley twins amiable as ever, but less inclined to chat. After yesterday's effort they had run out of inventive steam. They explained they were busy, but spared the time to ask: had he enjoyed reading about the silver mine? He had? Good, even if *enjoyed* might not be the right word. A true disaster for the village, and never forgotten, even after these many years; a piece of history, and of real interest 'unlike such poor events as happen now. A quiet place these days, Combe Tollbridge.'

He somehow didn't like to remind them of his own 'real interest' in less historic events, but agreed politely with the general sentiment, and drifted from the post office to Widdowson's Bakery. Here he sat fidgeting over his paper with coffee and gingerbread 'made by me, not by Angela you met in the Anchor' after Evan had sold him a fresh leaflet, giving the story of the miller, the half-sack of flour, the widow, and the widow's son who made the business thrive. 'Which I inherited from my kinsman Farley Ridd, cousin to Jan as you've also met,' said Evan Evans, before vanishing to the back of the bakery.

Nobody snubbed him, but Peter didn't feel as welcome in this clearly close community as he had before. He was glad to abandon his reading and return to the quay. The *Priscilla* chugged to a halt with much activity on deck 'on account of being later than expected – that half-hour's gone to more the full sixty minutes,' said Mike Binns. 'Ever unpredictable, the sea.' He climbed slowly from the van, and made a great effort to haul rattling ice-crates on their dolly to the foot of the gangplank for fishermen to load. 'You mind yourself, Dad!' roared Mickey in alarm. 'Wait for me or Jerry to do that!'

The family's care for the patriarch was evident. Mickey forced his father into to the driving seat 'and stay there!' while he and Jerry lifted heavy crates into the back of the van. The toot of a motor-horn in Boatshed Row had Jerry apologising as he rushed off, saying that this was his dad with the taxi. Jerry had been 'asked for most particular,' it was explained, so Gabriel would try to take his place 'if you'll pardon the old man for being a bit slow today' as Mickey, curbing obvious impatience, said he would try his best to do.

The bespectacled young man in the background was a receptive audience, trying not to get in the way of actors who had thrown themselves into a full-blooded performance they intended to celebrate and recall with pleasure once the audience had gone, the danger of bad publicity (they hoped) averted. The performance was excellent: no suspicion of hoodwink crossed the mind of Peter Twelvetrees: but, had Angela been there, nothing would have altered her view that he lacked the enquiring 'nose' that makes a true reporter.

'Well, now.' Having seen the others on their way Mickey Binns, dusting his hands, at last came up to Peter. 'They tell me you've an interest in our silver mine and matters appertaining, which is why you've the wish for a quick word with me on account of how, before I settled to the fishing, I was a mining engineer.' He gave Peter no time to reply. 'Knew the legend from my cradle, interested in rocks and minerals, dreamed of finding a seam of gold or a diamond pipe – but that was many years since, and when I was working I was more for copper and tin. These days it's the rare earths that are most in demand for batteries, magnets, computer chips; but in my time such elements warranted little more than a footnote, having no industrial use beyond help controlling sulphur in the making of steel.'

He mimed the stirring of a cauldron. 'It's all very different now, and I can't keep up with modern knowledge. My friends say I'm too modest, but tidn so. Whatever I could tell you really wouldn be of help to any story you might wish to write.'

'But I don't want to know about the mine! I mean – I've read the booklet, and yes, it's a good story. Maybe, if it was written up with the one at Combe Martin it could be bigger – but it's your rescue of the little girl I want to ask you about.'

Mickey stared, shrugged, and shook his head. 'Nothing much to tell, really. Spotted her floating on that pink thing, lad went down to pick her up, missed his footing, fell in. I didn take to the notion of the two of 'em soaking wet so I grabbed her while the others hauled young Simon up on the rope ladder. Warned him not to try climbing – did you know it was trying to climb the rescue nets killed almost as many seamen as being torpedoed, during the war? Shock and strain on the heart, after being weightless in the water too long. Not sure how long it takes, so we told him on no account to climb, just in case, and –' he shrugged again – 'and that's about all there was to it.'

He made it sound a very dull affair. 'But—' began Peter Twelvetrees.

'Look, it's all done and dusted, with no great drama and a happy ending, everyone back safe at home. No point stirring things up again. For a good story, try Combe Martin! Traces of all manner of engines and mine workings downalong –' he waved – 'or, in t'other direction, at Kilve –' he spelled this out – 'there's relics of the oil-shale industry that never caught on, being no more financially viable there than silver would be here, these days.' He didn't mention the curse. If Peter had read the booklet he would already know there was little chance of any commercial enterprise obtaining permission to explore (or, in local terms, to desecrate) the mass grave the mine had become after its collapse in mediaeval times. 'You see, in Tollbridge we've really nothing much to show you. And if you'll excuse me, I've my dad to look out for. If I don't join the old rascal on the fish round he'll be unloading the van himself, which at his age… Good to meet you!'

He waved again, strode as briskly as a man wearing sea-boots can stride across to the waiting van, and climbed in. Mike gunned the engine and drove off, with a cheery pip-pip on the horn as a last farewell.

Peter went back to the Anchor, and told them he'd be checking out that day.

The Mertons brought the news a few evenings later. Though they were no longer the social media junkies they'd worried they had become while living and working in London, once a day they permitted themselves a little peep into the cybersphere, at the top of Coastguard Steps. Jane had ruled that domestic checking on their computers risked a return to the pointless treadmill they'd moved to Combe Tollbridge to escape, and Jasper was secretly relieved to accept that ruling.

Like most of Tollbridge, they suspected that Angela had been right about Peter Twelvetrees and his supposed career as a newshound. Nothing had appeared under his byline on any topic in anyone's daily paper, and there was as yet nothing on social media.

'Not even *and finally*,' Jane told Angela, when the latter arrived mid-afternoon at Clammer Cottage with half of her latest cake for constructive criticism over coffee. 'At a guess, if he did write about it, it didn't sell. Like you said all along, stale news.'

'If he wrote anything at all: a real reporter surely wouldn't have let himself be so easily talked out of his story.' Then Angela smiled. 'Mickey will be pleased, though I'm not sure about Mike. He does seem to relish being the centre of attention so much more than his unfortunate son.'

'The competitive spirit,' suggested Jane, 'sharpened by a lifetime's acquaintance with Gabriel Hockaday. Mickey won't have had any such problem with his Hockaday cousins because Jerry and all those brothers could fight it out among themselves at home.' Gabriel and Louise had been blessed with five sons, Jerome (named for his mother) being the pin-horse or middle one, and closest in age to his cousin Mickey Ornedge Binns.

Angela sighed. 'I used to imagine having brothers and sisters, but what I couldn't help imagining was the down-side – made to share your books and toys, wearing hand-me-down clothes, always being compared with one of the others – or comparing yourself with them and feeling jealous, which would be even worse. On balance I think I'm glad I'm an only, even if the reason was so very sad for my mother.'

'How is Susan? Is the other half reserved for her?' Jane was admiring her portion of cake, so splendidly decorated with cherries and flaked almonds, in its plastic box.

'Yes, she phoned yesterday to say hello and ask how I was, so she'll be about ready to go public again. I know how hard she works and how she often forgets to look after herself properly when the research genius burns. She'll need building up, so telling her it's a new recipe and I want her opinion is the most tactful way I know to get some proper nourishment into her. Fruit and nuts are good for you.'

Susan had a sweet tooth and, as her friends knew, though her daughter sometimes doubted, willpower. Where weaker women might bulge, Susan rejoiced in curves that were just the wrong side of elegant. Mickey Binns admired their discretion, but never dared say so. Angela took far more interest in food than her mother, and worried far more than Susan about nutritional values, and the empty calories in hot chocolate dipped with Turkish delight taken on a too regular basis by a writer who didn't want to lose the thread by concentrating on anything other than work.

'Drag her to the pub next time she phones,' said Jane. 'Or *you* phone *her,* and fix a definite date. I plan to drag Jasper there myself – he's still tied up with whatever-it-is he's been doing for Barney Christmas recently, and keeps muttering that he doesn't want to be disturbed. We might almost be living in London. He's as bad as Susan! I have to practically force him out for exercise. You and I will have coffee, but I'll save the cake for after he surfaces and I make him walk up round the headland. Then I'll say you want to know what we think, and we should report to you in person. With any luck the fresh air will have cleared his head and he'll start behaving like a rational human being again.'

'I know,' said Angela. 'I know! Exactly like my mother, only with her it lasts longer. Do I take it the vegetable patch is still at the daydream stage?'

Jane sighed, and raised expressive eyes in silence to the ceiling.

On today's headland circuit the Mertons checked their phones for news, then hurried home to access the same information through mains technology with a printout facility. Paper is easier to pass from hand to hand than a tiny battery-powered screen at which, even when it works, only one person can look at a time.

'I should call this his last resort.' Jane watched Jasper fiddle with the printer. 'If he couldn't drum up newspaper interest by contacting them directly – as I suppose he must have done – then he hopes they'll pick it up when they see how many Likes he's getting.'

'Not enough of 'em fast enough to be worth anyone's effort.' The proprietor of Packlemerton's Publicity spoke with confidence. 'As we've been saying all along, it's old news. Simon and Co splashed the story right after the event, but with them treating it as one big joke, that's how people took it. Okay, Mickey Binns is the older generation, but not old enough to make it a good story. Now, if Mike had jumped in that would have been brilliant – or Gabriel, even better. That beard!'

'They've all got beards. But I do agree,' said the artist, wistfully, 'Gabriel would make a wonderful image. Father Christmas leaping to the rescue! What a pity it was from a boat, not a sleigh. The reindeer swooping in a gorgeous arabesque—'

'The goats kicking the poor bloke all the way down, you mean.' Jasper took the final page from the printer tray. 'There! After supper, we'll see what everyone thinks of this.'

Everyone thought Jasper's printout hilarious, as they chose quotable phrases to hurl in greeting when Mickey and his father eventually appeared.

'Here come the local hero! Three cheers for a fearless fisherman! Brave Binns in the briny – *Priscilla* saves Persephone!'

Mickey read the printout and shook his head. 'No wonder we don't know this chap's name as a writer. He idn much good. Give me Susan any day, and I never thought to hear myself say that.'

'Romance,' said Mike, 'being o'course not much in your line, son.' Mickey handed him the papers without another word. Mike grinned, and began to read.

Jasper agreed with Mickey. 'If he sells anything at all, it will be to come-and-go very niche-market cheapo magazines. Poor bloke.'

'He'll have a small private income, or still be living with his parents,' said Jane. 'That's how he can indulge in a harmless fantasy. Everyone likes to think they could write a book, if they only had the time – and if only I would illustrate it for them they just know it would sell – but a magazine article takes far less time than a book, which makes it so much easier to fool yourself that's what you do for a living.'

Mickey thought of how Milicent Dalrymple's new persona had removed her from general circulation for so long. 'Research takes time, done right,' he began, 'but—'

Mike looked up. The grin had faded. He snorted. 'Research done right? Why, he says Auntie Prill was your grandmother!'

'And so she was, Dad – or as good as, to my mind, just as old Ralph was my gramfer, giving me my middle name. You've always said it was a whole new life starting when you got evacuated here in the war. New life, new family – why not? It's understandable the chap should make the mistake, with the very boat named in Prill's honour.'

With this Mike had to agree, but grudgingly. For a man who could spin the wildest of yarns whenever the fancy took him he was surprisingly upset by the clumsy story given to the world by Peter Twelvetrees. No amount of persuasion from Jane and Jasper that this particular world had very limited horizons, or that the earlier versions posted by Simon and his friends had been played more for laughs than for facts, could suppress the old gentleman's grumbling both to himself, and to those around him.

It dawned on Mickey that his father regarded Peter's errors and poor writing as no less than an insult to the memory of Aunt and Uncle Ornedge, which Mike held as dear as that of Mickey's long-dead mother. Mickey couldn't defend the poor writing, but he tried his best to explain that much of Peter's confusion had been deliberately caused by himself and his friends – as Mike really should remember. Never mind the feelings of his son, there was the likely impact of unfavourable publicity on the economic life of the village to consider; and Mike, with Gabriel, had been among the first to consider it.

'He wrote pretty much as we hoped he would,' said Mickey, 'and tidn fair to blame him for doing what we wanted. So far as I'm concerned it's a job well done. Now the whole rescue business can be forgotten, apart from that Warning notice the Tollidays wanted, then we'll all get back to how we were before. At least there's nothing posted from *them* on social media – or is there?' he added hastily.

'All quiet on the western front,' Jasper assured him.

'I should think they're too embarrassed to mention it,' said Jane.

Mickey hesitated. 'More likely they want to spare the prof's feelings. A serious-minded chap like him's going to feel he's to blame, whether or not other folk would think it justified.'

'Justified?' Again Mike snorted. 'That child should never have bin left to his care in such a way, poor soul. He's a sick man that needs his rest – and she's a spoiled brat wanting to be the centre of attention every waking hour!'

'Probably another reason they haven't mentioned it,' said Jane. 'They don't want to do any more spoiling – encourage her to see herself as a heroine—'

'Which reminds me,' broke in Mickey, to forestall any mention of heroes. 'This notion of Cap'n Longstone's about a watch-keeping group – any thoughts yet, Jasper?'

Jasper shuffled on his chair. 'I'm sorry, but I've had a lot on my plate this past week – one of those we-want-it-yesterday jobs that comes out of the blue expecting miracles and – well, agrees to pay more for the inconvenience, which is good news for me, but it means I've only managed to check out a few basics for you.' He cleared his throat. 'In much the same way there are independent – private – lifeboats dotted about the country, I've learned there are various look-out arrangements at quite a few places round the coast. It could be done here too, if someone like Rodney Longstone would take charge of organising for particular – local – requirements, and of course that's where local knowledge comes in.'

He smiled at Mike and Mickey. 'The knowledge of experts like you two and – well, everyone else with a lifetime's experience of this village, the tides, rocks, river currents, whatever... All I can do is stuff like spreadsheets, cost analysis, check out the sort of equipment that we'd need – oh, yes!' He beamed at Captain Binns, Senior. 'I've had one thought that might appeal to you, Mike, if we can only work out the details.'

'Always ready for good news, midear.'

Mickey shot Jasper a warning look, which Jasper ignored. 'A drone,' said Jasper.

As his father beamed back, Mickey sighed with relief. 'Tell us more.'

'Mike told Jane that the Scrambler Tank was a – a consolation prize for being... a bit behind the times with his ideas.' The veteran Captain Binns didn't seem offended. Good. 'These days, drones are so versatile that everybody has already thought of anything you can possibly think of, ages before you've thunk, right?' Mike agreed. 'But did you ever think of air-sea rescue?'

At this Mickey, too, began to pay attention.

'Our patrol,' said Jasper, 'would obviously patrol high on the headland for the best view of what's happening at sea, but there are places where you can't go too near the edge of the cliff. Suppose someone in a canoe paddles along the coast but hasn't got to Tollbridge, and capsizes with a freak wave or a gust of wind – or doesn't look where they're going and hits a rock. If they're hidden from direct view by the cliff overhang, all we'd hear would be shouts – if they were able to shout – so how would we know what the problem was, or where exactly anyone was, to tell the lifeboat when every minute might count?'

Mike thought this over. 'The lifeboat,' he said at last, 'they're trained to look, you might say, with equipment on board – and there's not many places within shouting distance you couldn see, or make a fair guess, where folk in trouble were. If no shouts are heard, then we wouldn know of the trouble anyway, until too late.'

His son had a better grasp of the possibilities. 'You mean, send the drone out on regular patrol and use it as a – a marker buoy in the air should it find anything?'

Jasper nodded. 'The thing would be too small for search and rescue in any *physical* sense of rescue, but for search-and-signal-to-rescuers it seems ideal. Get it in fluorescent colours to attract attention – and of course the pilot, or whatever's the word for the man at the controls –' he looked at Mike – 'would fly it low for a wing-waggle to say help was on the way, then keep it flying about overhead while the canoeist or whoever waited.'

'A skilled job,' said Mickey Binns. 'Would need a lot of practice.'

'A great responsibility,' said Jasper.

'But so very worthwhile,' said Jane.

Mike Binns, who'd collected his old age pension for over twenty years and was well into his ninth decade, had the gleeful final word.

'And it's something can be done just as well sitting down!'

Chapter Fifteen

Some days later a letter arrived for Mickey Binns. As it was a minibus-and-taxi day, nobody was home when the mystery envelope landed on the mat. Jerry was driving the bus, Mickey the taxi; Mike was out with Gabriel and a group of anglers in the *Priscilla*, in quieter moments tormenting his brother-in-law with more information about drones than Gabriel, after last time, had thought it possible (or desirable) to impart.

Mickey delivered his last passenger to her sister's door, promising to leave Hilda's own shopping at home while she and Daisy bickered over tea and biscuits as they always did. Old Mrs Beacon shook her head at him for 'the imperence of 'ee, Michael Binns' but, as he drove away, smiled to herself. Local hero, indeed!

Mickey made for the harbour, wondering how weary two old gentlemen might be after a long day trying not to intervene while amateurs fished. He realised he was watching for any sign of a pink unicorn, or children playing unsupervised at the water's edge; he saw nothing, sighed with relief, and fanfared his arrival on the taxi's horn.

Persephone's parents had made a generous contribution to the Tollbridge Community Fund by sending a cheque and covering letter to the Reverend Theodore Hollington at his

Ploverton vicarage. The vicar duly banked the cheque, sent the Tollidays a receipt and passed a copy of their letter about the Warning notice to the council, for appropriate action. He called to offer Mickey private congratulations and show him the letter, but Mickey wasn't there and Mike, promising to give his son Mr Hollington's message, had vetoed any further talk of heroism. Mickey had jumped in, pulled her out, and returned her to her family; the matter was finished and done with, and it would never do to draw overmuch attention to what might have happened, because it hadn't.

Now Mike went indoors ahead of his son, bending to pick up the scatter of envelopes from the mat with no sign of the troublesome back he had shown Peter Twelvetrees.

'Odds and ends, mostly,' he announced. 'And another one. For you.' The tone of his throwaway afterthought hinted that curiosity had been piqued.

'Postmark?' Mickey knew how the game should go.

Mike looked down. 'Sheffield.'

'Not the bank, then. Interesting. A long way from here, Yorkshire.'

Mike looked again. 'Business of some sort. Typed address to Michael Ornedge Binns, company name printed along the bottom: Datchery, Harris and Brooks. One of your college 'sociates writing from the office without paying for the stamp?'

'Nobody I recognise.' Mickey waited in patience for the investigation to be done. If he asked too directly, Mike would take twice as long to respond.

'Nothing inside beyond the letter, I'd say.' Mike crumpled the envelope gently between his fingers. 'Fan mail for the hero, no doubt.' Having learned nothing useful, he did his best to ignore the letter and held it out, all too clearly bored by the whole subject.

Mickey took it with a nod, opening it with a careless thumb. 'Hope not. I wouldn know what to charge, if anyone's after my autograph…'

'Well?' demanded his father, as Mickey fell silent.

'*Well?*' persisted Mike as Mickey, having read his letter, went back and read it again.

'Sure there's not one of these for you, too?' Mickey was puzzled. 'But then, it was my name got the publicity, so I suppose… It's from a genealogist – probate researcher – an heir hunter,' he translated as Mike in his turn was puzzled. 'Saw that chap's post about me and the *Priscilla* saying I was named for my grandmother—'

'Hah!' said Mike.

'—and says they're looking to trace descendants of Bidlake Percival Ornedge because they may be entitled to share in the estate of another member of the family, if their claim can be proved. Which o'course—'

'It can't,' supplied Mike. 'I recall old Ralph's middle name being Bidlake, always made me smile, but you're no more a family member or a descendant than me. Not by blood nor by adoption.' He rushed into reminiscence before Mickey could speak. 'Ralph and Prill were a wonderful pair, no question. They took me in, gave me a proper home for the first time in my life. Got dragged back to London when the bombing quieted down. Can't think why. With eight in the house you'd think they'd want the space, and me being the youngest I'm surprised anyone even thought to notice I wadn there.'

Mickey had grown up with his father's story, and knew better than to suggest that Mrs Binns might have pined for her Benjamin. According to Mike his mother, in spite of nine children 'and another two that died' from unspecified causes, had little maternal instinct. Her husband, 'so she called him, but they'd long since pawned the ring, they told any of us as asked' had a strong right arm and a heavy leather belt. Both parents enjoyed drink above food, and were worse than useless at budgeting. Even Mike, young as he was, knew where to run when the rent collector came, and what lies to tell should he move too slowly.

Mickey always believed that his father's genius for telling the tourist tale took its first tentative steps in those grim formative years of London infancy. Moving to Combe Tollbridge, an exotic stranger in the company of Gabriel Hockaday, Barney Christmas and their fellows, he found that the continuing need to think on his feet very quickly honed already-sharpened wits and imagination yet further. In modern parlance, Mike Binns hit the ground running and had charged merrily through life ever since, with few stumbles beyond the loss of his wife in childbirth, and the sadness of having but the one child when Gabriel could boast five sturdy sons, and a tumultuous assortment of grandchildren.

After a respectful pause, Mickey said: 'You did all right, Dad.'

'Thanks to Prill and Ralph, more than any. Which idn to say the others didn't make me welcome, in their way, but when Gabriel pounded me for making eyes at Louise it was Aunt Prill who put a carvy-seed poultice on the bruises, and took care of me...'

'And it was Gabriel walked you home from school in the first place.' Mickey wrinkled his nose. 'A great one for treatment with caraway seeds, old Prill. If I complained of over-eating she'd give me the oil on a lump of sugar—'

'—and you had to make it last, or twouldn work so well.' Mike, who'd begun to display faint signs of melancholy, cheered up. 'Stick out your tongue after a minute on the kitchen clock and prove it!' He laughed. 'Else it was a tablespoon of physic from the big blue bottle in the corner, remember?'

'Top shelf, and hold your nose!' Mickey shuddered. 'Epsom salts, wormwood and oak bark – these days she'd have the child cruelty people after her. Yet here we are, survivors both, so no great harm done – and a lot of good,' he added gravely. 'Better than blood family, Ralph and Prill. Far better.'

'Did me the biggest favour in the world, keeping me away from mine. Talked about making it legal, but Prill worried they'd try to get me back again if lawyers wrote to remind 'em, so nothing was ever done. No papers signed.' Mike spoke with pride. 'Didn need papers to know I belonged. Never entered my head I might not.'

'I know, Dad, and so does everyone else in Tollbridge, but this chap who wrote the letter don't know. I'll write straight back and explain I'm not entitled.' Mickey grinned. 'Shows the Twelvetrees chap wadn altogether wasting his time, I suppose.'

'Made the lawyer waste *his*, though! Just you ask Evan Evans about legal letters, and how much they cost to write with their hizey-prizey language. Now, as to why this chap's wrote to you but not to me, even with both at the same address – well, it *could* be no more than saving money. But...' He frowned and fell silent, trying to work it out.

'But it could arrive by tomorrow's post – or, tidn unknown for letters to go astray and never arrive at all. Or – well, you're my father, meaning older than me, and perhaps this Datchery thought – well...'

'Thought I might be dead? Or too addle-headed with age to be worth the writing? For all your fancy education they've learned you little tact, Michael Ornedge Binns.' But Mike's heart wasn't in the skirmish: he was too busy thinking. Mickey saw this, and kept quiet.

'I owe a lot – everything – to Ralph and Prill,' said Mike at last. 'I'd never want to do them down, nor any that belong to them; and you'm of similar mind, my son.' Mickey had no time to reply. 'This chap's going to hear from you there's no claim in it for any by the name of Binns, but – what happens next? If he can't find the legal heirs, is he to keep the money for himself? That wouldn be right.'

'To cover his expenses?' Such a possibility hadn't occurred to Mickey. He wondered what others might occur to his father, whose imagination, unlike his own, knew no limits when the stimulus was strong. He turned the letter over in his hands. 'If the law would let him get away with such a trick he'd never have written me in the first place. And there's nothing obvious to say he'd try anything like that. The paper's good quality – none of your fluttery, flimsy stuff; the heading's got a bit of class to the design, very fancy, though tidn engraved—' he ran his fingers lightly over the print – 'which o'course these days not everybody cares to spend money on...'

He saw Mike's expression. 'So, maybe he photocopied it from someone else, or ran it off on his computer. Easy enough to do, but – if he's playing tricks for some reason, why play 'em on me? I'm not entitled, but he writes "members of the family" and after so many generations there must be plenty who are, and he'll have written to them too.'

'Maybe not. Didn write to me, remember. There's no Ornedge to my name, which is how he says he found you, but if Prill and Ralph were your true-born grammer and gramfer like he thought, then stands to reason I'd be their son, and better entitled than you. Tell you what, don't write just yet. Wait a day or so, then if my letter don't come I reckon we ought to start asking a few questions. I wonder who might know?'

Mickey was startled. 'Anyone in Tollbridge, not to mention Ploverton, could tell him where to look for Ralph's family, within reason—'

'For heaven's sake, boy, I could tell him myself! That wadn my meaning. Who would know how to find out about these Datchery people, is what I'm asking. The vicar, maybe, as it's a family matter – or maybe not. Always likes to think the best of everyone, Mr Hollington, and I'm in a mood to think the worst.'

'There's no reason you should – or not yet, anyway.' Mickey never worried as much as his father over unexpected paperwork: but Mike hadn't enjoyed the benefit of higher education, with all the burrowing through files and documents a university degree can entail. 'If they're lawyers there must be a directory, register, some sort of official list to be checked for how long they've bin at this game. A library with a good reference section, that's what we need. Probably not one of the smaller ones: Taunton or Exeter, most likely—'

'Losing half a day's work,' said Mike, 'but worth it for peace of mind.'

Mickey laughed. 'Five minutes, at a guess! All we've to do is phone to ask if they've such a register on their shelves, or in their computer—'

'Computer!' Dramatically, Mike smacked his forehead. 'Well, here's us a right pair of fools, forgetting there's folk with computers far closer to home who'd be glad to look things up if asked, like young Jasper, and Jane; Angela, maybe – and there's always Susan,' he couldn't resist adding, 'if she can spare the time, as she did for that professor when Jan Ridd asked.' Mickey said nothing. 'O'course,' Mike went on, 'Susan wadn acquainted with neither Prill nor Ralph – but she knew Prue Budd well enough. Doubtless she'd have no great objection to doing a spot of research on behalf of Prue's sister, seeing how she's a dab hand to find things out.'

'We'll ask Jasper.' Mickey wasn't going to rise to his father's teasing. 'But we'll do nought till tomorrow, after the postman's bin and gone.' With a resolute hand he folded his letter, returned it to its envelope, and prepared to carry it off to his room. Mike eyed him with renewed suspicion. 'And we won't mention it,' said Mickey, 'should the Mertons happen to be in the Anchor tonight.' Mike opened his mouth to speak. 'Tomorrow,' said Mickey. Mike shut his mouth. Mickey nodded.

'See here, Dad, this idn anything I've come across before, nor you, nor anyone that we know, though you read of it in the papers now and then.' Mike grunted. 'This Datchery made an understandable mistake, and I'm going to set him straight – but you've started me to think. I'd rather like time for thinking some more, before I get in touch.'

'You reckon there's trickery in it somewhere, too?'

'I said before, no reason there should be – but there's other problems might arise apart from trickery. I'm inclined to think it's an honest mistake. People do this sort of thing for a job; make television programmes about it, even. Mr Datchery will look for the proper heirs once he knows I'm not one – but families can be complicated, Dad. I know you think of us as local after all these years, and the Jerome half of me is certainly true-born Tollbridge, but there's the other half. How many brothers and sisters were still in London when you were sent away during the war?'

'You know well I was the youngest of nine still living.' Mike tugged at his beard. 'Could even have had a few more after I was gone. Can't say they were great ones for writing, and nobody had the phone in them days, and me too young to be writing to them without Ralph or Prill to help – which I seem to remember 'em asking a few times, and me always saying I'd rather they didn bother. So,' he finished happily, 'they never did, not being greatly given to book-learning or penmanship themselves, and a war on besides.'

'No.' Mickey fell silent in thought. 'I blame Susan,' he said at last, with a laugh. 'This new idea of hers – she fancies a life of crime, she says, or part-time at least, as a change from –' he glanced at his father – 'silk sheets and so forth.' He coughed. 'We've talked over a few thoughts, and she's made me see there can be a mystery in anything, if you stir things deep enough. So I can't help wondering what might be stirred up if anyone starts looking into our family tree. I've no notion how much poking about through marriages and – and ramifications these heir hunters have to do.'

'This Datchery idn looking for a Binns, but for an Ornedge. I doubt anyone in London would recognise Ralph's name after all these years, if they ever heard it – but you could be right. Why risk trouble when there's bin none since that one and only time during the war? When they had me took home, remember, and I bolted back here the minute I could – on my own, too! No idea how I did it – but then I always was sharp, as a youngster.'

'Come on, Dad, for such an old-timer you're hardly blunted yet,' Mickey assured him.

Mike preened himself, savouring the compliment. 'We'll have a drink on that tonight, son! And, yes, not a word from either of us about this business – not until after the postman tomorrow. Least said, soonest mended – but it does make a chap start to think.' He chuckled. 'I wonder how 'twould be to meet up with a whole mess o' my kith and kin I didn know I had – and whether they'd know anything about me. Would the older ones remember young Mikey that was sent away from the bombs to the seaside and never seen again, to tell their children?' Part of a little verse read by Auntie Prill from a bedtime book came drifting back. 'Did they tell 'em I was lost, stolen or strayed?'

Mickey, who had inherited his father's copy of *When We Were Very Young* and read it to destruction, laughed, then grew serious. 'Did *you* tell *me* anything of these "older ones" of yourn? Hardly a word! And no doubt it was the same for them, the same way I never really felt like asking you because, from what little you said, there were none of you too happy at home and – well, I wouldn want to remind you.'

Mike said nothing; a shadow crossed his eyes. Mickey smiled at him with an affection he found hard to put into words. 'True, they'd be my uncles and aunts, if still living, and their children my cousins – their grandchildren too, and probably greats as well, by now. But the Hockadays and Jeromes and the rest, I've known my whole life. That's family enough for me. I doubt I'd have too much in common with any of the name of Binns except – well, except the name of Binns! You and me can be the last little twigs on our branch of the family tree, and for myself I'm not bothered. I've had a grand life – as have you, ever since Ralph and Prill gave you a home—'

'And that's why I've no wish to see them or theirs cheated, if that's what might happen. If there's no letter for me tomorrow, we'll have a word with Jasper – or would Jan Ridd be better? Having bin a policeman, as I was about to say when we talked of going to the Anchor – but then, I don't know. Jan's retired, but asking him might somehow make it too… official, when we've both thought it best not to stir things up.'

From time to time Mickey would muse idly on his father's past, but never come to any serious conclusion. Mike had made a new life in Combe Tollbridge; the old life was forgotten, and didn't seem all that important. Until now it hadn't really occurred to Mike's son to ask himself how far an ongoing reluctance to make contact with the larger Binns connection might be something more than a childhood wish to escape from poverty, overcrowding, and harsh treatment to a life of fresh air, good food, and loving kindness among a close village community. Mickey had joked about Susan's intention to turn to a life of crime: was the joke closer to the truth than he knew?

And yet, how reliable after eighty years were a little boy's memories of his seniors' behaviour in the big city? Mike, as any tourist could testify, had a vivid imagination. It took very little to let it rip; with Gabriel Hockaday beside him there were few bounds it could not leap. When first he had arrived in Tollbridge it was wartime. Blue, navy and khaki uniforms; busy-ness and grim purpose; heartbreak and loss, grief and strain; rationing, the black market, spivs and crooks. Every stranger not in uniform was a potential spy; every paperboy's innocent whistle, every ring of a bicycle bell or toot of a motor horn could be a signal to the head of a criminal gang, or a message to be passed on by an enemy agent hidden nearby, living on iron rations, his short-wave radio tuned to the same frequency as that of the U-boat that lurked on the sea bed to surface every night, listening for coded information vital to the survival (or conquest) of Great Britain.

Mickey thought few Tollbridge children would have suspected as many spies, enemy agents or criminal gangs as story-telling Mike and his best friend. Egging each other on was what small boys did. Maybe Gabriel, the elder, had persuaded young Mike the family he'd chosen to leave had been left for even better reasons than he supposed. Honesty was not only the best policy: for Mike Binns it might be the safest. Oliver Twist had been cruelly trapped in Fagin's gang, but Mike had made his escape just in time, never to return—

'Look at you!' cried Mike. 'Grinning and girdling away to yourself like an ape, when there's nothing funny in any of this, not as I can see.'

Mickey returned to reality. 'You're right, there isn't.' He shook himself. 'So, we'll say nothing to anyone until tomorrow after the postman and then, letter for you or not, we'll be along to Clammer Cottage and talk with Jasper Merton.'

Mike, who had himself had time to think while his son was thinking, agreed the general principle but, as ever, wanted the last word. 'Or Jane,' he said. 'I'd forgotten she has a computer too – and she's a nice, obliging girl. Took a good likeness of me t'other day with her sketchbook, remember. Printed that photo, as well.'

Mickey decided to ignore him, and headed up the narrow stairs to his room.

Next morning the postman's van was observed passing the end of Hempen Row without stopping.

'He might have forgotten, and drop in on the way back,' said Mickey.

'No harm in asking now,' said Mike. He didn't say *I told you so*, but the sentiment was heavy in his voice.

'They weren't in the pub last night. I don't like to disturb him at work, when tomorrow—'

'—or tomorrow-day, or never-tide! He might well be glad of a change.'

It seemed any qualms Mike might have had about delving into the past had been overtaken by curiosity; or perhaps it was the thrill of the chase. The spies, enemy agents, and criminal gangs of wartime hadn't been altogether forgotten: there was something still childlike in Mike's eagerness to unmask Datchery, Harris and Brooks of Sheffield as the villains in whatever convoluted fantasy his imagination had woven.

'I'll fetch the letter,' said Mickey, and clumped upstairs to his room.

Jane was wrestling unproductively with creativity when the knocker rattled on the front door, which she opened with a smile that didn't fade when she recognised her visitors.

'Thank goodness I've an excuse to stop work for a while. Come in. Is it me or Jasper you want, or both of us? What can we do for you?'

'You've both got computers, so whichever can spare some time for a spot of digging's fine by us.' Mickey drew the letter from his pocket, and handed it across. 'We don't like to bother you, but it's a matter of finding out a bit about these folk – such as, are they really what they seem. And o'course I've no notion how long such an investigation might take.'

'Nor me, neither,' Mike chipped in.

As she pulled Mickey's letter from its envelope, Jane laughed. 'That makes three of us! I'm the practical one for most things but I have to admit, with Jasper running his own company he has a far better head for business, having to deal every day with all sorts of people. It's so much safer to *know* something about people you're dealing with rather than take what they tell you on trust.'

'Most of all when it's a question of money,' said Mike. 'Old Barney idn the only one with an eye to the pennies and pounds, and careful where they come and go – 'specially where they go.'

'I'll give Jasper a shout,' said a baffled Jane, the letter still unread.

The boss of Packlemerton's Publicity shouted back that he'd be about five minutes, and if anyone suggested putting the kettle on he wouldn't argue. Mickey worried again that they might be interrupting important work, but Mike followed his hostess happily into the kitchen and dragged a chair from under the table without waiting for an invitation to sit down.

'Bin a while since we had our breakfast,' he said hopefully. 'Susan told me once, in the old days they called it *bracksus* and elevenses, *forenoons*. Did 'ee know that, midear?'

'In New Zealand,' countered Jane, 'elevenses used to be *smoke-oh*. I don't know if it still is. My father had Kiwi cousins and they came to stay the year before he died, and told us. Now so many people are giving up smoking, perhaps they don't say that any more.'

'Smoke-oh or forenoons, 'tis all much of a muchness once it gets inside you,' said the philosopher, still hopeful. Jane laughed again, and rummaged for the biscuit tin.

When all four were seated comfortably with steaming mugs and welcoming plates Jane handed the letter, her quick explanation footnoted by Mickey, to Jasper. 'Can you do anything to help?' she asked.

'If it won't take too long,' added Mickey.

'Computers make everything quick, don't they?' Mike knew little about them, beyond the fact they used too many words he didn't understand. He liked, he said, to keep his mind lively, but he knew his limitations and was too old to learn another language.

Mickey in his college days had spoken of punch-cards, and brought home concertina stacks of green-striped paper with holes down each side. Mike had shown some interest at first, but lost it once 'mainframe' was explained. When home computers finally arrived at an affordable price he said that television had been hard enough, for a lad who'd grown up with the cinema screen; anything smaller would be too much effort for too little a reward, which as a fisherman he was used to anyway. No need to go asking for more.

When Jasper brought his laptop into the kitchen, Mike's eyes came out on stalks. He began asking questions Jasper had no time to answer as he typed, clicked and scrolled with the wireless mouse he had long preferred over any touch-pad. Mike watched and marvelled.

Mickey and Jane exchanged looks. This could of course go either way, but if investigations into Datchery, Harris and Brooks proved successful it would be no great surprise if a certain pensioner's erstwhile wish for a birthday drone were to be transmuted into a request for a Christmas computer.

'Datchery, Harris and Brooks – their website, see?' The laptop was turned for Mickey and Mike to read the display. 'They've been going eight – no, nine years. I'd say that's long enough for them definitely not to be on the dodgy side of things.'

'So how do they make their money?' Mike demanded.

'A percentage of the value of the estate if your claim's proved, usually.' Jasper clicked and scrolled some more. 'Sometimes it's a set fee, so much charged per hour, but – there you are: a whole page listing their rates.' Once more he turned the laptop so that Mickey and Mike could study the screen. He then pulled it back, saying he would 'name-check for any dissatisfied customers out there' but, after some minutes, could find none.

'The firm has a page of case histories –' he moved the cursor to the relevant tab – 'and all favourable, but then they would be, wouldn't they? Easy enough to cherry-pick the positive testimonials and ignore the people who feel they've got a justified complaint.'

Mike frowned. 'They could have wrote their own testimonials,' he pointed out.

'Maybe they did, but there's no negative feedback that I can find – or not without a lot more digging than I've had time to do. They seem to be a long-established firm, within the limits of the job description. Heaven knows how people managed to find missing heirs before the internet! I believe there were only notices in newspapers, unless you were a lawyer of some sort and received the official lists.'

'Then it looks like I've no cause not to answer this letter.' Mickey gave his father a reassuring grin. 'I'll be tactful in what I say, o'course, but I wouldn't want to do anyone out of what's rightfully theirs and not mine.' As he embarked on telling the Mertons the full story he saw Mike slide the mouse from Jasper's casual grasp and begin to manoeuvre it erratically about the table, watching the cursor freeze and jump in turn as plates and mugs interrupted the wireless signal.

'It happened to a cousin of mine,' Jasper began as Mickey, having answered such questions as the Mertons saw fit to put, at the end of his recital put a question of his own. Mike throughout had remained silent, absorbed in his new game. The three onlookers were quietly amused by the old gentleman's enjoyment of the new experience. Mickey wondered how soon he would be dragged off to a computer shop.

'Which is how I know a bit about it,' Jasper went on. 'I don't think it was the same firm as yours – there's quite a few of them around these days – but just like you, she got a letter out of the blue. Heir-hunting's become quite a thing, now so many public records are available online. Far easier to check 'em sitting at home rather than travel miles to some archive office and drag enormous files on and off shelves for hours: these days you just need to be able to do a decent online search. With so many families not living on top of each other the way they once did, people can soon lose touch and then, whoosh, some relative you've never heard of dies without leaving a will, and like my cousin, you get the letter.'

'Did she get anything else?'

'No, because she didn't take 'em up on it. They weren't crooks,' he hastened to add, 'but she'd already looked into our genealogy herself because she likes that sort of thing, so she knew her way around. She thought she'd play detective, same as you, and she phoned various relatives, including me, to ask if we'd had the same letter, which I hadn't. From our answers she worked out which branch of the family tree this dead person belonged to, and then she looked at census records and stuff like that to draw a chart – and she decided it probably wasn't worth it. One line of descent on the distaff side involved marriage to a Brown, which is as bad as marriage to Smith or Jones for tracing purposes – but, even with half the possible heirs so hard to find, even the possibles she found on the other side came to a couple of dozen, she said, all entitled to an equal share of whatever it was – which, from the family background, wouldn't have been much. But it makes a good story!'

'So who gets the money?' Mickey was thinking of Susan, and good story plots.

'The government, at a guess. The treasury? Don't know.'

'The Duchy of Lancaster, I think,' offered Jane. 'But don't let's get into politics, or the rest of the day will be ruined.'

'No it won't,' said Jasper, his eyes bright. 'Because I've just had a brilliant idea!'

Chapter Sixteen

'Yet another brilliant idea,' Jane amended.

'Well, an idea that's potentially brilliant, and might boost the tourists-are-good-for-trade campaign we're all trying to establish.' He indicated Mike Binns, raconteur extraordinaire, but addressed his son. 'Mickey, you were named for Ralph Ornedge, weren't you?'

'No room for Ralph as well, but Ornedge it is, and proud of it.' As Mickey spoke, Mike abandoned his game with the wireless mouse to smile. 'Old Ralph was as good as any grandfather to me, same as Prill was my grammer in all but name. What does a drop of blood here or there matter, save to the mind of a lawyer?'

'The name,' said Jasper. He retrieved the mouse and addressed himself again to his laptop. 'Should be easier to trace than Smith or Brown or Jones...'

Mickey coughed. 'Susan told me once it was a corruption, derivation, what-d'you-call-it of *aulnager* – something to do with measuring cloth sold at market in mediaeval times, she said.' He laughed. 'Sort of trading standards officer, I think.'

Mike now had some fun at his son's expense, making elaborate apologies for the burden he'd unwittingly imposed on him when Ralph by itself would have done almost as well, if he hadn't wanted Aunt Prill commemorated too.

'Susan was right.' Jasper emerged from his internet search. The teasing stopped. 'About the duties of an aulnager, that is, though the derivation of Ornedge seems to be anyone's guess – and I can't find anyone with that exact surname out there, which explains why Datchery and Co. were so glad to find Mickey's details when they spotted Peter Whatsit's blog. They wrote before they'd checked you out properly, Mickey – they must have thought they'd got lucky and just grabbed at the chance.'

'And now I'm obliged to write and tell 'em they're clean out of luck, which means they must start all over again finding the right person to make a proper claim.'

'Which is a pity, because it means Ornedge is a non-starter for my idea – which doesn't stop it being brilliant, if we can work it right. Hang on.' Jasper moused and clicked some more. 'Aha! Nowhere near as rare as Ornedge – scattered all over the country – just imagine if everyone replied and we had to impose restrictions! Wouldn't that be brilliant?'

'Would it?'

'A themed family reunion.' Jasper began putting thoughts into words. 'Everyone invited who has the same surname, a name with local connections. Not Ornedge, but – Mike, Mickey: wasn't your Aunt Prill our Prue Budd's twin sister?'

'Dear old Prue,' said Jane, as Mickey and Mike confirmed the fact. 'She and Elias were a lovely couple.' She gazed round the Clammer Cottage kitchen. 'I wonder what they'd think of me – us – living in their place and doing it up the way we have?'

Jasper sighed. 'Doesn't matter now: we've done it. But weren't the twins born Christmases? Some sort of cousins to Barney? He's always lamenting he's the last of the family and how, once he goes, there won't be anyone left in Tollbridge to carry on the name.'

'Often,' said Mickey. 'He claimed kin to speak at Prue's funeral, remember – oh, no, you weren't living here then. But he did. The last of the name, he kept saying.'

'Last o' the name unless,' said Mike, darkly, 'all them brothers and sisters he helped make their way in the world, and never thanked him nor come back, come back after all.' Mickey shot his father a curious glance. Did Mike have renewed suspicions about his own long-lost siblings? He'd deliberately chosen to lose touch with them, but Barney had made no such choice. Might he harbour similar misgivings to Mike over Jasper's brilliant idea?

'Of course we'd ask Barney what he thought before doing anything,' said Jasper. 'If he doesn't like it, we pick another name. Only, "Christmas" has such possibilities – like a trip to Bristol, with a group photoshoot on Christmas Steps. A Tollbridge Christmas market, maybe in the old school, or the Anchor skitt alley, or the Jubilee Hall if that's ever fixed – or somewhere in Ploverton, because they'd be involved, too. Only, we'd do it in summer, because that's when there are tourists in the area. Most people like to be with family at real Christmas – and anyway, it's not so easy to travel then. After all, Australians have to celebrate Christmas in the summer. We could have barbecues on the beach and tell everyone we were celebrating locals who emigrated to the Antipodes. We'd still have all the trimmings. Photos galore. Gabriel can dig out his red suit and ho-ho-ho all over the place; mince pies and cake from Widdowson's Bakery, Miriam can weave a giant stocking to hang from the *Priscilla*'s mast.' Everyone laughed. 'Or maybe not!'

'Maybe she could,' said Jane, 'though stockings are usually knitted, I believe – but don't people dress the masts of boats with flags when there's a celebration?' She appealed to Mike and Mickey. 'Someone who sews could make lengths of green bunting for a Christmas tree, with coloured stuff in between to look like baubles—'

'And the masthead light for a star on top of the tree.' Mickey was laughing again. 'Not sure we could run to an angel with a trumpet, though.'

Mike shook his head. 'In summer? We'd need brighter than a masthead light during the day, for best effect.' There was a familiar gleam in his eye. 'Given time to consider the problem, I've no doubt I could contrive something to suit. My first thought is, 'twould be more noticeable for the light to flash than stand still. Now, if port and starboard lights were rigged in the right sequence – no, stars are gold or silver, not red and green.'

'Red and green for baubles.' Mickey was enjoying the sight of his father quite as enthused as his host and hostess. Jane had slipped from the kitchen, to return with pencil and sketchbook; Jasper was once more looking things up on the laptop as his wife doodled on page after quickly-turned page.

Mickey smiled. 'I'd say our Jasper's idea idn so far off being brilliant, just like he said. If we could persuade Barney to go along with it – ask him to be guest of honour, speech of welcome, or similar – I reckon if we did it every year we could really put Combe Tollbridge on the map! And,' he added ruefully, 'for the right sort of reason, what's more.'

That evening, the Anchor buzzed quietly as people waited for Barney Christmas to appear. Whatever Barney's current business interests might be nobody knew but, long past official retirement though he was, they still preoccupied him more than they allowed him to socialise with his fellows, and he wasn't to be found every night in the pub as was the case with other locals.

Jasper had earlier paid a discreet visit to Boatshed Row and explained the latest idea for bringing visitors, their trade and their money to the village. Barney had in theory approved, but wanted time to consider all the implications. 'The village boiling with nought but Christmases? Who knows who might be among them, hoping to get their hands on my money?'

His young friend thought he understood the old man's concerns, and somehow missed the twinkle lurking deep in

Barney's eye. Mr Christmas had a reputation, and enjoyed living up to it: he still savoured the memory of telling the vicar he planned to establish a caravan site on Elias Budd's vegetable patch at Clammer Cottage. 'I've seen neither hide nor hair of any o' my family since I don't know when,' said the eldest of six. 'Wouldn recognise 'em if they walked in this minute. Just suppose I go soft in my old age, and start believing what anyone tells me about blood being thicker'n water—'

'Is it?' asked Jasper. 'In your view, I mean: now, while you're hale and hearty?'

'No,' said Barney. 'I'll leave my money where it suits, having made it myself with no help from a soul, and beholden to none. Ralph Ornedge left what he had to Prill, which is as it should be – and what little was left when Cousin Prill died went to Mike Binns, with a token to Mickey, seeing they'd no chillern of their own and a great sorrow to them both, until young Mike arrived from London town.' He spoke with sincerity now, all teasing forgotten. 'No, there's less occasions than folk like to think where blood can be argued thicker than water, just as there's no particular need for charity beginning at home.'

'You could certainly give it all to charity – but why not have a word with your solicitor? Some sort of trust, perhaps,' said Jasper.

Barney snorted with laughter. 'Costing even more money! Think I'm made of it?'

Jasper eyed him shrewdly. There had been a certain note in that laughter... 'You've already arranged something,' he deduced.

'Might have.' Barney sniffed. 'Might not – and I'll thank 'ee, young imperence, not to go tattering my private affairs all over town.'

'I won't breathe a word,' promised Jasper.

'I've uttered no word for you to breathe. I told you I'd want time to think, and so I do. No one takes Barnaby Christmas for granted. Tidn the way I am.'

'I know,' said Jasper. 'I don't – and I don't think anyone else does, either.'

'Just how it should be,' said the old man. 'Fancy a drink afore you go?'

Jasper reported this partial success to Jane, adding that he suspected Barney would in due course thoroughly enjoy being the centre of Christmas attention, but wanted to milk the present situation for all it was worth.

'We should let him play it at his own speed,' he said. 'If anyone tries putting pressure on him to agree he'll drag his heels from sheer devilment. You know what he's like.'

'Not as well as you do. If you say wait, then we'll wait. Have you told Mike and Mickey?'

'There was nobody home when I knocked on my way back from Barney's. We'll catch them later, in the pub: it's too late to stop either of them talking, so we'll just have to take it as it comes.'

That evening, the Anchor buzzed quietly as people waited for Barney Christmas to appear. Mickey had said little, but Mike had said more, and everyone thought that Jasper's Surname Reunion had real possibilities. And if Barney disliked the notion, there were other names 'equal-so-good as Christmas, if not better.'

Jasper hoped that Barney's blessing would before long be given to the plan. The publicity potential of Bristol's Christmas Steps crowded with visiting Christmases had a strong appeal. Each time he heard the thud of the Anchor's door, like almost everyone else in the bar he looked up, hoping that tonight would be one of the busy entrepreneur's pleasure-not-business nights. Only a few strong-minded persons such as Angela Lilley, the perfect barmaid, carried on as before: Angela because she was working, and others because they disapproved of making Barney Christmas (or anyone else) the centre of attention when he wasn't even in the place to be seen. 'No more than encouraging the man to keep on with his tricks, which are artful enough when all's said and done.'

Mickey Binns spluttered over his cider.

'Barney?' asked his father, turning his head. 'Oh!'

'Susan,' gasped Mickey; choked, set down his mug, and had to clear his throat.

'Good to see 'ee again, midear!' Gabriel Hockaday and Mike joined the rest of the bar's delighted chorus of welcome. 'So, what's your pleasure?'

She was very soon settled with half a pint in what Mike Binns maintained should be a farthing dish, being a smaller companion to the penny and ha'penny dishes she'd discovered during her various research endeavours.

'So you've finished looking things up for now, have 'ee?' was Gabriel's query.

'No more tiring out your eyes in front of a little screen,' said Mike.

'Well, less of it,' said Susan, 'and I'll be pacing myself far more sensibly once I get round to the actual writing.' She looked across to where her daughter exchanged pleasantries with Sam Farley. 'Angela worries when she thinks I'm too immersed in my research, but this time it meant a different approach to my usual background reading because I had to change the emphasis. But I've made lots of notes, and soaked up tons of atmosphere. It shouldn't be long before I can make a proper start.'

She smiled at Mike. 'But now I'm quite screened out, as you can imagine! And I wanted to ask your son when he'd be free to take me to Bristol in the taxi.'

'To Christmas Steps,' said Mike, and everyone except Susan chuckled. They all tried to explain at the same time, but in the end she made sense of it, and told Jasper he could well have had a very clever idea.

'But I don't want to go to Christmas Steps. I suppose one day I should, to satisfy my curiosity: I've never been: but it's the

Hippodrome I want to see – the music hall that was built as part of the Stoll empire, just before the First World War. It's right in the middle of town and the way I feel now, the last thing I want is to drive myself anywhere.'

'Glad to oblige,' was all Mickey said, as Mike shot him a quizzical look and Gabriel, far too obviously, said nothing. 'Day after tomorrow all right?'

It was. At the appointed hour the taxi drew up outside Corner Glim Cottage.

'There are backstage tours I could take,' said Susan, 'but I want to wander about at my own speed, soaking up the atmosphere.' She smiled. 'I'm sure there are booklets or leaflets on sale. If Tollbridge can do it, the Bristol Hippodrome certainly can.'

'But they don't have Lorinda Doone writing for them.'

'Lorinda Doone won't be writing my new series. I'll need another name for that.'

'You going to tell me what it's about, so I can make a few suggestions? Or maybe you'd like young Angela to dream something up.'

'Please don't mention it to Angela! It can really stifle an idea if too many people know about it. She's so much better organised than me; you know how she's sometimes a bit… deflating, without realising. Disapproving. But I've told my agent, and she *does* approve – and of course I'll tell you, if you won't tell anyone else. After all, it was something you said that set me off in the first place.' There was a faint colour in Susan's cheeks, but as Mickey was concentrating on the road ahead he didn't notice.

'Always glad to be of assistance,' he assured her. 'So, what did I say?'

'You – you quoted that bit from Sherlock Holmes about Irene Adler.' Susan didn't go into details. 'And I remembered the end of the story, when Irene disguises herself as a man and follows Holmes back to Baker Street so she can say goodnight, and she does, and he doesn't recognise her.' She paused. Mickey grunted to show he was paying attention.

'In the letter she leaves for him to find with her photo, she says she often dresses as a man and enjoys the freedom it gives her, and I thought – but she was a singer, not really an actress. Was it more than ordinary stagecraft? Who taught Irene Adler how to be a proper male impersonator?'

Again she paused. 'So, who did?' asked Mickey, as was clearly expected.

Susan laughed softly. 'Well, it's something for which I can honestly thank Angela and I will, when the time comes. It was while we were trying to sort the museum, and I unearthed the Friendly Society daybook and took it home to repair it.'

'Done it yet?'

Susan blushed. 'Well, no – but I will, before I give it back. It makes fascinating reading! One of the entries is about a Ladies' Day outing to a music hall, and lists their favourite acts, and how a good time was had by all.'

'And they saw Irene Adler?' Mickey, baffled, was doing his best.

'Of course not. The act that most impressed everyone was Vesta Tilley.' Mickey said nothing. 'Perhaps the greatest male impersonator of them all, Mickey Binns!'

'Sounds vaguely familiar,' he conceded.

'Mike and Gabriel's generation would recognise the name, I bet.' Then Susan giggled. 'To be honest, I only know of her because I wrote a Victorian Dalrymple with my heroine a workhouse orphan, who goes on the stage and gradually becomes legit and ends up marrying a lord. I read round the period for background, and Vesta Tilley was seriously famous as a performer for – oh, decades. And she became Lady de Frece! She was amazingly convincing in male costume. She was so thorough, and took such pains, she even wore men's underclothes on stage, and used to spend hours plaiting her hair – she never cut it – so that it lay flat in coils under a wig. She had a string of hits like "After the Ball" and "Following in Father's Footsteps" and –' here Susan shot Mickey a sly glance – 'one of her most famous, "Burlington Bertie" where she wore white tie and tails.'

'Now, I've heard of that!' He sounded pleased. He cleared his throat. '"I'm Burlington Bertie, I rise at ten-thirty / And saunter along like a toff—"'

'Aha!' cried Susan, delighted he'd fallen into the trap. 'No you haven't. That's "Burlington Bertie from Bow" and was a spoof sung by another music hall star called Ella Shields. Vesta Tilley's song came first, and it's entirely different.'

'Trick question,' grumbled Mickey.

'I didn't ask a question,' said Susan.

After three seconds of frosty silence, Mickey burst out laughing and Susan joined in.

'So your idea is that Vesta Tilley taught Irene Adler how to act a successful boy, right?'

'Right. The time period fits. Their paths could easily have crossed more than once – but they don't need to. Once, just for a few weeks, would be enough for Irene Adler, with her quick wits and acting skills – but she's not the heroine of my new series. My heroine will be Vesta Tilley. She toured the country from music hall to music hall – she performed at the Bristol Hippodrome, which is why we're going there today. She toured America, and retired to France. Think of how many crimes and mysteries she could encounter in her travels! The people, the characters, the settings! Quite as much variety as Milicent Dalrymple could wish for – only, as I told you, Milicent won't be writing the series.'

'What series – I mean, what's the title?'

'Still under discussion. Possibly *Vesta Investigates*, maybe *Vesta the Investigator* – either would work, I think. Don't you?'

'I'm no judge, midear, but yes, reckon I do. And who's to write this series, whatever it's called in the end?'

'I thought about "Matilda Powles" because that was Vesta's real name, but it's too far down the alphabet. The number of readers who start at "A" and work their way along the shelf until they find something they like, would surprise you.'

'After all these years not much surprises me.' Mickey chuckled. 'I was in a bookshop once – second-hand, o'course, selling some textbooks,' in case she thought he might have been buying one of her titles, 'and a chap comes in and says he's going on holiday. Wanted the thickest paperback they'd got, didn't care what sort so long as it was fiction, handed over the money and said, now he wouldn't mind leaving it behind when he came home, on account of he'd not paid the asking price when new. A bargain, he said.'

'Oh.' Susan was almost speechless.

'True as I'm sitting here! I'd cross my heart and hope to die, only I'd prefer not taking my hands off the steering wheel to do it in case that's what happens.'

She thanked him; there was a pause; and they both started laughing again.

'So,' said Mickey, as he drove on, 'further up the alphabet than "P" and no doubt you'd prefer earlier than "Dalrymple", too.'

'Well, not much later.'

'Not "Susan Jones", then.'

'Very boring,' said Susan Jones. There was a longer pause, as Mickey considered the problem. He took a deep breath.

'How would you feel about "Susan Binns"?'

Also available

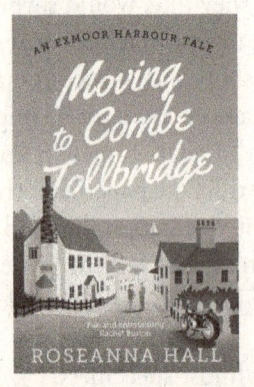

**Moving to Combe Tollbridge
(An Exmoor Harbour Tale, Book 1)**

When a cosy country cottage goes up for sale in Combe Tollbridge, a small fishing village tucked away on a quiet corner of the Exmoor coast, young couple Jane and Jasper decide to make the move.

But while Jane is returning to the place of happy childhood memories by the sea, another recent newcomer to the village, Angela, has sadder reasons for her move.

Receiving a warm welcome from the colourful residents who call the village home, all three soon become embroiled in rural life, and find it not as sedate as they might have once imagined...

OUT NOW

About the Author

Roseanna Hall is the pseudonym adopted by Sarah J. Mason for her new 'Exmoor Harbour Tales' series, to distinguish these books from the seventeen 'Miss Seeton' mysteries she has written as Hamilton Crane, and a further eight mysteries under her own name.

The first Roseanna Hall was Sarah's grandfather's grandmother. Roseanna married John George and, in 1843, gave birth to grandfather's mother, Elizabeth. Elizabeth George might have been a good name for an author, but sadly it's already taken.

When not busy at the keyboard Sarah will relax with craft work. Her current enthusiasm is for weaving inkle bands, but she also enjoys patchwork, tapestry weaving and, from diagrams in a Danish textbook, she taught herself to make 3-D beaded animals. She's especially proud of her peacocks.

She supports her local hospice shop by checking 500-piece jigsaw puzzle donations. Please don't ask about the earwigs.

Note from the Publisher

To receive updates on further releases in the Exmoor Harbour Tales series – plus special offers and news of other humorous fiction series to make you smile – sign up now to the Farrago mailing list at farragobooks.com/sign-up